Kiara,
One of
favorite people too!
I love you!

SHALLOW

YESSI SMITH

xoxox,
your fav tia and
author
Yessi Smith

SHALLOW
by Yessi Smith
Copyright © 2018 by Yessi Smith
All rights reserved.

Cover Designer: Jill Sava, Love Affair With Fiction
Editor: Eli Peters, EP Editing
Formatting: Jill Sava, Love Affair With Fiction

DEDICATION

For Marisol, Kiara, Alyssa, and Caitlin because you're my favorite girls ever.

For Denise (and Callie, Tyler and Nicole), who cares if no one (including me) can actually pronounce Sedlacek? Hahaha! You're the absolute best.

CHAPTER 1

Brinley

Lıke the rumbling thunder just outside my window, chaos trembled inside my chest. Pressure from above, from within and without, built and intensified.

"I'm sorry," my mom said, the melody of those words was soft, yet eloquent. It was the only sign she gave that today was one of her good days.

My dad's eyes, as large and green as mine, bore into me as I shrugged away their apology.

"What's the big deal? You're getting a divorce." My voice came out cheerful, muting the loud cries in my mind. "People divorce all the time."

I shouldered my heavy book bag and walked past them with a smile I perfected long ago. Manicured fingers wrapped around my wrist, stopping me from making my quick escape.

"It's not like you won't still be my parents," I told them, placating them, keeping my guarded heart from the outside world.

My mom's fingers unfurled from my wrist as she dropped her hand.

"You'll just live in different houses, and I'll take turns seeing you. See? Not the end of the world."

We'll just lead different lives. The lies I've perfected will change and I'll adjust with the same calculation I brought to everything I did. Further building the walls, brick by brick of fabricated warfare. Impenetrable. Unrecognizable.

"I knew you'd understand, honey."

That understatement came from my mom. Her pale hand palmed my sun-kissed cheek, and I leaned in to it to absorb the temporary warm compassion. I didn't know when I'd feel it next.

The woman who carried me inside her for nine months, whose heartbeat I recognized as intimately as my own. She brought me into this world and should've known me better than anyone. Only she didn't. No one did. Sometimes, I wondered if *I* even knew who I was.

She kissed my forehead. Her lips pressed against my skin that at the moment felt too tight. Like I'd outgrown my own flesh and was just waiting for the scales to shed.

Indecision crossed my dad's face. I felt myself spinning in the vortex of his emotions. His sadness tore into me. His shame collided and began to crumble my composure. Grief stormed through my system, setting my heart ablaze. As if on cue, thunder rolled over us, making the walls tremble.

I wondered if God himself knew this was coming. If

the continuous storms of the past three days were his way of warning me. If the flashes of light breaking through the ominous clouds were his signal, telling me to brace myself.

The worst was yet to come.

"Are you sure?" he asked, his arms going around me, pulling me to his solid chest.

My mom turned at the entrance of my bedroom door and waited, again, for me to reassure them. The discord gave way to the tidy calmness I knew how to embody and a serene smile spread across my face. Stepping away from his narrow frame, I pushed a long strand of blonde hair behind my ear.

"I'm fine, Dad," I promised, lifting on the tips of my toes, so I could plant a loud kiss on his cheek.

He wasn't that much taller than my five-foot, four inches, but he loved the show of his little girl standing on her toes to reach him. I guessed it made him feel like I wasn't growing up, that I would stay his baby forever, but the truth was I wasn't anyone's anymore. I hadn't been for some time. I belonged to myself, isolated on an island I'd built throughout the years.

"I can't be late. I'm meeting Nicole for a final cram session before our math test."

With long strides, I waltzed by my mom who patted my butt as I made my way out the door through the narrow hallways. Outside, I breathed in the weighted air and walked to the old Honda my parents gave me two months ago for my seventeenth birthday. Once inside, I turned the ignition over, hearing the low hum of the engine come to life. I let myself disconnect for the duration of my drive and allowed the rage to take center stage. Loud music filled every crevice of the small vehicle, making my ear drums whine. I gripped the steering wheel, knuckles whitening. I ignored the small vibration of my phone resting beside my leg, alerting me of incoming texts. I knew, as soon as I pulled my car into the school's parking lot, I'd have to rein it all in. An hour and half, that's all I had to myself.

That time where I could be alone, where I could be me, was mine and I guarded it through lies. This morning was no different than the others. I had a routine and before my hike, I'd change in to the clothes and boots I pack every night. When I finished, I'd go back to my car, replace the comfortable clothes with ones that revealed only as much as I wanted others to see and head to school where I went back to being Brinley Crassus. The meticulous, yet deliberate girl my friends looked to for direction. The girl whose subdued laughter drew the right kind of attention from the students and teachers at Sedlacek

College Preparatory High School. The girl whose GPA was above par. The girl who headed the cheer team, tutored other students and humiliated classmates to deviate negative attention from herself.

The most popular girl in school, who was as much feared and respected as she was hated.

The girl everyone believed had everything.

The lie sunk below my skin and stained my blood with beautiful blends of color. Blissful shades that hid the unseen battles I'd faced. They entwined themselves around me and dressed me up in all my fears.

Pulling into the muddy spot I normally parked over, I changed clothes quickly. When I pushed my door open,

I stepped out of my car and in a small puddle. I jumped twice, soaking my boots. I would've danced in the puddle longer, but I didn't have enough time to play. Not this time. My parents and their divorce announcement took away precious time that would've allowed me to linger. With my book bag carrying my most valued possessions straddled over my shoulder, I crossed the sodden path through the wooded trail and hung a left toward the unbeaten path I discovered over the summer. California natives, like the tall redwoods, lined both sides of me with the early morning rays of the sun streaming weakly through the trees. Forgotten shrubs spilled onto the muddy pathway and a few times I lost my footing as the vines tugged on my boots.

Two miles I hiked where I lost myself even further to the static electricity of the dark heavy sky. Two miles I trudged while last night's rain trickled through the lush leaves hanging overhead. Two miles where the scent of the looming storm pacified me.

Two miles to the cave — my cave — while I carried what was most essential to me, I put as much distance between what I was and who I wanted to be. I crossed small creeks, crawled beneath low hanging untamed tree limbs, climbed over fallen trees and when I finally reached my destination, the weight of so many impossibilities lifted.

I took in a greedy breath of air and let it linger in my chest before I let it out on a loud whoosh. But before I could go into my cave, a figure came out. Surprise and fear made me huddle behind a nearby bush, but I kept my eyes trained on the intruder.

A man wearing nothing but low hanging jeans that

hugged his lean waist turned in front of the mouth of the cave. He yawned, lifting his arms out wide over his head. Muscles stretched and quivered with the motion. He combed his fingers through his disheveled hair, letting me see his face. I couldn't take my eyes off the man. No, not a man, but a boy on the brink of manhood. A boy I recognized from school. *Roderick Roher*. When he lifted his face to the sky, I stammered back a step, tripping over exposed roots and fell with a hard thud on a bed of wet leaves. His head snapped in my direction and I hugged my body closer to the bush and held my breath.

He scanned the area. When his eyes zeroed in on where I hid, I rushed to my feet and ran.

Roderick wasn't like me. He wasn't like the group of friends I had.

He was a loner. Whether he was on the school's outdoor patio or sitting on a chair in the back of the classroom, he seemed comfortable in his own skin. Completely alone, never uttering more than the necessary words to anyone who spoke to him.

He wasn't one to waste words and to be honest, he didn't need them. Not when his eyes said everything he didn't.

A loner, but not lonely. Seemingly angry at everyone but at no one in particular. Until those heated eyes met mine. Whether it was in passing or from across ten football fields, they always told me I was the true enemy. The one who held so much unforgiveable under her skin.

Today, it was my turn to be angry with him though. He ruined my morning routine. Without it, I didn't know how I'd get through the day. How I'd plaster on a fake smile until night fell and I could crawl into my bed.

I should've stayed. I should go back. Demand he leave my cave where the darkness infiltrated while I wrote words that set me free. Words that bled from my heart onto a blank piece of paper no one would ever read.

But I couldn't go back. I couldn't risk him asking questions that would allow him or anyone else understand that side of me. So, like a coward, I fled to my car and put on the same clothes I originally dressed in this morning. I combed my damp hair and after drying my face, I touched up the makeup that would further hide me from my classmates. With my nerves rattled, I didn't bother with the radio but instead let the silence scream through my head. Allowing everything I wanted to say pound through my veins and poison my heart.

When I got to school, I felt worse than I had when I left the cave. I hated that he'd stolen my peace. Hated even more how I couldn't get past it. With anxiety braiding a tight knot in my stomach, I pulled out my phone. Ignoring my text messages, I went instead to Google where I searched the symptoms for various brain disorders.

Mania.

Hallucinations.

Hysteria.

Depression.

Violent tendencies.

Dementia.

I searched through every disease, every dysfunction I could find just as I'd done numerous times before. I took down notes, tried to learn as much as I could while I tried to piece it all together. It didn't ease the growing tension, didn't make me feel any better. In the end, I had more questions than answers. Questions neither of my parents wanted me to voice, which left me on my own to do research on a disease I knew nothing about. Not even a name.

Letting out a long string of air, I stared forward in a daze until I spotted my friend Nicole's sculpted figure waving from her perch on the sidewall. I readied myself. Every day was a fight I had to win because high school and the people I surrounded myself with were more like a prison than a sanctuary. Only six months separated me from graduation. I'd made it three years without anyone ever knowing me, ever getting close enough to really see me. Except for maybe Danny, who was the only friend I came close to trusting. When school was over, I would move to Los Angeles for college where I could finally unleash the girl I'd kept hidden from the world. With all the consequences that might follow, I was, after all, my mother's daughter.

Chestnut brown hair tumbled past Nicole's slender shoulders, framing the delicate features of her face.

"I've texted you like a thousand times!" Nicole exclaimed seconds before I even shut my door.

Eager hands pulled me toward the bleachers that rested on the sidelines of our football field. I didn't bother speaking, knowing she'd already rehearsed whatever urgent matter she had to tell me. Waving at a handful of kids from my class, I felt the stormy clouds from above follow me like a crown of thorns. The wind howled in my ears. Thick tendrils of hair played across my face, so I piled it up in a quick bun. With hunched shoulders, Nicole shielded herself from the oncoming storm while her hand stayed tucked in mine.

She led us away from the school from prying eyes and meddlesome ears. The cold metal of the bleachers creaked when we sat on it and I looked past the field to the bending trees. Sinister clouds gathered closer, sudden lightning illuminating the broody day and setting the stage for the stifling atmosphere.

"Look." She handed me her phone to show off a picture of a pretty silver dress with light frills on the bottom. "This is it! This would be perfect for you to wear to the Fall Ball."

Pinching my fingers together on the screen, I made the image bigger. It was simple with a slight dip in the neckline and cinched inward at the waist so the fabric molded to the model's figure.

"It's perfect," I said, scrolling down to see the price.

"Yep," Nicole agreed. "Which is why as your best friend, I already made an appointment for you to try it on today after school."

"Shut up!" I smacked her shoulder, but the lightness faded when I saw the price.

There was no way my parents would give me that much money for a dress, and no way any other dress could compare to this one.

"After school," she said, bubbling from the inside. "Skip whatever club or meeting you have and we'll go to the boutique. Then you can help me find a dress for myself."

"Nicole," A warm smile tilted my lips upward as anxiety twisted in my gut. "I can't today. I already made plans to tutor someone at her house." It was a lie, but I couldn't tell her the truth. The cave had become my safe haven. I had to go back and sit in my darkened oasis, to let the words pour from me. It was the only thing that could cleanse my ugly soul.

"We're seniors, Brinley. It's your last year on the Fall court. Just like every other year, you're going to win, but this time you'll be crowned queen." She squealed. "You have to look the part, so ditch whatever loser you're tutoring and come with me."

This was the part of Nicole that made me keep her at arm's length. She was one of my closest friends, but I didn't trust her, *couldn't* trust her. Not when she was so quick to belittle others. Not that I was any better.

I ignored the tiny sprinkles of water that began to fall from the sky and dampen my skin. "I can't today."

"Saturday, then?" she asked with a slight twitch of her lips. "Or are you all booked up that day too?"

This time my smile came more natural and it took over my face. "Saturday," I agreed. "After lunch?"

"Hmmm…" She tapped a forefinger to her chin. "I'll have to check my schedule. Yep, Saturday, Jacob and I have a hot date. A nooner." She waggled her brows at me. She and the oldest twin in our group of friends had been dating off and on for close to a year. At the moment they weren't dating, but it was during their offseason that they saw each other the most. "He'll be done in like five minutes, so I can still meet you. I'll call and reschedule at the boutique."

Laughter spilled from my lungs at the same time the sky opened up with a roaring clash of thunder. In unison, we flinched at the deafening sound and with a quick glance at one another, we ran back to school. Our feet hit the soft ground, splattering mud on our jeans, but still our moment of happiness hung over us, hiding away the charged air.

CHAPTER 2

Brinley

HOMEROOM BEGAN WITH a blaring shriek of the alarm. A few of us shuffled to our desks while others stayed standing in small circles talking to one another. Mr. Fischel, our homeroom teacher, was pretty laidback and let us use our time in his room freely. He didn't mind what we did as long as we weren't too loud. I waved at my friends when they called my name and although I wanted to go over some last minute problems for my upcoming math test, I went to them.

Danny held out his arms for a hug. He was one of the few friends I felt comfortable around. He was as pure as they came, was the thread that kept me together when the frayed edges threatened to come apart.

"You're wet," he accused.

"That's what happens when you're outside when it

rains," I teased.

"I saw you and Nicole running from the football field. Next time you plan on playing in the rain, wear a white top," he replied.

"No bra, right?" I asked.

"You get me." He tapped his shoulder against mine and when I leaned in to him, he hugged me closer to his side.

Danny was one of the good guys. Unlike the twins, Jacob and Joseph, who spent most of their time taunting those they felt were below them. If it weren't for Danny playing different sports so well, he probably wouldn't be part of our group. Sometimes, I wondered why he even bothered with us. He was so much better than the rest of us.

"Ready for math?" he asked.

I nodded. My brain was loaded with the varying tricks and lessons we'd been taught the past few months of school. Equations and formulas. Variables and graphs. So many problems without a solution for the real troubles of our young lives.

These teachers, whose goal I assumed was to enlighten us, to sharpen our minds, didn't realize how suffocating these tests were. They judged us based on the progress behind a paper with scratches from our pencil, as if that was all we amounted to. As if their insignificant lectures, would have any bearing in the grand scheme of things.

"Of course she is," Mariah replied, her tone dry. Her eyes swept over me from top to bottom, and I had to fight the urge to squirm under her scrutiny. "She's kinda perfect."

It was said as a joke, but I knew better. Mariah was

one of my friends who hated me. The feeling was mutual.

"She is perfect." Danny pressed a kiss to my temple.

Warmth pooled in my chest, and I hugged him closer to me. This was the kind of friendship I wanted when I was younger. The kind of friendship I turned away from in order to have these fake friends. And the status they held that would hide away all my truths.

"You're kind of my favorite person in the whole world," I whispered so only he could hear me.

His lips spread in a huge smile. "Whoa, I'm your favorite person in this great, big world?" he teased, his voice just as low as mine. "That's intense. I don't know if I'm ready for that type of commitment."

I smacked his shoulder and when I glared at him, he threw his head back in laughter. Yeah, he was definitely my favorite person in a world that seemed to hate me.

CHAPTER 3

RODERICK

I STEPPED IN to the cold office. When the receptionist, Mrs. Jeffries, saw me, she held out a finger while she finished on the phone. I listened to the chatter of the other staff while I tapped my pencil on the side of Mrs. Jeffries's desk. When she hung up, she turned to me with a slight tilt of her head.

"I uhh..." I ran my hand through my hair, hating this day. It always came too quickly, although days seemed to trek by endlessly. "I need my lunch card." I stared at her, daring her to make me feel bad about myself. The scholarship kid, who couldn't eat lunch if it wasn't given to him for free.

Mrs. Jeffries stood from her chair, arching her back as if she'd been seated in the same position for hours. She held her white cardigan to her chest as she left the front office. A few minutes went by, and I continued to tap my pencil on her desk while I waited.

"Roderick," she called.

Rather than handing me my lunch card, she stood behind her desk with her hands digging through her purse. She handed me a few loose bills.

"What's this?" It came out gritty and rough.

She shook her head. "There seems to be a problem. Your aunt…" she ran a hand over the back of her neck, "your aunt must've forgotten to renew your card. I'm sorry, but I can't give you a new card for free lunch if she doesn't renew it."

I blew out a long string of air. She didn't forget; she just didn't do it. With me no longer living under her roof, I guessed she no longer felt any responsibility for me. A week, I'd been gone a week from her house. That was all it took for her to let me go completely.

"Just forget it." I forced down the bile that rose with my anger.

She waved the bills at me again. "Here, take it," she said. "I'll call your aunt and remind her to fill out the paperwork online. Meanwhile, just take the money. Please. You can pay me back later." She smiled and although the lines on either side of her lips deepened, her features also softened.

Heat spread to my cheeks while I studied the money she held out to me. "She's at work, has meetings all day. I'll talk to her when I get home," I said. She waved the bills again, and this time I pocketed the money. "Thanks," I muttered and turned to leave.

I wasn't sure how much Mrs. Jeffries had given me, but whatever the amount was, I had to make it last. Just as I had to keep anyone at school from calling my aunt. I couldn't be outed. I had to graduate so I could have some sort of future away from this shithole beach town. Until then, I had to scrape by with what was given to me because I could only sneak into my aunt's house when she wasn't around to steal food and do small loads of laundry so many times before she figured out what I was doing. Besides, I didn't want to do that anymore anyway. Didn't want to rely on someone who didn't want me in her life.

I made it to my English class before anyone else and took a seat in the back. Always in the back. Even when teachers gave us assigned seats, I dragged my chair to the back, away from everyone. For the most part, teachers and students alike left me alone. I liked it that way. There was strength in going unnoticed. In not being seen. There was peace in being invisible.

It was why after a week of sleeping in the woods, I was so happy Saturday afternoon when I found the cave while hiking. It's secluded, far enough from the beaten path, I couldn't imagine many people knew about it. It was the perfect home until I graduated high school. With the money I earned from my part time job at the ice cream store, I hoped I could save enough to get a bus ticket out of this town and to San Diego where I had a full scholarship at the art university. Getting in, getting a full ride, to the school that was on the top of my list meant everything to me. It meant freedom, and the ability to immerse myself in writing.

When the bell rang, my classmates scrambled in to the room and slid behind their desks. Seth, a kid I knew from several other classes, took a seat beside me. I didn't acknowledge him, and he didn't acknowledge me, but since our freshmen year when I stopped a group of baseball players from using his head as a ball, he's sat next to me when we were in the same class. It made pairing up with someone for group assignments easier. Unfortunately, we were paired up a lot in English class. It was like our teacher didn't know how to assign work without making us work together.

"Move," a light voice from beside me said. "I said move." Her voice rose and just like the other kids in my class, I turned to see Brinley kick Seth's seat.

The school's prestigious princess. The almighty who everyone bowed down to. She sat on her self-proclaimed throne with her pom-poms, where no one could touch her. But I saw her. Saw through her charade. She was as vulnerable as anyone else. She just knew how to hide it better than others.

It took years to figure out how much she hated being called out on her nasty attitude, but once I saw how she reacted to it, I did it often. It brought me pleasure to see her cheeks redden and her eyes widen. To watch her fall from her throne onto her ass.

Seth pushed his chair back, but I put my hand on the back of the seat, not letting it move further. I didn't know why she was turning her venom on Seth, and although Seth and I weren't friends, I wasn't about to let her give him crap just because she thought she could.

I was the only one who stopped her. The only one whose anger matched her selfishness.

"He doesn't have to move," I said. "Go to the front, princess. Where you always sit."

Brinley glared at me, but then her lips twisted in a sneer

as she lifted her chin up. "Do you smell something?" she asked loudly, her nose scrunching up. "Smells like"—she took a couple inhales—"like someone hasn't showered in days." She glowered at me.

From across the room, her friends laughed while everyone else seemed to hold their breath. My temper was known throughout the school, and this girl was playing a game she wasn't meant to win.

"Brin," one of her friends, Danny, called from a few rows down, "what are you doin' over there?" He patted the empty chair next to him.

From what I'd seen of him, he wasn't a bad guy. Just hung out with the shittiest of the shittiest.

She lifted a single shoulder in a half shrug and pouted, her thin lips pulling down in what I assumed she thought was a cute gesture. It was cute. I hated how cute it was. "I wanted to sit with Roderick today."

I tensed at the sound of my name coming from her lips. It'd been years since she called me by my name rather than freak. Such a stupid, cliché name. Not that I would expect more from her or her friends.

"My mom always goes on about charity," she smiled, and it wasn't one of her practiced smiles that she gave her friends, but one that looked a lot like hurt. One that looked like she was trying to hide one of her greatest truths.

"Brinley," Danny said. It came out as a warning. One she ignored.

"Maybe I'll sit with you tomorrow," she said as if her presence was some sort of grace I should be thankful for. As she leaned over my desk, her face inches away from mine, she whispered in my ear, "The community center has showers, you know?" and softly chuckled at her own joke.

Her warm breath fell on my skin and it sent an electric shock down my spine. I gripped the side of my chair and when she didn't pull away, I felt my insides begin to quake as if an earthquake and cyclone were about to rip me apart limb from limb.

"This is cute, princess," I whispered back, keeping my voice steady when I turned to look at her, but with how close she held herself to me, our noses almost touched. "You think you can embarrass me? You use everyone around you to make yourself feel better, but it never works, does it? When it's all over and the laughter dies, you're still you. A fake. And everyone in this room knows it."

Through gritted teeth, she sucked in a breath. Her eyes widened, and for the briefest of moments I could've sworn hurt flashed behind them before anger replaced everything. She leaned back and patted my cheek as I worked my jaw back and forth.

"I'd love to go to the Fall Ball with you." She looked around the room, her eyes wide with innocence. "I'm sure someone here can let you borrow an old suit or something."

Around me students laughed. I opened my mouth but clamped it shut when our teacher, Mr. Scott, finally came in the classroom a few minutes late.

"Find your seat, Brinley," Mr. Scott called out.

With a satisfied grin on her perfect little face, she turned on her heels, but I clasped a hand around her wrist. She jolted as if my contact stung and when she pulled from my hold, I let her go.

"Yeah." I huffed out a laugh as I leaned back on my chair with my palms resting on the back of my head. "I get it, poor people make you uncomfortable. Like I said, fake." I smiled.

Her breaths came quickly, red spilled across her chest to her cheeks. When she shot up her middle finger, I barked out a laugh. A few students turned to look at us, but when Mr. Scott coughed to get our attention, Brinley scurried away with her chin dipped down.

"Brinley," he said and she snapped her attention to him. "Since you and Roderick seem to be getting along so well, I'll be pairing you together for our next group project."

Brinley stayed frozen in place, her light green eyes darting from our teacher back to me. I almost laughed at her despair but beside me Seth slinked further into his chair. No one would want to pair with him, and he'd be forced in a group that didn't want him.

Fury gripped me like a vice as I watched her walk across the room. In a hushed tone, she spoke to Danny, who looked over at Seth and nodded at whatever she said while Mr. Scott handed out a small packet of papers to us.

"I'm giving each of you a piece of paper," he said. "It's a copy from an excerpt of a book I have at home. If you had Honors English with me last year and did all of your assignments, you'll recognize the words. Or maybe you've already forgotten." A few students laughed. "Either way, it doesn't matter. When you pair into your groups, I want you to skim through the page, not read the passage, but look for a word that stands out to you – just one word. On one of the copies, I want you to circle that word. Both you and your partner have to agree this is the word that means the most to both of you. Understanding so far?" he asked and paused to see if anyone had any questions. When no one replied, he continued, "Once you've circled that one word, I want you to go back and read the passage and circle any words that amplify or give meaning to the first word you picked. It can be expressive or evocative. Next step is to list all your words on a separate piece of paper in the same order they appeared in your reading. With these words, you're going to write a poem. If a word you circled doesn't fit, you don't have to use it. You can eliminate parts of a word, like an ending if it helps clarify your poem. If you get stuck, go back to your passage and read it again. The point isn't to make the words work to form a perfect poem, but to give meaning to your words. When you have your poem complete, go back to the paper you were given, erase the circles around any words you didn't use and make sure only the words you are using are circled. You can work on that paper or the extra one that was given to your partner for the finished product. When you're done, you're going to go back and add a drawing that connects your image to your poem. And guys," he chuckled, "I don't want some Google image on here. You're drawing it – together or you can pick who's the better artist. But this is your work, and I want to see your creativity."

Eager to start, even if it was with Brinley, I tapped my foot on the floor. Restless. Always in need of creating.

"While you get into groups, I'm gonna pass out some examples from previous years to give you ideas," Mr. Scott continued. "This, my young students, is called

Blackout Poetry. You're the poet, make me something beautiful."

I shook my head at how lame that sounded, but I couldn't deny it. Mr. Scott, with all his dumb jokes, was my favorite teacher. English had always been my favorite subject but some teachers could make their lessons worse than torture. Not Mr. Scott. He enjoyed teaching, but more than that, he loved to see his students learn and grow. Become engaged and creative.

"Take your time," Mr. Scott continued. "This isn't due until next Friday, so there's no rush. I want to see your best work. Points will be taken off for lack of creativity and neatness, and if I find out you are not working together as a team, but doing the project alone. If you finish early, you can come sit with me and critique the novel I'm working on."

That earned a groan from everyone but me. Me, I was curious what Mr. Scott had to say. How he'd word his story, the prose he used, the rhythm of his sentences.

When the girl who normally sat in front of me left, Brinley took her spot with Danny taking the seat next to her. Brinley turned her table around so it faced me.

"Hey man." Danny knocked on Seth's desk and turned his own desk around to face Seth's. "Since these two got themselves paired together, looks like you're stuck with me."

Seth sat upright in his chair and nodded. Danny could've partnered up with anyone. In fact, there were at least four girls who frowned in our direction when he sat in front of Seth.

I scoffed. Ignoring me, Brinley stared at her paper, her big eyes jumping across the page. I studied her –

the way she twisted her blonde, almost white colored hair around a slender finger. The way she sucked on her bottom lip. The way she sat – her head bowed, back straight, always the picture of perfection.

On the outside, she was pretty. The prettiest girl in our school... probably in our whole town. It was the only reason I could think of that people would flock to her, to seek her approval. It was what was on the inside that made her so detestable.

She hadn't always been like that. The weirdest part about the change in her behavior was, she never had to be mean to be noticed. Not like Nicole or Mariah. I couldn't help but wonder what happened to the little girl who picked wild flowers for every boy and girl in her elementary class on Valentine's Day. What happened to the twelve-year-old girl who held my hand when I went back to school after my parents died? The girl who promised me I wasn't alone. The girl who told me she'd hang on for me, even when I wanted her to let go.

CHAPTER 4

Brinley

ONE OF THE examples Mr. Scott gave us made me smile. If I were partnered with Danny, as I usually was in this class, I would've giggled. But because of who sat in front of me, I kept my thoughts to myself. Guarded, always guarded.

Broad black lines covered the entire page aside from the scattered words that formed the sentence, "it's easy to scribble Out words the clever Part is figuring out which ones you should Leave".

It's easy to scribble out words. The clever part is figuring out which ones you should leave.

I shuffled the paper to the side and grabbed our assignment. I scanned the page for one word; the word that resonated the most with me. My stomach fluttered happily in my belly because this was what I thrived on.

Words. Finding hidden meanings.

"Here we go," Roderick said, pointing to my paper.

With his pencil he circled the word *shall,* and a few spaces over he circled the *ow* in the word *below.*

Shallow.

"Cute." I smirked to cover the pang in my chest. Another mark on my already bruised heart. This one I deserved. Actually, I deserved most of them. Heck, I'd worked hard at becoming the person I despised. I flipped my pencil around to erase the circle he drew around the two words. "But we're supposed to only circle one word."

"You got me there, princess." He yawned. When he stretched his arms above his head, it reminded me of this morning. Of the boy sleeping in my cave, who took my favorite part of the day from me.

"Doesn't your aunt own a washing machine?" I turned my nose at him, but kept my eyes trained on the dirt on his shirt. "Your clothes are disgusting, like you've slept on dirt or something."

He narrowed his eyes at my challenge, and I could see the veins in his neck pop out.

"Ohmygosh!" I gasped in mock horror. "You're not homeless, are you? If you are, if you're sleeping outside instead of being safely tucked in your bed, the police should know about this." I nodded my head, showing him I'd come to a solution.

Fear darkened his features and softened me. Damn, I felt sorry for being so vile. For being exactly what he'd accused me of, fake and shallow. It made me wonder if the mask I had to wear was worth the pain I'd caused.

Reaching out to him, I squeezed his hand. He clenched his fist and his hand shook in mine before he pulled away.

"I was joking," I said and cleared my throat, so I could continue. "I didn't mean anything by it, but if you're in some sort of trouble…"

"What?" He snorted. "You'll hold my hand? You won't let go, right?" An ugliness that didn't belong to him made his lips turn sinister. An ugliness I put there. "I slept outside last night. You see," he continued in a patronizing tone, "there's this thing some people do called camping. It's where you sleep on the ground and are surrounded by nature. If you do it right, there's no showers or burger joints. You rely solely on yourself."

"Sounds awful."

Lie. It sounded *amazing*.

I turned my focus back to the paper. Tears pricked the back of my eyes, making the words in front of me blur. I didn't know where they come from, and while tears weren't foreign to me, they rarely made such an abrupt appearance. I swallowed past the thickness in my throat and only spoke when I knew I'd claimed the tears back.

"Let's just get this over with, okay?" I mumbled.

I felt the heat of Roderick's eyes on me. Eyes so clear, they reminded me of the crystal pond I found in my cave. Mine, not his. He camped there last night. A onetime deal because I wasn't willing to share my spot.

Beside us, Danny and Seth laughed. Danny reached across both desks with his fist out and after a few seconds of awkward silence, Seth bumped it.

"What's so funny?" I asked, turning to Danny. Away from Roderick and his prying eyes.

Although I was pretty great at being mean, I felt awful

when I realized Seth would no longer have Roderick as his partner. Knowing no one else would want him in their group, I asked Danny to partner with him. Danny being Danny, he agreed as if it weren't a big deal. It was though. In the world we created in our school, it was a huge deal.

Danny showed me his and Seth's paper and I squinted to see the word they decided to circle.

"Hungry?" I asked.

Seth shot me an embarrassed smile.

"It's like you can read his mind." I winked at Seth. "I have to bring sandwiches and snacks to Danny's games so he can eat when he's not playing."

"And practices," he added. "It's the only reason I upgraded her to best friend status."

My heart clenched at Danny's words. Expanded against its cage. Because I knew beyond his words were a deeper meaning. He cared about me, maybe even loved me. In spite of what he saw.

"I'm touched," I deadpanned, but my smile grew when he leaned in to smack a loud kiss on my forehead.

"Heart of gold, this one." He tilted his chin toward me.

Seth looked down, worrying one of his papers with his fingers, no doubt not believing anything good lived inside of me.

"Never misses one of my games," Danny continued.

"Well, I do have to go to the football and basketball games since I cheer and all that."

"Yeah, you cheer for track too?" he asked. "How about the summer soccer league I play outside of the school?"

I squinted my eyes, drawing my lips together in a thin line. "All these sports you play." I fanned my face, pretending to be impressed with his athleticism. "How'd I end up with a jock as my best friend?"

"I only pick from the best." He looked back at Seth. "Rain or shine, she's there with food and water, just for me."

I snickered, but the tension in my gut amplified. I wasn't good, everyone knew that. I was fake. *Shallow.* No matter how much he went on about me, Seth, Roderick, and everyone else knew the truth. The truth Danny was blind to.

"You're like some sort of mutant," I joked, hiding further behind the safety of my walls. "If I don't feed you, no one else will and I'm afraid you'll die on the field. Then poof," I slapped my hands together, "there goes the future I have planned for us."

"Yeah." He rolled his eyes. "I can't wait for the big slobbery dog and all five of our kids."

"Seven," I countered.

"No." He leaned forward, putting me in a headlock. "We compromised and you agreed. Five kids, or no deal."

My body shook in quiet laughter, and my smile widened when I saw Seth laughing with us. A few minutes ago was the first time since fourth grade that I saw him smile. It was just who Danny was and it wasn't a surprise that he'd managed to not only make him smile, but also laugh.

"Five kids and two dogs," I argued between short gasps of breath. "And I get to be a stay-at-home mom."

"Fine, but you're making homemade pasta. None of those store-bought noodles." He let me go only to hold my face in his hands. Our eyes locked on one another, and I saw the humor behind his eyes. "Homemade," he said slowly, enunciating each syllable.

"Homemade," I repeated, even slower.

"And naked," he continued. "I want you naked."

"Naked? They're not even born yet, and already you're planning on traumatizing our kids."

"Pretty sure no one would be traumatized if they saw you naked," Seth said under his breath.

Danny, Roderick and I jerked our attention to him, our expressions mirroring our own surprise at his words. When he bowed his head down to hide the blush that crept over his face, I laughed so hard, tears spilled from my eyes and my stomach cramped.

It was the first time I'd laughed like that in what felt like years. It was liberating. But I clamped on my bottom lip and suppressed the emerging joy when I peeked over my shoulder and saw my other friends looking at us in disapproval.

Because Brinley Crassus didn't laugh without restraint. And she sure as hell didn't have fun with people like Seth and Roderick.

"I can't believe you have to work on a project with that freak." A sympathetic look washed over Nicole's features when she squeezed my arm.

"It's no big deal," I said before taking a healthy bite of my tuna wrap.

"He's not bad on the eyes, but what the hell were you thinking going up to him?" Her sculpted eyebrows shot to her hairline. "Mariah said you were all over each other before Mr. Scott got there. There isn't something going on between you two, is there?" Disgust marred her features.

Annoyed, I set my lunch down and folded my hands in front of me. What was I thinking? It was simple really. I wanted to ruin his day, just as he had mine. And I did it the only way I knew how, not realizing it would backfire.

"Me and the freak together?" I asked on a laugh. "I was having fun with him."

A slow smirk crossed my face and she laughed just as I knew she would.

"You're such a bitch sometimes," she said through her laughter.

I rubbed my chest, right over where it hurt the most. She wasn't wrong. She wasn't right either. I was mean, but it also wasn't who I was.

Danny took a seat beside me and tucked me under his arm. "Definitely not a bitch," he said.

"What about you?" Nicole's lips parted to form an *O*. "You got stuck with the loser because of her."

"Seth's cool." He kissed the side of my head before releasing me and taking a bite of his pizza.

"Seth's cool?" Her voice rang in my head and she spun her head to face his table where he sat with one other kid. Neither of them were what anyone would call *cool*.

"Yeah," he answered between bites.

"Maybe you," she pointed across the table, "should be sitting with him then."

Our friends laughed, Jacob's ringing louder than anyone else's. Enjoying the attention, she tapped a red fingernail against her lips and waited. When Danny shifted beside me, I reached for his leg and squeezed. He looked back at me through sad, brown eyes but shook his head at my silent plea.

He was leaving me. Alone. With friends who didn't like me. Who on most days I didn't like either.

"I think I will." He stood from his spot beside me and with our friends mocking his retreating back, he went to Seth's table and took a seat. Within seconds their table erupted in laughter.

It didn't sound cynical or ugly like ours did, but genuine. Happy. I wanted to be a part of that kind of happiness again. The kind I found earlier in English class. The kind Danny always seemed to find and expose. But more than that, I wanted to be a part of something real. Something that would rub away all the fake, all the shallow.

Mariah giggled, causing my attention to snap back to her. She eyed me curiously, so I took another bite of my lunch, hoping whatever she thought she saw wouldn't interest her anymore.

"Your boyfriend will come crawling back soon enough." She smoothed her hair back and pulled it in a pony. "Unless you're worried Seth and his lame friend have more to offer than you do." She arched a brow.

Fury burned hot in my veins, but I kept my face calm. My eyes leveled on hers.

She knew Danny and I weren't together. She knew just as everyone else in the school knew, he had never had a girlfriend. Too many times his sexuality had become a point of conversation when he wasn't around. Too many times I'd tuned them out without defending him.

"Aw c'mon, Mariah, leave the poor faggots alone." This came from Jacob. His eyes were cold, his lips pressed together in a thin line while his twin tapped a beat on the table beside him.

Shame was thick in my throat, but I swallowed past it when I stood from my seat.

"I need to study for my math test," I said. "I'll see you guys later."

"Brin, we were just joking!" Jacob called after me.

I kept my stride even, my shoulders back, and my head high. I was impenetrable.

"Don't be mad because we don't like queers!" Jacob shouted, laughing at his own joke.

I felt the eyes of everyone on the outdoor patio on me. It made me queasy. I shivered, pulling my tan sweater tight around my chest. When I turned to face Jacob, I forced a smile on my face.

Danny watched, waited. Hope and fear shined behind his eyes. I couldn't let him down. I couldn't let myself down either.

"Jealousy is such an ugly trait," I sing-songed back at Jacob. "Just because gay men don't find you attractive, doesn't mean you're not pretty."

Laughter erupted around us. Jacob grinned back at me and when I shot him the middle finger, he shook his head.

We were still friends. I was still on the top of the

pedestal. Untouchable.

While we still had time before lunch was over, I headed to my next class. It would give me the time I needed to regroup and study. I turned the corner and ran straight into a wall.

Or not a wall, but a chest. A hard one with broad shoulders and corded arms.

Fingers dug into my arm, steadying me so I wouldn't fall. When I peered up at Roderick's face, he took a step back and shoved a piece of paper in to my chest. The paper fell, gliding back and forth slowly before it hit the floor. I took the paper from the floor and choked on a cry when I saw the word he'd circled.

Afraid

Yeah, I was afraid. Of everything and nothing. All at once the fears slammed together in my gut, making it difficult for me to breathe.

But he was the one who had circled it. A word that had to resonate with both of us.

He was afraid too, he just hid it behind thicker, higher walls than I had built.

CHAPTER 5

Brinley

AFTER LISTENING FOR any noise, I eased into my cave quietly, hoping and praying Roderick wasn't there. It'd been a long day at school. A bad one, all born from my decision to taunt Roderick for a sin he didn't know he'd committed. Made worse by cheer practice where I had to listen to Nicole and Mariah question me in front of everyone. Where I had to put them in their place with snide comments that made me feel even uglier.

While the cave itself didn't look different, it was. Everything was different because of Roderick, who had claimed my secret hideaway. Two garbage bags full of clothes leaned against my rock. The rock I hunched away from as I wrote. The same rock I rested my back on while I poured over the words I'd written. A flashlight rested beside rumpled sheets and a pillow lay across the hard ground. My ground.

Not only had he invaded my cave, but he made my spot his personal bedroom.

I beamed the flashlight from my phone around the rest of the cave, looked for somewhere else I could settle in to write. Because if he was staying, which it looked like he was, he wasn't pushing me out. I needed this cave. I needed something that was mine. I needed to breathe.

A small corner, away from his things looked to fit the part so I kneeled down with my book bag in front of me. Once I found my notebook and pencil, I pulled them out. And breathed.

Inhale.

Exhale.

Something any one of us can do without thinking or direction. Something that too often seemed so difficult for me.

I set my phone beside me, allowing the flashlight to illuminate the small area I sat in. Thinking, I peered forward, not really looking at anything but the words that played behind my mind. With a content smile, I drew my pencil to the notebook, but stopped when something on the wall caught my eye.

Curious, I grabbed my phone and shone the light toward the wall. My chest constricted with the weight of what I saw.

Alone isn't such a tragedy
when you're trapped in a past
that holds no future.

I stood on shaky legs and when I reached the wall, I traced the lettering with my fingers. The handwriting was jerky but bold, as if whoever had written the message wanted to be heard, to be seen.

Roderick. It had to be him. Since I found this place during summer break, no one else had come by. I hadn't told anyone about it. Not Danny and definitely not Nicole. It was mine, but it looked like I was going to have to share. And at the moment, with my eyes glued on Roderick's words, I didn't mind.

A black magic marker sat beside the wall. After a quick glance around, I picked it up. My heart hammered in my ears, deafening me to everything. My tongue peeked out, wetting my lips. With one palm resting on the smooth surface of the wall, I wrote my own message to a loner who'd made today hell. He hadn't done it on purpose. Hell he had no way of knowing the disaster he'd start by being at my cave and not giving me the time I needed to write.

A broken soul
can turn cold.
No one can make it alone.

It was the closest I'd ever come to telling anyone the truth. The closest he'd get to an explanation on why I was no longer the girl he remembered from our childhood. Why after years of friendship, I'd not only turned away from him but began calling him a freak until the name caught on and everyone started calling him that. The ache in my heart grew. My breaths fell rapidly, my chest heaving with the effort. But no one was there to hear me. To tell me it would be okay.

I wasn't alone though, I reminded myself. I surrounded myself with people, so I wouldn't be alone where my mom's illness snapped at my heels. No matter how much I tried to outrun it, it was always there.

Reminding me what my future might hold.

Distance. I had to distance myself from it. From everyone who might look. I had to stay in the limelight, where everyone could see me outshine the ugly, the dark. Until it no longer existed.

My head swam. My vision blurred. Holding a hand to my stomach, I sucked in a desperate breath. Then another, trying to pull myself back.

Alone isn't such a tragedy

I ran Roderick's words in my mind, staring blindly at the wall, doing my best to make sense of it all. My limbs shook so hard I could barely hold myself upright.

Alone isn't such a tragedy

A sob broke from deep within my soul. It smashed down every barrier until the tightness in my chest lifted. Relief washed over me and I rested my pounding head against the cool wall. When I felt better, I pulled back and read over the mismatched poems.

My words and Roderick's words bled together.

It wasn't perfect. It wasn't eloquent and probably not very poetic. But it was us. Him and me. Roderick and Brinley in our rawest forms.

Not wanting to be here when Roderick came back, I grabbed my stuff and ran out of the cave. Rather than going back to my car the way I normally would, I deviated through the woods. It made the hike longer and if the sky opened up once more I'd be drenched by the time I made it to my car. If Roderick came back while I was hiking, he'd see my car but hopefully we wouldn't see each other. I didn't want him to know it was me who left him that message. Not now, maybe not ever.

A rush passed through me. Alive, that's how I felt.

My body hummed with the feeling. I never felt this way before, this vulnerable. I didn't want to lose it. Not any of it.

When I reached my car, I started the ignition and left. Hoping and praying Roderick would continue writing on the wall, making it more than two distinct poems, but some sort of message to one another.

DINNER WAS QUIET with just my dad and me. My mom's good day was as fleeting as a sand castle built on the shore at low tide and by time I made it home, she'd locked herself in her bedroom.

Her illness stole her from us. Most days, I didn't have a mom just as my dad didn't have a wife. I couldn't blame him for leaving her, not when he found someone else that made him happy. He wouldn't desert her though, he'd continue to take care of her. He would no longer be staying in our house, but would move into his girlfriend's place when the divorce was finalized. Until then, I could continue pretending we were still the family we once were. The mom who would braid my hair and tell me fun stories on the drive to school. The dad who'd grill outside every weekend with our neighbors and run across our backyard with me on his back.

I couldn't remember if they'd been the happy couple

I imagined them to be, but to me… to the little girl I once was, we were perfect together.

But my mom's illness swept in without warning or invitation. It changed me. It changed all of us. You couldn't find the evidence of her disease written on her skin. No, it went deeper than that. Her body was strong while her illness stayed buried deep within her mind, crippling her from the inside out.

I didn't know what it was that she had. My mom rarely spoke of it. My dad spoke of it even less. It was something we existed with, something that haunted all of our todays and tomorrows.

"You know, you can move in with me if you want," my dad said, breaking the silence.

I wished he hadn't spoken. Even though I was tempted to take his offer, I couldn't. Eventually, my mom would break from her fog and come back to us. When she did, even if she wouldn't stay long, I couldn't tell her I was leaving her too. That she would be alone in the home I grew up in.

"I spoke to Linds, and she'd love for you to live with us." His face was so hopeful, so eager. "Or you and I can get our own place. Just you and me, kid. What do you say?"

"You only want me to move in with you so you don't have to clean if you're living by yourself," I joked.

Eyes so similar to mine lit with mischief. "You are pretty handy with the dishwasher and laundry. And you know, no one knows how to vacuum like you do."

I pointed my fork at him. "I knew it! But nope, Dr. Crassus, you're gonna have to make do with Lindsey and without my expertise."

His face sobered. "It could be like old times." He held a fisted hand to his mouth when he coughed. "Or not exactly like old times, but…"

"Old times were fun, Dad," I interrupted, my heart cracking in half at what he wanted from me. "I love the memories we have from when I was younger, but this is our life." I shook my head, strands of platinum blonde hair danced across my face. "This is my life," I corrected, "and I'm happy with it. I'm happy in this house. It's my last year before going off to college, I don't wanna move out just yet. For now, this is my home. I'll visit you though. All the time," I rushed on. "We can even do sleepovers on the nights you're not on call or working in the emergency room."

"I want you happy, baby girl." It came out low, barely above a whisper. "More than anything, I want you happy, and I know this hasn't been easy for you. Seeing your mom withdraw from us, yell at us. It's not who she is and she hates that she can't control it or protect you from herself. She wants you to move in with me."

Shock jarred me. Hurt made everything worse. My mom wanted me to leave her. She didn't want me to live with her anymore. That… that was worse, far worse than anything else she'd ever done. Worse than the times she couldn't control the rage and would hit me. Worse than the times she cried endlessly for days. Worse than the times she slept for countless hours and refused to eat. Worse than the times she hurt herself, cutting and bruising her own skin to lessen the pain in her head. Me, her daughter, she didn't want anymore.

But she needed me.

I forced my lips upward in a smile and narrowed my

41

eyes at my dad. "You get sleepovers, Dad. We'll binge watch those dumb superhero movies you love so much. Deal?"

He grinned, and the gesture made him look younger than his fifty years. "What color nail polish should I buy for these sleepovers?"

I giggled. "Is the nail polish for me or you?"

"Both of us." He held his hands out in front of him and examined his fingernails. "I think yellow is my color."

"Obviously." I rolled my eyes.

"You're good to me, kid. You know that, right? Most kids would hate me right now."

"Well," I tapped my chin and continued to tease him in the hopes of keeping the mood light. "I almost started hating you, but Nicole showed me this gorgeous dress I absolutely have to have for the Fall Ball. Then I decided I needed to be on your good side, so you'd hand over the money."

"Oh, so this is bribery?"

"At its finest."

"How much is your love going to cost me?" He raised his brows and God, I loved him. His sense of humor, the way we joked with another, how easy it was to fall in to his charm, and forget all the hurt.

I coughed while also giving him the cost.

"What was that?" He stuck his pinky finger in his left ear and twisted it around. "Your old man's hearing isn't as great as it used to be. A hundred and eighty dollars? Is that what you said?"

I widened my eyes while I chewed on my bottom lip, giving him my most innocent look. "Yeah."

"Face of an angel." He shook his head. "How can I

say no when you look at me like that?"

"What?" My mouth dropped open where it hung for a few seconds before I snapped it shut. "You're actually gonna give me the money?"

"Yeah, kid." He grinned. "The dress is yours. You're going to need shoes too, right?"

"I..." I should've been happy. This was what I wanted, still my gut twisted in agony. "Dad, you know I was joking, right? I'm not angry with you or Mom. I get it. I don't need that dress." I shrugged. "There's others I can pick from. I was just teasing you."

"When was the last time you asked me for something that wasn't school related?" He paused. "It's been so long, I can't remember. You're getting the dress you want, shoes and makeup too. If you want to get your hair done, let's do it."

The tension in my shoulders and back subsided. Not much, but enough for happiness to filter through. "Technically, this is school related," I pointed out as I played with the last bits of my food.

"Then I can probably write it off come tax season."

I snorted. "You're such a dork."

"Noted. Make an appointment at the hair salon. Get your nails and hair done. Don't they have people who do makeup at the mall? Get that done, too. This is your last Fall Ball. Make it special."

I jumped from my seat, left my food – it wasn't like I could eat much anyway – and ran to my dad where I crashed into him for a hug. "Thank you."

With my arms around his neck, he stood up and hugged me back. Resting his chin on the top of my head, he said, "You're gonna need a dress for prom too, huh?"

I smiled in to his chest. "Yeah, you probably should've thought about that before agreeing to spend all this money on the Fall Ball."

He planted a loud kiss against my hair. "Looks like I'm gonna be broke by the time you graduate."

"You can always pick up extra hours at the hospital," I suggested.

"Get out of here, brat. Go do homework or better yet, call Nicole and tell her how you have the best Dad in the world."

I looked at him from over my shoulder as I made my way to my bedroom. "You're pretty okay."

He tossed a dishtowel at my departing back and hit me on my shoulder. I shrugged it off and watched it fall to the floor.

"Stop making a mess or you're going to have more stuff to clean while I study." I gave him a quick wink before I turned down the hall that led to my room.

My mom's room, the room my dad and her had shared since before I was born, remained closed. I lingered in front of it with my hand on the door knob, willing myself to open it. Knowing I wouldn't be welcome if I did. I rested my forehead on the wall, my heart fought against its cage, trying to escape. But we were stuck. Not like the prison that made up my school, but a certain kind of hell that brought me both love and hate, tears and joy, hope and despair.

With my dad leaving, the hope, the love, the joy, would go with him. While my mom still had good days, they weren't enough. They didn't last long enough for me to enjoy them. For me to find peace in them.

I should move in with my dad until I graduate. She

wanted me to. He wanted me to.

No one who knew my situation would blame me. But no one knew my situation.

On a sigh, I walked to my room. Immediately, I pulled out my phone to put on some music but instead tapped on the text icon when I saw I had a few messages I'd missed during dinner.

> *Danny: Hey Brin u ok?*
>
> *Danny: U seemed kind of off... just wanted to check on u*
>
> *Danny: U can talk to me. Uk that right?*

I clutched the phone close to my chest and wondered how it'd feel to tell him, tell someone about my mom. How her mind had been slowly disappearing since the summer before eighth grade. How she hid from the world on her bad days, and how I hid from her on her worst days. How I hoped she'd find me. Not with a fist closed in unrestrained fury, but with arms open in love.

How I went to doctors for yearly tests because her condition was genetic and discovered that one day, I could be just like her.

I just wished I knew more. Wished I could ask my dad the questions I needed answers to, but he hated talking about the disease that took my mom from him.

Silence was how we dealt with her disorder. My dad hadn't even been the one to tell me what my future could hold. No, it was my mom during one of her manic episodes. I could still remember the way her fists rained across my body as she let slip my greatest fear. It wasn't her fists that hurt me that day. It was her words.

It was my dad being gone while working at the hospital with the erratic schedule kept. He was never there to protect me from my mom's fury. Not that he knew about the abuse. It was just another secret I kept to shield him.

It was my dad's silence that gutted me. He didn't even have the courage to tell me, and I didn't have it in me to ask him and further break his heart.

It was the whispers after the tests were run, when my dad talked to the doctor in private. Where I couldn't hear anything about my future.

Because I didn't want him looking at me with the same sad desperation he gave my mom, I never spoke about it. Never let him know that I knew one day I could wind up just like my mom and how terrified I was of the future. I only let him see the parts of me he wanted to see, while I searched for answers on the Internet. Which only confused me more because nothing I found matched my mom's symptoms.

I swallowed hard, pushing back the tears. Another text came in.

> Danny: Txt me back. u don't have to talk if u don't want to. Tell me u r ok. I just need to know u r ok.
>
> Me: I'm ok. Bad day, that's all.

I imagined myself telling him the truth. Would he be there for me? Be shocked? Horrified? Would he turn me away and share my secret with our school? They would laugh at me, all of them. Especially those who I pretend are weaker than me, the ones I preyed on because they were easy targets. Then they'd realize I am the weak one, never them.

> Danny: Want me to come over? I'll grab a bag of the small chocolate bars you're addicted to.

That made me smile. He cared, I knew he did even if I doubted it most times. Because of that, I had to give him something, so he wouldn't keep prodding. Half the truth would have to do.

> Me: I'm good, promise. My parents are getting a divorce. They told me this morning before I left for school. Guess they thought that was the perfect time to announce our new family dynamics.

Within seconds of hitting the send button, my phone rang. I shook my head when Danny's name showed up on my screen.

"Hey," I answered.

"Hey yourself, sweetheart," he said. "Look, I know you don't wanna talk about it. You never want to talk about anything that's bugging you, but I needed to tell you I've got you, okay? Divorce sucks." He pulled in a breath before he continued. "Been there, done that, wrote the damn book. Divorce sucks. I'm here if you need anything."

"Okay," I whispered in the phone. "Thanks, Danny. I don't know what I'd do without you."

He chuckled. "You don't know what you'd do without me? I'm the one who'd be lost without you. You make everything better."

"With my sandwiches and snacks?" I teased.

"With your sandwiches and snacks," he agreed. "And your friendship. Remember sixth grade when you threw a rock at that older kid who was picking on me?"

My heart stilled. I'd forgotten about that. About the fearless girl I used to be.

"Yeah," I breathed in the phone. "You've been a leech ever since."

He laughed. "And you'll never get rid of me." He paused, and the silence between us felt heavy. "You know, you're the only person who comes to my games to cheer me on?"

A knot built in my stomach and grew. I'd never thought about it before, but I couldn't remember a single time I'd seen his parents at his games. No aunts or uncles, cousins or grandparents.

"How many times have you stopped by practice to see how I'm doing or if I need anything?"

"And that makes me a good person?" I asked, needing to know if there was absolution for all the wrong I'd done with only a little good.

"It makes you a good friend." He breathed heavily in the phone. "You're pretty good at being mean, but usually you're only mean when you're defending yourself or someone else. Like how you stuck up for me when you were leaving lunch."

"Jacob didn't mean…"

"Tomorrow," he interrupted, "why don't we sit with some of my friends?"

"You don't want to sit with our group?"

"Do you?" he asked. "That's not my group, Brin. It's yours."

"Why do you sit with us then?"

"To sit with you, so you aren't alone," he replied.

Alone. In a group full of the loudest most popular kids, Danny stayed by my side, so I wouldn't be alone.

"There are other tables, other people you can be friends with," he urged.

"I like our table." I liked how the other students respected us, feared us. I wasn't ready to give that up. Not yet, maybe not ever. "Sit with whoever you want." Hurt made my voice sound small. "I'm good where I always sit. I'm not alone." It came out defiant, childish.

"I'm with you. Wherever you sit, I'll be next to you."

I shook my head, not understanding why Danny was so good to me. Sixth grade was a long time ago. I wasn't that girl anymore. I'd proven that time and time again when I'd stay quiet while my friends made fun of the only person who was willing to stick by me.

"All I'm saying," he continued, "is you've been there for me, let me be there for you."

Tears welled behind my eyes, and my throat constricted as they built. "I'll let you know."

I wouldn't. I couldn't let anyone in.

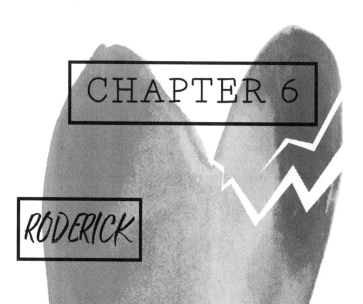

CHAPTER 6

RODERICK

My shift at Giorgio's ice cream shop was slow. With the storm looming overhead, the clouds opening and closing with such unpredictability, I wouldn't have expected anything less. Even the surfers stayed away from the beach on days like this. I was surprised when Giorgio sent me home an hour after I started. And then told me not to return until the following week when the forecast was expected to clear.

With my head throbbing and my stomach growling, I stepped into the rain. Of course, the rain had waited for me to leave work to start its descent. At least it meant I could bathe outdoors with the shampoo, conditioner and soap I'd taken from my aunt's house when I left. Maybe then Brinley wouldn't have any snide comments about my hygiene. I should've gone by my aunt's earlier to take some food too, but I hadn't expected Giorgio to cut my hours.

Already I'd gone through last week's paycheck when I went to the laundromat to do laundry instead of doing it at my aunt's house. Where I wound up buying a guy who looked even more lost than me two sandwiches, potato chips and a drink.

Shit.

Anyone who knew my situation would think I was stupid for leaving my aunt's house, but no one knew about my situation. Despite our many arguments, I knew she cared about me, that wasn't the problem. She'd taken me into her house, given me a place to stay, and that was where the problem lay. It was her house and even after five years, I still felt like a guest. One who, according to our latest argument, had overstayed his welcome.

By the time I made it back to the cave, I was drenched. Trekking through town and then the woods had exhausted me. Tired but determined to not give the school's princess more ammunition, I rummaged through one of my bags and grabbed my razor, toothbrush, and toothpaste. I took it back outside where I'd left the soap, shampoo and conditioner. After stripping my clothes, I bathed in the ice cold water raining down from the sky. My teeth shattered against the hard lashes of rain while I bounced from one foot to the other. Once my body and hair were clean, I put soap on my face and shaved with trembling fingers. Without a mirror, I could only hope I'd do a decent enough job.

Thunder rolled and I turned my head to the sky when it illuminated with brilliant lightning. Between the gloomy clouds, lightning flashed from the sky to the ground, negating the darkness from the storm.

Turning on my tip toes, I ran into the cave and dried myself with a towel. Quickly, I dressed into the clothes I'd taken with me before I left my aunt's house. When my limbs continued to shake, I put on my hoodie and without eating, I hunkered down for the night with a thin blanket tight around me. But still the shaking wouldn't stop.

I closed my eyes, willed myself to sleep. Thunder bellowed, lightning flashed across the cave. Throughout the night, the rain never stopped. The chilly wind howled as thunder made the earth beneath me vibrate.

Inside of myself, I drowned.

THE ALARM ON my phone sounded and with a groan, I sat up. The few hours of sleep I'd gotten weren't nearly enough, but I got up from my makeshift bed. Wet.

Everything around me was wet – the cold ground, my sheets, and myself. At least, I'd gotten up in the middle of the night to put my bag of clothes, my book bag, and my phone on higher ground when the rain started careening in. But I'd been too tired to look for another spot to lie in.

Grabbing my phone, I turned off the alarm. It had half battery left. Hopefully my homeroom teacher would let me leave it with her to charge for the day again.

I took off the wet clothes that clung to me like second skin and dried myself with the towel that was still wet and cold from the dropping temperature last night. After putting on clean clothes, I brushed my teeth using a bottle of water to rinse my mouth and put on deodorant. Lifting both my arms, I sniffed, hoping I didn't smell like the desperation I felt.

I still had a few hours before I had to be at school, so I started doing the homework I hadn't finished at the laundromat yesterday. There wasn't much left and I finished it quickly which left me with some time to waste before I had to start walking to school.

After grabbing a granola bar, I went to the wall furthest from my bed, so I could continue writing what I started the night before last.

It was my mark on a world that seemed to stop caring about me when my world fell apart. Sure, it was my parents who'd died, but they took me with them, or at least they took the good, working parts of me. All that was left was the gnawing anger I couldn't rid myself of.

Words had a way of calming me though, of helping me make sense of the nonsensical. So I wrote, anywhere and everywhere. The wall was my latest project. I promised myself I'd fill the cave with myself, so anyone who ventured inside would know me. Know that once I had existed. That once I had mattered to two people who would always matter the most to me.

When I got to the wall, I sucked in a sharp breath and stared at the feminine handwriting beneath my own words. Neat, tidy, perfect. Each word was probably thought out, mulled over before she wrote her poem beneath mine. Or maybe it was a spontaneous reaction to my words. A warning of sorts.

A broken soul
can turn cold.
No one can make it alone.

Except I had been making it alone for years. Whoever wrote the poem didn't understand the peace found in being alone. Even on the best days, I still missed my parents. Always would. But that's why alone fit me so well.

Not in the cramped house I lived in with my aunt. Where she asked too many questions and left even more unanswered. She cared about me, but not enough to dig and expose all the ugly, shattered pieces.

A broken soul

I wondered if she knew what it truly meant to be broken. To have nothing or no one to call your own. To live in a home that wasn't yours. In a body that wrapped around your bones too tight, suffocating everything until you couldn't breathe. Until even your heart wanted to give up.

Even though I didn't know her, the girl behind the broken soul, I didn't want her to give up. Whether she was younger or older than me, I wanted her to live.

With fingers numb from the blinding cold, I grabbed my black marker. I imagined her fingers wrapped around it, leaving her own mark in my life. Already, I felt better knowing I wasn't alone. The loner who sought solitude, wasn't alone, but had a faceless friend who felt as drained in existence as I did.

A broken soul
but not an empty shell.

The human heart
YOUR heart
beats with everlasting resiliency.
With threads of strength
sew yourself back together.
You can do it alone
or we can do it together.

I stared at my words, hoped it brought her strength to fight whatever she was up against. And I hoped she'd fight with me. So, I wouldn't have to be as alone as I kept telling myself I wanted to be.

CHAPTER 7

Brinley

LAST NIGHT WAS one of the worst. My mom shrieked from her room. Her cries echoed into the hall while her fist slammed against the wall. Even two rooms down, I heard her. Heard my dad try to calm her. And for what? In a month, maybe less or more, he'd be gone. And it would just be my mom and me.

It wouldn't be like the nights he worked at the hospital. Those nights were hard, but at least they hadn't been permanent. There'd always been the promise of his return. But now, there was no reprieve. There would be no placating her. Just more bruises from trying. While my dad wore most of the bruises, I had my share. Once he was gone, no longer a buffer between us, the scars would all belong to me.

I buried my head beneath my pillow, slapped my

hands over my ears. Still, I could hear her.

But no one heard me. No one heard my cries, my wails, my sobs of injustice. Only hers.

My dad's red-rimmed eyes greeted me as he handed me a cup of coffee. Averting my eyes, I took it from him and poured it in a travel mug. With my book bag hanging over my shoulder, I kissed his cheek and made my way to the door without either of us saying a word.

I paused at the entrance, took in my dad—his wrinkled clothes, the frown etched across his face, and the way his shoulders slumped down in defeat.

"Love you," I said when I pulled the door open.

"Think about what I said last night," he called after me. "It can be just you and me, kid."

I shook my head, sadness sinking into my skin, into my soul.

"Love you, sweet girl," he said as I closed the door.

His voice sounded the same as I felt.

Lost. So damn lost and sad. Broken.

Not able to wait until school finished, I drove to the park. In my car, I waited in front of a large tree on the opposite side where Roderick would cross when he made his way to school. Once I saw him, his figure in nothing but a short sleeve shirt and shorts huddled against the freezing wind, I waited for him to round the corner so I could drive to my spot.

I parked without looking around and sprinted toward the cave. My cave, his cave. Ours.

I was out of breath by the time I made it and was taken aback when I saw wet clothes and sheets draped over rocks. I hadn't even realized I was standing in a puddle until I looked down. It'd rained last night, but stuck in my own misery, I hadn't thought about how it would affect Roderick.

Shame slammed into me. It wasn't a foreign emotion to me, but it was a bitter one to swallow.

Roderick had slept here, cold and wet while I cried myself in and out of sleep in my warm bed. It wasn't fair. None of it was.

Without thinking, I took his wet clothes, his sheets and pillow case, leaving the wet pillow drying on a rock and hiked the two miles back to my car to drive home.

By the time I made it home, my dad had left for work, and I was six minutes away from being late for homeroom. Not wanting to worry my dad with an unexpected call from the office, I sent him a quick text.

> Me: Not feeling great... sore throat and head-
> ache. Came back home to rest. I'll head back to
> school later today when I'm feeling better.

I tossed Roderick's laundry in the washing machine and added detergent before closing the lid on the quickest cycle.

> Dad: Stay home if you're not feeling well. School
> will still be there tomorrow. Or next week.

I grinned.

> Me: A week?!? Think of all the work and gossip
> I'd miss. Wait... don't think about it! I'm already
> breaking out in hives.

Leaving everything in the wash, I went to the kitchen and poured myself a glass of orange juice and mentally kicked myself. In my haste to clean Roderick's clothes and sheets, I hadn't looked at the wall to see if he'd written me back. All I could think about was making sure by the time he got back from school his stuff was clean and dry. Without ever knowing it was me helping him—the girl he called *princess* with such heated hatred.

I didn't know his situation, why he wasn't living with his aunt anymore, and maybe I was out of line in grabbing his belongings, but at the moment it felt like the right thing to do.

An incoming text went off on my phone.

> Dad: How'd I end up with a kid with such a smart mouth?
>
> Dad: Seriously, listen to your old man. Stay home and rest. I'll bring home some antibiotics in case you need them

My dad, the doctor, who prescribed antibiotics to his daughter without even looking me over. For all he knew, it was my time of month and cramps were raking over my body. But then again, I'd never stayed home from school unless I had a fever or some sort of stomach flu. Even then I argued I had to go to school. Because home… most days, was hell in and of itself.

> Me: Thanks, Dad. Now go be a doctor and save some lives or something
>
> Dad: Cape on. Time to be a hero

Rolling my eyes, I snorted.

I settled on the couch with my glass of juice and a book I'd been wanting to read. The words merged together, making them more than words but a life, a new one that now belonged to me. I became the heroine, living a life so different than mine. Not better or worse, but different – with its own struggles, with love and sadness, laughter and tears. By the time the washing machine dinged, the hero looked a lot like Roderick.

Setting the book down, I shook my head as I made my way to the laundry room where I transferred all of Roderick's stuff in the dryer and again set it to go through a quick cycle.

My mind, relentless in so many ways, kept circling around Roderick and why I'd made him out to be a hero of any sorts. Especially mine.

We didn't like each other. Not anymore. Not for years.

We weren't friends, barely spoke unless it was to toss insults at one another.

Yet I'd found solace in him. In his words. So much so, that I was no longer angry at him for taking my safe haven, but worried. With his name and face floating in my mind, I made him a peanut butter and jelly sandwich. And then another one. I grabbed him some snacks, including apples and pears that were once his favorite.

I wondered if they still were. Or if, because of me, we'd drifted so far apart that I no longer knew anything about him. Just as he no longer knew anything about me.

But words. We had that in common. Something we hadn't shared before.

With food and clean clothes and one of my pillows in two garbage bags, I sent my dad a text to let him know I was heading to school and then made my way back to the cave. After putting everything on a rock so it wouldn't get wet, I went to the wall. Our wall where our hearts bled freely, uniting us.

A broken soul
but not an empty shell.
The human heart
YOUR heart
beats with everlasting resiliency.
With threads of strength
sew yourself back together.
You can do it alone
or we can do it together.

Tears swam behind my eyes and I let them fall. One after the other, they swam down my cheek and dropped from my chin to the ground. I didn't swat them away or wish them into inexistence. Because this time I wasn't alone. I had Roderick.

I had his words.

CHAPTER 8

Brinley

"So HAPPY YOU could join us today," Mr. Scott said as soon as I slipped into class, over twenty minutes late.

"Sorry," I muttered, keeping my head down, my eyes downcast. They were still red from the tears I'd shed at the cave and then again in my car. My skin looked too pale and my hands were shaking. I'd tried touching up the makeup I'd applied earlier that morning, but really all I cared about was getting to this class so I could see Roderick.

"Wasn't feeling that great," I said.

I sat down in front of Roderick's table and after taking out my folder, I turned to face him. Angry eyes bore in to me, so I looked back down, letting my hair hide my face and took out the paper we were supposed to work on.

"Sorry I'm late. Were you able to get anything done

without me?" I whispered.

"No," he ground out.

With my head still tipped down, I peered up at him to see the muscles on his jaw tick.

"It's a group project, princess. I don't give out free rides and I'm not working on it without you."

"Sorry," I repeated under my breath.

Beside me, Danny looped an arm over my shoulder as he pressed a kiss to the side of my head. I leaned into him, into his strong embrace.

"You okay?" Danny asked.

I nodded.

"We only have a few minutes before class is over," Roderick hissed. "Think we can get some work done?"

"Hey man," Danny said. "Lay off her. She's having a tough time."

"Having a tough time?" He barked out a laugh. It was harsh and coiled around me, tightening around my skin and bones.

"Yes." I snapped my head up. Our eyes crashed against one another and he took a sharp inhale when he saw me. With my chin sticking out, I tucked a strand of hair behind my ear and stood up. "Even the shallow princess has feelings. Shocking, isn't it?"

Grabbing my book bag, I stuffed my work in it and left with Mr. Scott calling my name. I ignored him. Ignored the curious looks from my classmates. When I heard the door open and close behind me, I expected Danny to be the one who followed me.

Not Roderick. Never Roderick.

But it was Roderick's hand that landed tentatively on my shoulder. His fingers that dug into my skin when he stood in front of me. His pleading eyes that asked too many questions.

I blinked back the tears, swallowed past the lump in my throat.

"Brinley." He said my name so quietly I wasn't sure if he'd actually spoken or if I'd imagined it.

I stared at his unmoving lips.

"Brinley." This time his lips moved and I moved with them.

I wrapped my arms around his waist, not sure if he'd welcome the embrace. Part of me wanted him to shove me away, but when his hands snaked across my back, I rested my head against his chest where I listened to the steady beat of his heart. Only it didn't remain steady. While his arms locked behind me in a secure hug, his chest heaved as his heart picked up a rapid rate.

I kissed his chest and pulled away with a somber smile playing on my lips. "I'm sorry."

He caressed my face with the back of his hand. "That's four times you've apologized today."

I laughed. "And to think, princesses don't apologize. Guess that means I've been dethroned."

He searched my face, his eyes dancing across my features, but he wouldn't find what he was looking for. Not when I had to shut down before I let him in any further.

"I-I shouldn't have hugged you." I stared at my shoes as I schooled my expression. "That was a mistake, but you came after me." My voice broke. "Don't come after me again, Roderick."

"Right." He shifted from one foot to the other. They were covered in mud, probably still wet. "Why can't I go after you again? We used to be friends. Even if I hate you, I hate seeing you hurting even more."

I flinched at his words. He hated me. *Hated.* And I deserved it. I'd done everything to push away the people who would look too closely. Because no one could know what I tried so desperately to hide. No one.

"Brin." Danny came beside me. I went into his open arms, buried my face in his chest.

"We're not friends," I told Roderick.

We couldn't be. I knew his secret, and it'd be safe with me. I'd never tell a soul and would do whatever I could to help him without him knowing. But my secrets? I didn't trust them with anyone.

I DREADED LUNCHTIME, something I'd never hated before, but today was different. I didn't want to sit with my friends. I didn't want to sit alone either. Alone was the enemy.

Roderick's words, his written promise, to fight with me, ran in my head as I stood in line for a turkey burger. Absently, I put a hand in the front pocket of my jeans to touch the paper I'd written his poem on. It brought me strength. Made me want more for myself, from myself. I wanted to fight with him just as badly as I'd wanted to stay in his arms.

But he hated me.

And I hated me.

More than that, I hated what I might become. I had to keep pretending though, keep pushing.

"Hey Brinley, you okay?" I spun around to find Seth's worried gaze on me.

"Yeah, thanks." I licked my lips. "I'm sorry, you know? Of course you don't." I shook my head on a humorless laugh. "Why would you know I'm sorry for all the times I've been mean to you, but I am, Seth. So sorry. That's not me. Or it is." Another laugh. "But it also isn't."

His brows drew together, eyes boring into me as if he were trying to figure me out. "It's okay. I'm an easy target." He shrugged his shoulders as if that made everything my friends and I had done to him and to others like him alright.

"You're one of the good ones." I turned around and followed the line forward before I peered back at him. "Not at all like me or my friends," I added.

He smiled and nodded. Maybe he understood, maybe he got it better than me.

After paying for lunch, I went outside where I normally sat with my group of friends, but rather than going to them, I stood there. Frozen.

From our table, Danny watched me. Patiently waited for me to make a decision. He'd mentioned earlier he didn't want to sit at our regular table, but again I had insisted. And now… now indecision warred.

"If you want, you can sit with us," Seth offered, his voice shaking with nerves.

"Why would you want me to sit with you?"

"I think… I think you're one of the good ones too."

66

My hands shook around my tray and God, I wanted to hug him. Tell him how badly I wanted that to be true.

"I'm not," I replied, "but I'm going to start trying to be."

He inclined his head to the side, another invitation to join him and his friend Jeremy. A slow smile creeped across Danny's face. Even though he sat at our regular table, if I went with Seth, I knew he'd follow. Licking my lips again, I took a deep breath. I could do this. Sit with the kids everyone made fun of. Open myself up to ridicule.

We only had six months before graduation. Six months before I went off to college and started a new life outside of this beach town. I wanted to become someone new. Someone I liked. Why couldn't I start now instead of waiting six months?

I smiled back at Seth, my reply on my tongue, when Jacob ran into him. Seth's tray tilted, but he caught it before it could fall.

Jacob chuckled. "Loser," he said loudly in Seth's ear. He wound an arm over my shoulders. "Let's go, Brin."

My heart wanted to stay with Seth, to sit with him and shrug out of Jacob's hold, but I knew better. Knew where I belonged. I sent him an apologetic nod. He looked directly at me. His lips pulled down in a scowl. And I saw it. This was my fault. Because I'd been talking to him.

Taking my usual spot next to Danny, I sat at our table and fiddled with the wrapper that covered my turkey burger. I was hungry, but not really. Jacob and Joseph high-fived each other while everyone at the table laughed. All except Danny, who rested his hand on my lap, grounded me to the here and now when all I wanted was to go back to the cave. To hide in Roderick's words.

But I had them. Etched to memory in my mind and on a piece of folded paper in my jeans. I wanted to be resilient. I wanted to sew myself together. Stronger, braver. And I wanted to do it with Roderick.

"Did you see that scrawny loser's face?" Mariah asked on a laugh. "He was all…" she made a dumbfounded look.

Fisting my hands, I reminded myself to breathe.

Inhale.

Exhale.

They – these people I surrounded myself with – they didn't matter. What I did mattered. What I didn't do mattered.

"You're welcome, Brin." Jacob's smile was big, showed off perfect white teeth.

"What am I thanking you for?" I asked.

His brows shot up in mock horror. "For Seth. Just 'cuz your gay-ass boyfriend likes him, doesn't mean he should be talking to you."

Danny's grip on my lap hardened. I took his hand in mine, twining our fingers together when I leaned on his shoulder.

"You and I are so much alike, aren't we Jacob?" I asked.

He nodded on a grin.

"We make fun of people to show others how beneath us they are." I brought Danny's and my joined hands to my lips and kissed the back of his hand. "The truth is, we're the ones beneath them. We're the ones not worth a shit, but it's easier, isn't it? To distract others so they don't see us?"

Joseph's eyes widened. Jacob shot up from where he sat, slamming his hands on the table.

"What are you sayin', Brin?" Joseph asked through gritted teeth.

"Isn't it obvious?" I shrugged. "Danny and Seth and everyone else we ridicule are the good ones. The better ones. Jacob and I," I shook my head, "we're the assholes." I looked at each of my friends that sat around me at our table. "We're all assholes."

"Yeah?" Jacob rested his fists on the table and leaned in to me.

I didn't back away, didn't turn to Danny when he let go of my hand and stood beside me. I held my gaze level with his, threw my shoulders back. "Yeah. You know it, don't you? That's why you pick on Seth, why you talk crap about Danny. You'll never be even a fraction of who they are."

Joseph was the first to react. A fist flew above me, almost making contact with Danny's face. Danny grabbed Joseph's wrist, pulled him across the table while the rest of us jumped from our seats. But it wasn't Danny, Joseph or Danny's football team that suddenly surrounded us that held my attention.

Jacob strolled past the few tables to where Seth and his friend sat. They stayed seated while I watched, wanting to look away, afraid to do so. Because I'd caused this, hadn't I? Egged Jacob on.

Jacob uncapped his soda and after taking a quick swig, he poured it over Seth's food. If that weren't enough, Jacob then splashed the little that remained in Seth's face. He took it. Seth took it all with a brave look that I couldn't help but admire.

I respected him for it. For not jumping out of his seat. For not feeding in to Jacob's actions.

I moved without thinking. Moved without realizing where I was going until I stood behind Jacob. Bracing a hand on his shoulder, I pulled him to the side. He shrugged out my hold.

"That's enough," I whispered. "You've proven my point."

When I turned, Jacob gripped my wrist, tugged me to him. Danny was by my side within seconds and grabbed Jacob's shirt by the collar. I let him deal with him, let myself walk away only to take my unopened sandwich and put it on the table in front of Seth along with some napkins.

"I'm sorry," I said, my voice low. "I'm so sorry, Seth."

I couldn't look at him, wouldn't look at him as I took the wet tray from in front of him and left it on top of a trash bin. With the sound of screaming and whistling behind me, I left not bothering to look back. Familiar footsteps sounded behind me and I turned around when they got closer.

"Hey." Danny hugged me. It was a tight embrace, one I didn't want to end, but I did. I was done being the shallow princess. I was done being someone I hated. Even if it left me alone.

"Go sit with Seth," I said buried against his broad chest. "I just made him an even bigger target. He needs someone who can defend him."

He kissed the top of my head. "What about you?"

I tucked my hand into my pocket, touched the poem I hid there. "I'm fine."

Or at least I would be.

CHAPTER 9

RODERICK

I watched it all unfold from my spot under a tree. Brinley looked scared but fierce. Determined.

The only kink in her armor showed when she watched Danny walk away. But she maintained her composure. When she pulled out a piece of paper from her pocket, relief flooded her. She held the piece of paper to her chest as she walked to her next class.

When I couldn't see her anymore, I followed her. She leaned her back against the wall and dropped her bottom to the ground. Her eyes never looked up from the piece of paper she held. I waited for her to open it, to read what was so dear to her heart.

Slowly, meticulously, she unfolded the paper and dipped her head down to read its contents. Pretty lips twitched until they finally stretched in a smile. It was her smile that undid me. The pure joy and relief she found in words I couldn't read.

Digging into my book bag, I took out a granola bar. I hadn't eaten since this morning when I scarfed down a bar for breakfast. Since money and food weren't things I had readily available, I was saving this bar for dinner.

Long, rushed strides carried me to Brinley. She peeked up from behind her paper. A blush crept over her cheeks and she folded the paper quickly.

"Here." I tossed the bar at her.

It landed on her lap. She looked at it and then at me. Her eyes squinted and I shuffled under her scrutiny.

"Thanks," she mumbled.

Silence thickened the air between us. It grew, expanding in my chest. I wanted to leave, but didn't want to leave her alone.

"Wait!" she called out when I turned.

From her spot on the ground, she handed me half of the bar. The gesture alone made me hungrier than I was moments ago. I tipped my head in a silent thank you and after taking the bar from her outstretched hand, I ate it in two bites.

My stomach grumbled. I placed a hand over it to quiet it. Not the least bit appeased with the little I'd eaten the past few days, it twisted in protest.

"I'm gonna get a refill." I shook my empty bottle of water and bent down to grab hers.

At the water fountain, I steadied myself, my breathing. One act of kindness, one show of who she once was didn't mean the Brinley I knew from so long ago was back. But it was a start.

It made me wonder if I had her wrong all along. If

she hadn't ditched her friends to find new ones, but to surround herself with people who'd never care enough to see past the charade and find her scars.

The idea struck me hard, straight in my knotting stomach.

While I had thought Brinley had deserted me, maybe it was me who'd deserted her.

When I returned her bottle now full of water, she handed me back her half of the bar, which she had tucked back in to the wrapper.

"I can't eat." She motioned toward the bar she held out to me. "My stomach hurts."

"You're sure?"

"Yeah."

This time I ate slower, washing down each bite with a swallow of water. I hoped that would hold me over until tomorrow because now... now I didn't have anything left to eat until I could scrounge up some snacks with the loose change I'd been picking up.

"Sit." She gestured to the empty spot beside her. After opening up one of her folders, she said, "Why don't we work on our assignment? You know, since I was super late to class and then stormed out in the most dramatic fashion." She eased her lips in a smile that fell when I didn't return it.

"What's going on with you?" I asked, searching her face for something, a hint of what she kept hidden.

She eased her head against my shoulder. I stiffened. Not because I didn't like her there, but because I liked it too much. I liked the feel of her closeness the same way I liked how she had felt when she'd wrapped her arms around me and rested her head on my chest. With a jerk she pulled away. It didn't feel right, her pulling away from me. I cupped the side of her face and moved her so that she rested her face back on my shoulder.

"Circle shallow," she whispered. It sounded broken. *She* sounded broken.

She closed her eyes when I took our assignment from her. I hated circling it, hated that I was the one who'd called her shallow. There was more to her than that. More to her than she wanted anyone to see.

I let my eyes dart across the paper, looking for a word that was true. A truth she kept hidden.

Depth.

"I think I was wrong about you," I whispered, my breath brushing across the top of her head, making a few strands of her blonde hair dance.

She peered up at me, slowly blinked a few times. I tapped the paper with the eraser of my pencil.

"You pretend to be shallow so no one can see your depth," I said.

"You don't know that." Her words bled from her lips. She wanted to believe me, wasn't sure if she could. "You don't know me anymore."

"I do," I resolved. "You're still the same girl who helped me through the hardest time of my life."

"Yeah." She huffed. "That girl left you when you still needed her."

"Only to save herself." Long fingers brushed over her arm. Goosebumps spread wherever I touched. "I'm sorry I didn't see it before. I'm sorry I wasn't there for you when you needed me. I dunno, maybe I was still too lost to see it, to see you. But I see you now, Brinley. Whatever you need, I'm here."

It was true. Another truth I could give her. One I hoped she wouldn't hide from.

"What if you can't save me?"

"What if you can save yourself?" I countered.

What if you can save me?

CHAPTER 10

Brinley

Shunning your friends in front of everyone isn't something I'd recommend. It had a way of casting you out, making all your insecurities more visible.

The only reprieve I had was the short moments I spent with Roderick. His words healed a part of my soul I thought was tainted indefinitely. He wanted me to save myself. I wasn't sure I could.

Heck, I didn't know if I could live the words I clung onto. But I wanted to try. Didn't I deserve it—for myself, to try? To be resilient and strong.

They weren't words I'd thought of for myself. It didn't mean they couldn't be true.

I'd proven I had some sort of strength, hadn't I?

Danny, being the best friend I could ever ask for, stayed with me the rest of the day. Even in classes he didn't belong. The teachers let him though. There weren't many people who could resist his charm, including teachers.

He was good, better than good. Made the remainder of the day bearable when all I wanted to do was hide.

If I thought I'd been dreading lunch, it had nothing on the dread that settled on my shoulders as Danny walked me to cheer practice. Mariah and Nicole huddled together, both of them shooting me angry glares when I walked into the gym.

"I'll be at football practice," Danny said from beside me. "I'll come get you when I finish."

I nodded. "Okay."

He tipped my chin up, kissed both of my cheeks before he closed his arms around me. I loved his hugs. Loved how safe I felt in his arms.

"You're okay, sweetheart," he murmured in to my hair. "No one's gonna give you shit."

"Yeah?" I looked up at him, at my best friend. "You gonna kick a bunch of cheerleaders' asses if they do?"

He laughed. "You've got this, babe."

I did. I could do this. The past four years I'd built my life on pretending I was better than others. Now, I just had to show them the truth. I was nobody, nothing special. Just a scared girl that lashed out for all the wrong reasons.

"Thank you." His arms tightened around me.

I squirmed in his hold to hug his neck. On my tip toes, I kissed his cheek.

"You have nothing to thank me for."

Pain crossed his features, made my heart spasm in my chest. "I have everything to thank you for."

Our coach blew her whistle and after another quick squeeze, Danny let me go. I felt too exposed without him. Too vulnerable when he left the gym to go to the football field.

Our coach gathered some of her things while the girls stood in the center of the basketball court. Shoulders back, head up, I went to them.

"If Danny hugged me like that, I'd make sure to turn the poor guy straight," Mariah said when I reached the group. Her voice dripped with malice.

"You can't turn someone gay or straight," Nicole said.

She looked at me, her eyes shining with the same uncertainty I felt. I wanted to go to her, talk to her. She turned away, shut me out before I had the chance.

"You're either gay or you aren't," Nicole continued.

"Why are you two obsessed with his sexuality?" I questioned.

"Why aren't you?" Mariah quipped, her tone dry.

"Danny is Danny." I shrugged. "He's my best friend. That's all I care about."

"What a great friend you are." This dry remark came from Nicole. She stared at my white tennis shoes. "As long as he's there for you, you don't really care about anything else. That's what makes you an asshole. Not teasing others."

I jolted at her words, felt them in the pit of who I was. I wasn't a good friend. Not to her, not to Danny. I took care of myself first. Always. But that didn't mean I didn't care about them. That I didn't hurt when they did. That I didn't try to be there for them.

"Teasing others?" I focused on that. It was the only tangible comment I could respond to. "Is that what we call harassing people? Leaving nasty notes in people's lockers? Writing lies on the bathroom walls? What about Facebook? Where we continue to *tease* them because taunting them at school isn't enough?"

Nicole folded her arms over her chest. "This is high school. We're supposed to do that." She paused. "And if we don't, then someone else will."

"Then I'll let someone else do it for me."

"Then you'll be the one targeted."

My bottom lip wobbled. I forced a smile on my face. As if I didn't care. As if being on top where others couldn't pry, didn't matter.

It did though. It mattered too much. Because if they found out what I was hiding, my life would be over.

"Brinley!" Our coach called out. "You're on."

I didn't feel the lightness I normally felt before we started. And as I walked the girls through our routine, I didn't care for perfection. Didn't care if they knew the moves. My only goal was to exhaust myself. Maybe then, I'd find sleep tonight.

CHAPTER 11

Brinley

"Hey." The familiar voice of Seth stopped me as I made my way out of the gym.

Mariah slammed her shoulder against him when she walked by. He held his ground, barely moved, but kept his chin tucked down to his chest.

"Hey back," I said.

I waited. Letting him decide if he wanted to talk to me, or if he hated me the way he should.

He stared at his shuffling foot for a long time, so I finally broke the silence.

"Danny's still in practice," I said, looking to the field. "He should be done in about five or ten minutes. Wanna sit with me while I wait for him?" I gestured toward the picnic table a few feet from us.

"Yeah." He stalled. "Sure. My mom should be here to

pick me up any minute."

We let our book bags rest on the bench while we sat on the table. The silence was awkward. Deafening.

I fidgeted with my fingers, hoping Danny would finish soon. Lightning struck the next town over, but at least it wasn't raining here. Yet. From the gray clouds moving toward us, I knew it wouldn't be long until the sky opened up.

"Thanks." He nudged my leg with his. "For today. Danny said you stood up for me, before Jacob... you know," he finished with a smirk.

I tapped his leg back with mine. "I should've done it a long time ago."

"No one's ever done that for me before." He scrubbed his face with his hands several times. "No, actually Roderick has a few times, but no one else has."

"Roderick stood up for you before?" Disbelief caught in my throat, made my voice sound squeaky. I coughed to clear it. "That was cool of him."

"Yeah, our freshmen year and a few times after that." His fingers toyed with the fabric of his jeans. "I guess I should stick up for myself but..." he trailed off.

"You shouldn't have to."

"Yeah, I guess."

We were quiet again.

"What do you like to do?" I asked quickly. "You know, hobbies."

He shrugged. "My grandpa taught me how to cut wood a few years ago. I like making stuff."

That surprised me. To be honest, I expected him to say video games or computer stuff. Which was a dumb, stereotypical assumption. I knew that and felt ashamed about it. Woodwork sounded fun though. Making something from nothing but pieces of wood was far more intricate than joining words together to tell a story.

"That sounds really cool. What do you make?" I asked.

Another shrug, but this time his eyes lit up. "Furniture mainly. I made my grandpa a rocker to put on his front patio."

I covered his shoulder with my hand. "You did not! For real?"

He smiled, exposing two dimples I'd somehow missed throughout the years. "Yeah, I did. He loved it."

Excited, I hopped on my bottom, angled my knees toward him. "What else?"

"Grandpa and I made some picnic tables over the summer that we donated to that playground that opened up by the beach."

My mouth opened wide, and I snapped it shut with a loud click. "The ones with the cool designs carved into them?"

Red stained his cheeks and he nodded, keeping his head dipped down.

"I love them. I took so many pictures on my phone to show my mom." My voice caught, I coughed to clear my throat. "She loved them, too."

"Thanks." It was said with a hint of pride. He ran his hand over his phone. "I have pictures of other stuff I've made," he said but it came out sounding like a question.

"Oh, Seth, you have to show me!" Anticipation coursed through my veins and I tipped my hand out for his phone.

The dimples on his cheeks deepened as he unlocked

his phone. After going to his gallery, he handed it to me.

A gorgeous deep mahogany table. A swing hanging from a tree. A detailed figure of a pelican and another of a sailboat.

Creation after beautiful creation, I went through his pictures and saw the craft, the talent that hid beneath his skin.

I gasped. "This one." I turned his phone to him, showing him the picture of a small bookshelf. It was smaller than the one in my bedroom, but the details in the trim were outstanding.

He swiped to the next picture and with a grin, showed me the carvings he'd done on the side.

"Seth," I breathed out. "This is amazing. Do you sell these? Can I buy this one from you?"

"I made it for my grandma." This time, pride shone deeply in his face. "The one in the nursing home was falling apart."

"I bet she loved it."

"I could make one for you if you want."

I took in a sharp breath, bracing a palm against my chest. "Really?"

He nodded.

"I'd love it!"

A horn honked, and we both turned when a red car pulled up close to us. The passenger window rolled down and a woman waved.

"That's my mom." He stood up and I waved back at his mom. "I just wanted to say thanks, you know." He darted a quick look to his mom and then me. "So, thanks, Brin." When his arms came around my neck, I hugged him back, digging my fingers into the back of shirt.

In that moment, another part of me cracked. This boy, who I'd tormented throughout high school didn't just forgive me, he'd offered me his friendship during lunch. And when things went completely wrong, he took even more abuse. Still he made the effort to hang out with me and thanked me for helping him through something that should never have happened.

I watched him leave with my heart lodged in my throat, with despair stuck in my chest. I continued to stare long after his mom drove away.

Minutes passed by without me noticing.

All I heard, all I saw was Seth giving me more than I deserved.

"Mind if I sit with you?" Roderick's voice broke through the silence. "Maybe there's enough room on the table for freaks?" He tilted his head, offered me a smile, but it didn't look real. Sad, forlorn, that's what his smile screamed out.

Wrapping my arms over my stomach, I nodded. "You're not a freak."

"And you're not shallow."

I blew out a breath, drew in another one and held it in my lungs.

"What's going on with you?" he asked the same question he'd asked earlier.

The worry in his tone echoed in my head. It wasn't something I expected, not from Roderick when I'd done everything to shut him out and watched from a distance as he surrendered into himself. Without any friends to help him. Without me, who long ago told him I'd be there for him.

I patted the empty spot beside me. He joined me on the table where his shoulder brushed against mine. I reveled at the contact.

"Do you want to work on our blackout poem?" I asked.

"No."

Good, I didn't want to either.

Leaning over my knee, I reached for my book bag and pulled out a bag of chips I'd bought in case I ran into Roderick and could come up with an excuse to give it to him.

"Aha!" I exclaimed, ripping open the bag.

I shifted the open bag to him and he reached in. I followed suit. We ate together in silence, but it didn't feel uncomfortable like it had with Seth. There was tension radiating from his stiff posture to mine. There was anxiety from my tapping foot to his. But there was also a sense of calm, of contentedness that I felt deep in the marrow of my bones. Maybe it wasn't real. Maybe I put it there to make myself feel better, but I felt it all the same. Wrapped myself in the peace and let it infiltrate my system.

The wind picked up, blew swiftly, making my hair whip around my face. On a laugh, I pulled it up in a pony.

"I like your hair loose." Roderick reached for me, touched the ends of my hair. "I like it up too. You're pretty either way."

Leaves on the ground swirled in front of us. The heaviness of the storm grew closer. I was ready for it, or at least I thought I was.

"You think I'm pretty?"

He shook his head on a laugh. "No."

My stomach dropped at his cruel joke. Of course he didn't think I was pretty. He had no reason to think of me at all.

"I think you're beautiful."

I shifted my head to stare at him, and the way he looked back at me – his blue eyes pulling me from my despair – was everything.

"You've always been beautiful, but right now," he paused, "There's something different about you, something that makes you even more beautiful than usual.

"I want to be different. I want to change." It came out low, shaking with uncertainty.

I wasn't sure if he could feel the intensity vibrating in my system, but he swallowed hard as I inched closer to him.

"I want to be a better person."

Reaching for him, I combed my fingers through his jet black hair and when he closed his eyes on a groan, my lips parted.

"I like your hair." It came out breathless, as if my lungs fought against what came naturally to them.

I leaned in to him, my face inches from his, our lips a whisper apart. His eyes flew open, shocked but filled with the same want that filled me. His breaths fell on my face and I snuck out my tongue to taste my lips where his breath had caressed.

"Brinley." The way he whispered my name made me want more. Want everything.

I dug my fingers in to his scalp. "Kiss me, Roderick," I breathed.

His lips touched mine. Gently. Tentatively. Like a smile in the breeze. His lips felt soft against mine. With my fingertips, I touched his cheek, the sharp angle of his jaw. When his tongue brushed across the seams of my lips, I took him in.

This kiss… our kiss was like a dream I'd been waiting for my whole life.

CHAPTER 12

RODERICK

I KISSED BRINLEY Crassus. And what's more, she kissed me back.

It didn't last long. Just a few light brushes. When we parted though, I missed the feel of her soft lips on mine. Her warm tongue tangled with mine. I wanted more. Needed more time to explore her, to savor her.

Brinley blinked several times before she focused on my face. Her attention drew down to my lips and I heaved out a sigh when she grazed them with a single fingertip.

"You kissed me." Her lips tilted up in a smile.

I smiled back. "You told me to."

A blush crept up to her cheeks. It was cute and irresistible. I inched into her and kissed her nose. Tears welled behind her eyes and I hated them. Hated that something hurt her enough that she even had tears to shed.

With my hands bracing either side of her face, her eyelids fluttered closed as she drew out a sweet breath I immediately wanted to inhale so I could breathe Brinley in and hold her in my chest. Instead, I pressed a kiss over one eyelid and then the other.

She traced her hands over my arms and wrapped her fingers around my wrist. Eyes the shade of evergreen trees widened.

"You're cold," she whispered as if it were some sort of secret.

I laughed. "It's kind of cold outside," I joked.

She looked down to my chest, over the short sleeve shirt I'd put on since I didn't have any long sleeves that were wearable. She ran her hands over my chilled arms. I shivered at her touch.

"We should go inside, into the gym." She angled her head to the side. "Get out of the cold. I'll text Danny, so he knows I'm there."

I helped her off the table, keeping her hand in mine. I didn't want to let go. It'd been years since anyone had shown me any affection, years since anyone had held my hand or touched my face. I wasn't ready to let go. Maybe I never would be.

"What. The. Hell?" The grating sound of Nicole's voice reached us.

Beside me, Brinley's body jerked as if she'd been struck by the lightning that wasn't too far from us. Not wanting to embarrass her further, I dropped her hand. Her eyes danced across my face and when she looked away from me resigned and hurt, I felt it in my gut. In my soul.

I'd let her down. Only a few hours after telling her I'd be there for her.

"What's up, Nicole?" Brinley kept her voice bright as the fake smile I hated so much took over her face.

She was still beautiful, always beautiful. Even when I wanted to hate her, she was beautiful. But that wasn't the smile I wanted. No, the smile I wanted was the one she'd given me after we kissed. But I'd wiped it away without meaning to.

I reached for her hand, but she shook me away, dismissing me the same way I had dismissed her moments ago.

"Is the freak giving you trouble?" She sneered in my direction.

Brinley cast a quick look in my direction. Her eyes narrowed at me and I waited for the Brinley I'd grown accustomed to, to belittle me. To make me feel like the nothing I was.

"No." She peered back at her friend. "Roderick and I were hanging out while I waited for Danny to finish practice. Then I kissed him." She jutted out her chin, waited for Nicole to reply while I stood frozen in place with my mouth hanging open.

"Well, was it at least a good kiss?" Nicole asked with a smirk.

Brinley touched her parted lips. "The best."

"There you have it!" Nicole threw her hands in the air, either in frustration or joy – I couldn't tell. "My best friend has officially lost her damn mind." She grinned, but it felt misplaced. "Talking to losers, calling my non-boyfriend an asshole. Hell, calling all her friends and herself a bunch of assholes and now, kissing freaks."

Brinley's lips twitched and dumbfounded, I waited to see what she said next. "Seth is cool. If you talked to him for like five minutes, you'd see he's the better guy over Jacob."

Nicole made a face. I shoved my hands in my pocket and waited. Brinley looked at me, her expression still sad, still dejected. Because of me.

"And Roderick isn't a freak. But you and me," she pointed to herself and Nicole, "we are a bunch of assholes." She giggled, and even though I couldn't tell if it was real or pretend, it sounded like music to my ears. "All of our friends are assholes. You gonna try to deny that?"

"No." Nicole shook her head. "But it's nice being the asshole on top."

"Yeah, except I don't want to be that anymore," Brinley said, her voice low and shaken. "I'm tired of being that person."

"So that's it?" Nicole asked, her eyes turning red as tears welled behind them. "You were the first friend I made when I started here. You've been the only friend I could talk to, and you're just going to throw it away?"

"You know, we don't have to break up just because I don't want to be a jerk anymore." Her sass... the sass that lit me on fire when we were just kids returned and I wanted to kiss her again. And again.

"Jacob and Joseph aren't happy with you. I just wanted to find you and tell you. That's it."

Brinley reached for her friend but let her hands fall to her side when Nicole turned away. "Are we still going to the boutique Saturday?"

"No, not after what you did. Not after you pick the same people we've been making fun of and turn on your friends."

Brinley nodded, her fists clenching and unclenching beside her as she watched Nicole leave.

When Nicole was out of earshot I went to stand beside her and put a hand on her shoulder. "You don't need her."

She looked up at me, eyes glaring as if she could see right through me. "I don't need you either."

I ran my fingers over her face. She didn't move or flinch, just continued staring. It was as if the girl from my past had left. She was here for only a few minutes, but already I missed her.

"Go, Roderick. You hate me, remember?" she snapped. "Alone, that's how you like it? Go be alone."

She turned away from me and faced the field where Danny ran toward us. Immediately, he took her book bag from her and rummaged through it until he found what he was looking for. With a sandwich in hand, he smacked a kiss on top of her head. She leaned in to him, didn't bother looking my way.

Danny eyed me curiously.

"You two talkin'?" he asked.

"Something like that," I replied.

He nodded. "If you hurt her…"

"You'll hurt me," I finished for him. "Got it."

"We're not talking," Brinley said, her voice louder than it needed to be. "Let's go, Danny."

She took his hand, never once giving me a second glance. She walked away leaving me with my heart flayed open, bleeding on the ground.

THE CAVE I'D made my home was cold, but someone – the same someone who wrote poetry with me – had cleaned my wet, dirty clothes. Had cleaned my sheet and given me a new pillow while my old pillow remained wet on the rock.

She'd left me food and some bottles of water and soda. I bit into the pear first. It was my favorite and reminded me of my mom. How we'd eat pears every morning together and let the juice drip down our chins. The memory of it, of her, swallowed me, but rather than getting angry, I let it take me whole.

I remembered the ringing melody of her laughter. How she'd wrap her arms around me in a hug and splatter kisses on my face as I tried to squirm away. How she'd help me with my homework with a patience unlike any other. How she'd tease my dad about him being the better cook, so she wouldn't have to prepare dinner. How he'd wink in my direction and joke about the times she'd tried to poison him just to get out of cooking. How his eyes always followed her, love so evident in the way he watched her.

I choked on a sob, letting the sadness tear into me, destroy me while keeping the anger at bay. I owed it to my parents to think of them without the memory being tainted. Later, I could let the fury seep back in.

On shaky legs, I went to the wall with my flashlight after I finished eating the pear. I illuminated the wall, hoping to find a reply to my poem.

The kiss, the argument with Brinley had shaken me. But worse yet were the words she slung at me with such vehemence, as if she knew I didn't want to be alone. Maybe she'd tasted the desperation on my tongue.

Taking a deep breath, I looked at the wall, looked for the girl's handwriting and drank in her words.

Together.
We fight together,
desperately together.
We both dwell in darkness,
our souls broken into jagged pieces,
but look!
Look how perfectly we fit together.

I slammed an open palm against the wall. Wanting to cover her words, her plea. We weren't in this – in anything – together. We were two strangers who'd never met. Two strangers who wrote messages in poetry form.

It didn't mean anything.

I was still the loner. The only difference was I no longer wanted to be alone.

Heaving in a heavy breath, I looked around the cave for somewhere else I could sleep. Somewhere higher where the rain and puddles couldn't reach. When I found a spot, I took all of my belongings to it. The small ledge wasn't a smooth surface. It would be harder to sleep on, but at least I'd stay dry.

I wrapped the blanket over me and lay on my side, away from the wall, from the poem. But it called to me.

This girl, she'd cleaned my stuff, made me peanut

butter and jelly sandwiches and brought me snacks and drinks. She didn't know me anymore than I knew her. But she needed me, needed my words, and maybe I needed her too.

Cold, even though I'd bundled up beneath my now clean sweatshirt, I covered my arms over my chest and went to the wall where I picked up the marker and scrawled back my own message. Hoping she'd have the answer.

In all this togetherness,
why do I feel so alone?

I stared at it for a few beats. Stared at her poem, at her plea for us to fight desperately together. It was a nice thought. A sentiment that burrowed itself deep into my bones. Taking my phone out, I took a picture of her words, so I could keep it with me to read it over and over when hope dwindled. Then I read it again for a final time before I went back to bed.

My head rested on my new pillow as my lungs filled with a familiar scent. That night, with the cold rain lashing outside, I dreamt of Brinley. Of her lips. Of her smile. Of her soul connected with mine.

CHAPTER 13

Brinley

I HADN'T LOOKED up my mom's symptoms and poured through various articles since I started writing on Roderick's wall. I hadn't even written in my journal, just his wall. My wall. Ours. But in a way, I was still exposing my wounds, healing them through the words I shared with him. I savored his poems. The one I read yesterday morning about how he felt alone, and it hurt me to the core. His sadness, his loneliness hung on my shoulders, seeped into my pores, trembled in my veins.

I felt it. How utterly alone he felt. I wrote to him then. Words I hoped would reach him, give him the hope he gave me when he first replied and offered to fight with me.

He barely existed
in a world full of people.

Laughter and easy smiles concealed
the fears she hoped no one would know.
They hid behind masks,
their pen their only weapon.

Reading it now, I realized I had given him nothing. My words, my poem was meaningless. Maybe I had nothing to give him. Perhaps I was only fooling myself in thinking we'd fight together when he was better off without me. He'd asked why he felt alone. I left him in silence and it haunted me.

All day yesterday, I wanted to reach out to him, to take back the words I'd said after he dropped my hand and hurt me. Throughout the night, it wasn't my mom's loud screams I heard but Roderick's hushed ones.

As I'd done the previous mornings, I waited for Roderick to walk to school before I made the hike to the cave. I wasn't sure if he would've replied. If he was upset with my non-answer.

But he had left me a message and as he'd done before, he left me breathless.

Write so you can hide
from the terrors of this world.
Write so you can live
with the terrors of your heart.

I lived in hiding, but I wrote so I could come to terms with my fears. So I could give them a reason, a voice. So I could fight back for myself. Because that's what I did. I fought for myself, thought only of myself.

But at some point during the week, I started thinking about Roderick. About how badly I needed to help him. It wasn't a want, but a need.

Without even knowing it, he saw me. With the few

words I gave him, he pieced me together and he figured out more about me than I'd been willing to share.

He was helping me, giving me a peace I'd never known before. Every time I read the words he'd etched on the wall, he saved me from myself. I needed to do the same for him.

It was irrational. Reckless. Dumb. It didn't make any sense, this need to be some sort of beacon of hope for him. But I felt it in my soul. It was real and something I had to do for him.

I took the marker to the wall and rather than think out my words, I bled. Begging him to bleed with me.

Infuse me
with your thoughts.
Consume me
With your words.
Bleed into me
and I'll bring you back.
There is no hiding from the terror,
only fighting
desperately together.

My chest rose and fell in rapid succession. I dropped the marker to the wet ground, wishing we could do more than just fight with words. That we could fight with his hands in mine.

I wanted his demons, his sadness, his anger. Just as I wanted him to have mine.

CHAPTER 14

Brinley

A WHISTLE BLEW from the field and in my cheerleading outfit, I stood beside the bleachers and waited for Danny. Sweat had collected on my back and under my sports bra from our pep rally. I couldn't wait to get home and wash away the grime. The rally had gone well though, and we managed to sell even more tickets for the Fall Ball.

I hadn't wanted to promote it, celebrate the fact the day of the dance was fast approaching when I no longer thought I'd be going. Chances were, I'd be crowned queen, just as I'd won court every other year, but this time I'd win without the friends I relied on standing behind me and cheering me on. This time I wouldn't feel like I was on top.

Danny was also nominated. I hoped he won. Not Jacob. Although it was a stupid tradition with a silly title that didn't mean anything outside of school, I wanted Danny to have it. To know his peers respected him exactly as he was. He deserved that.

Football practice was over after only twenty minutes when everyone finally gave up on the rain relenting. It didn't seem to want to stop and the forecast was now saying the rain would most likely continue until next week. It seemed someone had infuriated Mother Nature and she was punishing us all.

Joseph and Jacob ran passed me, identical ugly sneers on their face. I ignored them, like I'd been doing since the incident during lunch.

Our quarterback, Ari, tugged my pony tail when he stopped in front of me. I rounded my shoulders back, keeping my fingers by my side, playing with the bottom of my skirt and hoped the twins hadn't set him up to do something to me.

"Hey, cheer girl." Ari smiled.

He'd never smiled at me before. Never teased me with a nickname. We'd spoken on several occasions, what with him being football captain and me heading the cheerleading squad. At school events, we'd been paired together quite a few times and were friendly, but this felt different.

"Hey Ari," I replied.

"We're gonna go grab some burgers at the diner," he said. "You should join us."

I'm sure my face mirrored the confusion I felt, and it made him laugh. Danny came beside me, grabbed the sandwich from my hand and after taking it out of the plastic bag, he took a big bite.

"Yeah," Danny agreed with his mouthful. "You

should come with us."

"You're gonna eat a burger after eating a sandwich?" I asked.

"A sandwich?" He unzipped my bag to look inside. "What do you mean *a* sandwich? You always make me two."

"You're not having two sandwiches and then a burger." I placed both palms on my hips and narrowed my eyes at him.

"No." He agreed, taking the other sandwich from my bag and putting it in his. "That's for later tonight."

Ari laughed. "You gonna grab a ride with Brin?" he asked Danny.

After closing his bag, Danny took my bag from me, slung an arm over my shoulder and guided me to the parking lot. "Yep."

"Yeah?" I pinched his side. "I don't remember agreeing to go with you guys."

"You'll have fun."

"Until it starts to rain again and I have to drive in it," I argued, but it was futile. We both knew I was going. And maybe like he said, I'd have fun.

It sprinkled on the drive to the diner, but I let Danny drive while I daydreamed in the passenger seat beside him. It wasn't hard to imagine where my thoughts went.

Roderick. I wondered if the first thing he did when he got to the cave was read my message. Or if he waited to do other things, like homework, before he'd read it. I wondered what he would think about what I wrote to him. How he would reply.

I wondered if when he thought about the girl who wrote him poems, he smiled the way I smiled when I thought about him.

When Danny parked my car, he reached over and nudged my knee with an open palm.

"You alright?" he asked.

"Yeah."

"I know Joseph and Jacob have been giving you shit and…"

"It's fine," I interrupted.

It was mostly true. They'd tried to make me feel bad, to make fun of me, but they didn't get very far before someone interfered. Someone I wasn't friends with, someone who had no reason to stand up for me.

"Okay." He squeezed my leg. "How are things at your house?"

I hesitated, wanted to give him some semblance of the truth. "There was a lot of yelling last night. My mom…" My voice cracked. I couldn't continue. I couldn't talk about my mom, I hadn't been able to mention her name in years. It was a wonder I'd been able to get out the little I had said to Seth about her.

"She's having a hard time with the divorce?"

I nodded, set my lips in a thin line and said, "She has a hard time with everything."

He narrowed his eyes, tried to make out what I meant by that. I squeezed his hand and then turned to open my door.

"You promised me a good time," I reminded him. "Talking about my parents and their problems isn't my idea of a good time."

He grabbed my hand, tugged me to him for a hug over the center console. "Talk to me when you're ready to, but tonight… it's on. You're gonna have the best night of your life."

When I got out of the car, he tackled me from the side and lifted me over his shoulder with my butt in the air. Used to his antics, I rested my elbow on his back and my chin on my open palm while he carried me into the diner with his friends laughing and shouting at us. He sat me down gently on a bench and then slid in beside me.

I was nervous to be surrounded by Danny's football team. I knew them, some I'd hung out with at parties or talked to in class, but I'd never been with just them. Without my group of friends. But I was glad they weren't there, that Jacob and Joseph hadn't made it to the diner.

Restless, I tapped my foot on the floor. Danny placed a calming hand on my knee and I felt his warmth and strength through the fabric and forced myself to relax.

Around me, the guys joked about everything. Nothing was off limits. Including my cheerleading outfit. It wasn't said maliciously though. And even though I felt my cheeks warm, I didn't feel teased, but part of a joke. Part of a group.

I felt like I belonged.

Like I wasn't alone.

CHAPTER 15

RODERICK

DESPERATELY TOGETHER.

I weaved her words into the fiber of my soul and clung onto it. She was right. There was no hiding from the terror, from our fears. We could only fight.

Desperately together.

This nameless, faceless girl I was beginning to depend on. I liked her. Liked her writing, her heart. Liked the way she reached for me. The way she held on.

She wanted my words, maybe even needed them as much as I needed hers. Again, she'd brought me food along with some sodas and bottled water. She even left me a note saying she had taken my dirty clothes to wash and would bring them back in the morning. I should've felt ashamed that she'd done that. Once already she'd done my laundry and I was grateful to have clean, dry clothes. There was no need for her to do it again, but she did it anyway.

It should've embarrassed me that someone I didn't know was washing my clothes, bringing me food, but instead of embarrassment, all I felt was… cared for.

I tipped her note over and wrote, *A thousand thank yous will never be enough.*

I wasn't sure before. Now that I knew she came to the cave in the mornings, I wanted to wait for her, so I could see her. But I was afraid I'd scare her away. So although the desire to meet her and hug her to me to make sure she was real grew inside me, I would leave for school in the morning just as I'd been doing all week.

But the emptiness had lifted. I wasn't alone. I had an angel with a beautiful mind that was fighting alongside me. She wanted to bring me back. A part of me wanted to warn her there was no coming back for me, but I wanted her to try. Desperately, I wanted her to try.

It was daunting how well she knew me after only a few scribbles on the wall. I traced my fingers over yesterday's poem. It touched too close to my heart, made me too aware of who I'd become. And I wondered how she knew? What had given me away?

He barely existed
in a world full of people.

It hurt to read it, to know it was true. At one point, Brinley had been the one who kept me afloat, the one who promised me the hurt would get better. The one who'd make me laugh, and the one who would let me cry. Then the day came that she no longer needed the friends she had, including me, but new ones. The popular, outgoing friends who weren't hurting or lost inside themselves.

She pushed me away, just as she did all her other friends. I wasn't cruel enough to discard people like she did. I simply withdrew into myself, and no one followed.

When the rain started to come down lighter, I took off my clothes for a quick shower. Beneath the broken sky, the rain pelted against my shivering body. With my teeth chattering, I lathered soap over my body and let the cloud's sadness cleanse me.

While I dressed, I wondered what would happen if I went back to my aunt's house. Would she let me live with her or was she happier without the broody teenager she was forced to take care of?

Sitting on the ledge that made up my bed, I picked up my phone. The battery was mostly full since I hadn't used it much since I disconnected it from my charger in home room.

My aunt stopped texting me a few days ago. There were no more frantic messages to come back to her house. No more pleas asking how I was doing or where I was. Just like she always did, she gave up on me before she got any answers. But at least she kept paying for my cell phone. At least I still had that.

Gripping the phone between my clenched hand, I shuddered in a breath. I shouldn't text her. Wouldn't text her.

Instead, I logged onto Instagram where I was friends with people I never spoke to. I didn't care to see what any of them were up to. I wanted to see Brinley. Always, I was drawn to the girl who stopped caring.

We'd barely spoken since we kissed. I tried to talk to her and explain why I'd let go of her hand, but she wouldn't listen. She shut me out, pushed me away the same way she did before. This time, I was going to push back. Harder, until she caved and talked to me.

I craved to feel the smoothness of her lips against mine, taste the sweetness of her breath on my tongue. Of course, I did. I was a breathing, living guy and Brinley was... Brinley. Perfect in all her imperfections.

But more than that, I wanted her back in my life. I wanted her to talk to me about her tears, to trust me, maybe not to make things better, but to try to *help* her feel better. I needed her to know she wasn't alone. She had me, even if I didn't have her.

I went to her page and felt a pang in my chest when I saw her in a picture with most of the football team. Danny sat beside her. His arm around her shoulder and she looked back at him with a silent laugh falling from her lips.

He saw her, long before I did. He saw that the Brinley we knew growing up was still there, struggling to be set free. Throughout the years, he'd waited patiently for her, while I'd tried to hate her. He saw the hurt she hid from the world where I only saw the shallow girl she put on display for the world to see.

All this time I thought she'd let me down, when it was me who had disappointed her.

I was done disappointing her though. I was done with her pushing me away.

When I walked back to the wall, it wasn't to the mystery girl that I wrote, but to Brinley.

I bask in your warmth
while the cold drains me
and it balances out.

Back in my bed, I stared at the photo of Brinley with

the guys. She was sunshine, and now that she'd rid herself of her other friends, she would outshine us all.

CHAPTER 16

Brinley

THE REST OF the week went by quickly, even though I no longer had the friends I'd once coveted. Instead, I made new friends. I opened myself up to Danny's friends from the different sports he played. At lunch, Danny and I sat and talked to Seth and Jeremy who was just as shy but as nice as Seth. Even the drama and band kids stopped to talk to me.

I stayed quiet around Roderick, only talking to him when we had to work on our assignment together while I continued to go to the cave and feed off our mutual words. He tried though. God, he tried. He met me after class, walked with me in mutual silence, watched me from across the patio where we had lunch.

He tried and I let him.

School was different after the lunch incident. And it

was especially better after going to the diner with Danny and the football team. It was as if by shedding away the fake, the ugly, the shallow, everything I was afraid of disappeared. And for the first time in years, I had friends I enjoyed hanging out with.

Jacob and Joseph tried to make my life hard, but the other kids – my new friends – were there for me while Nicole only spoke to me during cheer practice. I couldn't figure out why the other kids accepted me. Why they let me in their groups when Danny tugged me along. But I was grateful for them.

More so for Danny. He'd proven to be the best friend I never knew I had.

"So the Fall Ball's next weekend." Danny drew his eyebrows up, twice.

"Yeah, I'm not going," I answered.

"Not going?" Danny questioned.

He stopped walking me to my car, his hand holding onto my arm.

"You're nominated for queen," he reminded.

"It doesn't matter."

"Is someone giving you trouble after… everything that happened on Tuesday?"

"No." I laughed. "I don't know if you threatened the whole school, but everyone's been cool."

"Everyone's been cool because they finally got to see the girl I see. You stood up to Jacob, to all of your so-called friends, and they saw you for who you are, and they love that girl. Who wouldn't? I love that girl."

I sniffled, wrapping my arms around my chest. "How'd you know that girl even existed?"

"I'm like Yoda, little Padawan. I see everything,

before it even happens."

"I don't think that's how that green little freak works."

Danny laughed and put his arms around me, but it wasn't his arms I wanted holding me in a hug. Roderick, that's where my mind always circled back to.

Roderick.

Roderick.

Roderick.

We continued writing to each other. Each message or poem more personal, revealing more of ourselves, while in the real world I maintained a safe distance. As if my thoughts could summon him, his huddled figure ran across the parking lot. He looked in my direction but turned away as he wiped his nose with the back of his hand.

"So tomorrow?" Danny asked.

I glanced back at him, my forehead scrunched up in confusion. "What about tomorrow?"

"You and I are going to the boutique. Nicole told me she made an appointment for you to try on a dress."

"Nicole? You're still talking to her?"

"She's not as bad as you think," he defended.

"No." I shook my head. "That's not what I meant. She barely talks to me, won't return my calls or texts. I'm surprised she's talking to you. Happily surprised," I amended.

"She'll come around." He said it with such confidence, I had no other choice but to believe him.

"Does this mean you're gonna be my hot date for the Ball?" I asked, letting myself get excited over the dance again.

Like Nicole said, it was our last Fall Ball. Whether or

not I won the silly title, didn't matter. Just that I showed up, danced, and had a great time.

"You know it." He smoothed down his shirt as he straightened his back.

"Okay, future king of the fancy Fall Ball, but don't you have someone else you want to take?"

"Sweet Brin," he kissed my temple, "I think we both know I can't take anyone I'd want to take."

My heart caught in my throat and I wanted Danny to keep talking. To confide in me what he kept closest to his heart, so he wouldn't have to carry the burden alone.

I swallowed. "If you could take whoever you wanted, who would you go with?"

"You." He grinned. "The prettiest girl in the school, who also happens to feed me."

I laughed. Yeah, Danny loved the food I took him. And until we graduated, I'd continue making him sandwiches and taking them to practices and games. Never once would I miss one of his games. Just as I would continue to leave Roderick food and snacks.

It was nice seeing him take out one of the sandwiches I made him and eat it along with a pear, which from the look on his face was still his favorite. At least I knew, twice a day he was eating, even if it wasn't a hearty or very fulfilling meal. Next week, I'd get in the kitchen and make him stew. Something I could put in a thermos to help him fend off the chill at night. The sandwiches would work for lunch though.

With my plan brewing in my head, I smacked a kiss on Danny's cheek. Just as we reached my car, the sky opened and rain started pelting against us.

Roderick. My mind immediately went to him. He

wouldn't have made it to the cave by then.

"I gotta run!" I shouted over the thunder.

"See you tomorrow?" Danny asked.

"Yep, tomorrow."

Danny shut my door behind me and I drove away, toward the cave. I found Roderick walking against the wind less than a mile away. His shoulders shook while he kept his face down. I pulled my car to the side of the road and rolled down the passenger window, but with the angry storm beating around us, Roderick couldn't hear me when I shouted his name.

After rolling the window back up, I jumped out of the car and raced to him. Reaching him, I grabbed his hand and tugged.

"Come on!" I yelled.

His brows drew together in confusion.

Maybe I was confused too. Here I was, bringing home the boy I'd been keeping at a safe distance, where he would be able to uncover all my secrets.

"We're getting soaked! Get in the car."

I pulled his hand harder and this time, he listened. Once inside the car, I turned the heat on even more. Roderick rested his head against the window with his hands shaking on his lap. I took his hands in mine and brought them to my mouth where I breathed hot air on them while I rubbed them furiously between mine.

"What are you doing, Brinley?" He sounded exhausted. Exhausted and dejected.

"Getting you out of the rain and warm," I replied.

I took off my jacket and although it wasn't much, I put it over his shuddering chest and drove us to my house. The entire drive, rain continued to fall as if it never intended to stop. When we got to my house, I urged him out of the car before I sprinted to the front door. With his hand, still cold, in mine, I led him through my bedroom and into the bathroom.

"Take off your clothes and leave them by the door so I can dry them," I instructed as I turned the water in my shower on hot. "I'm gonna grab you some of my dad's clothes, so you can put them on after you shower."

He grinned. It was slow and tired, but it made my heart leap so hard I thought it'd slam straight out of my chest.

"You trying to tell me I smell bad?" he joked and then sneezed.

"Yes, now go."

I closed the door behind me and waited for him to open it, so I could get his clothes. When he did, I raced to the laundry room, dumped his clothes in the dryer and turned it on. I grabbed one of my dad's folded shirts and gym pants from the top and raced back to Roderick with a clean towel.

Outside my bathroom door, I knocked. "Can I come in?" I called out.

"Yeah." The gruff sound of his voice sounded from the other side.

Inching the door open, I crept in, keeping my eyes on the floor as I settled the clothes and towel on the bathroom sink.

"Clothes and towel are right here," I said without looking at him.

"Thanks for not sneaking a peek." His voice was light, and I loved the tease behind it. "I'm really shy about being naked."

I felt my face inflame and fanned myself as I hurried out, Roderick's laughter following my every step.

His laugh was rich and full and made butterflies burst in flight deep in my belly.

I leaned on my bed and moved to rest my head against one of my pillows, but quickly remembered I too was wet. After changing into fresh clothes, I went back to my bed with my head swimming. I knew why I'd chased after Roderick, why I'd brought him back here and chanced him running into my mom, but now that he was in my bathroom – naked – I wasn't sure what I was supposed to do next.

TV, I decided, flipping it on with the remote control that rested on my nightstand. We could watch TV.

A few minutes later, Roderick shuffled out of the bathroom, his inky hair disheveled from the towel.

"Come." I patted the side of my bed.

His eyes and nose were red, his face pale. Despite how awful I'm sure he felt, he arched a single brow up in question.

"It's gonna be raining for a while," I argued. "Might as well make yourself comfortable before you go back home."

"Home," he repeated. It sounded empty, and I wished I could take it back.

"Here." I handed him the remote control when he sat on my bed.

He stared at it for a long time before he edged his back on the bed and lied down beside me. Instead of looking through the channels, he put the remote between us and turned on his side so that he was facing me.

Our shoulders brushed against each other when I

shifted my body to the side. Face to face. When I covered us both up with my blanket and comforter, he sighed.

"I'm sorry I hurt your feelings the other day," he said, his voice small. "I swear I didn't mean to. I thought… I thought I was protecting you."

"Protecting me from what?" I asked.

"From being seen with me. The freak." A sad smile tugged on his lips.

Reaching for him, I ran my fingers through his damp hair. "You're not a freak, and—" I licked my lips, wishing for the hundredth time I hadn't been so harsh with my own words, "you don't have to be alone if you don't want to be."

My chest tightened at his pained expression.

"I don't want to be alone anymore."

"Then you're not alone. I'm right here," I replied.

With a nod, he closed his eyes and placed a hand on my waist. My heart drummed loudly in my ears at the contact, but I continued to play with his hair until he fell asleep. With our faces close, our breaths mingling, I fell asleep beside him.

CHAPTER 17

Brinley

THREE DAYS LATER and I was still upset I'd woken up alone. At some point the rain had stopped, and Roderick had left me alone on a bed that now felt too big.

He'd taken his clothes from the dryer and folded my dad's clothes, leaving them on my bathroom sink. Right next to it was a piece of paper he must've torn from one of my notebooks. He'd scribbled *A thousand thank yous will never be enough* across the paper. They were the same words he'd written to me when I did his laundry earlier that week. Like the crazy girl he made me out to be, I kept both notes in a drawer in my night stand and every night I traced the letters over and over before I went to bed.

Although I wanted to go by the cave over the weekend, I stayed away. I wasn't sure what Roderick and I were to each other. I wasn't sure if I'd end up chasing him away if I showed up at the cave. Or if we'd somehow end up chasing each other off. I still needed him, still needed the messages we passed onto one another on a cave's wall. So I played it safe, away from the cave while my mind wandered continuously to him and how he was.

Monday morning I waited by the same tall tree to watch Roderick walk to school, so I could hurry to the cave and see what'd he'd written, but I never saw him.

Drumming my fingers on the steering wheel, I drove to school and wondered if he'd moved back into his aunt's house because of all the rain. While it had slowed down for short bits at a time, it was still pretty relentless.

"Ah, there's my favorite girl," Danny called out when he saw me just before second period. "Did you show your parents how gorgeous you look in your new dress?"

I blushed at his praise, secretly delighted he thought I looked so good. Even happier that I did what he and my dad told me to do and bought the dress with shoes that paired beautifully with it, along with making an appointment for my hair and nails. My makeup I could do myself.

"Yeah," I answered.

I'd shown my dad as soon as he got back from his shift at the hospital. After he hooted and hollered about how pretty I looked, he demanded I take it back. He even threatened to lock me in my bedroom if I didn't because according to him, there was no way he could beat off all the guys who'd fall in love with me after seeing me in it.

My dad had also made the weekend better by hiring a nurse to take care of my mom when he wasn't there. Which helped, especially at night when she seemed to reach her worst. The nurse was nice, patient, and made sure my mom kept a safe distance from me when she was lost in her mind. But for the few moments Sunday that my mom returned, the three of us enjoyed chocolate chip cookies. What was leftover was wrapped in my bag, some for Roderick and the rest for Danny, who'd already eaten three before lunch.

"We're gonna look pretty great together." I winked.

Danny had rented a black suit, and he filled it out with his wide shoulders and broad chest. Whoever Danny was hung up on would surely see him and not be able to look away.

There was a time I would've wished it were me. It would've made things simpler if we were attracted to each other. But matters of the heart are rarely simple.

Looking past Danny, I tried to find Roderick. Normally, I wouldn't see him until we were in the classroom, but I was both anxious and eager to see him. To spend time with him again.

"Who are you looking for?" Danny asked.

"Roderick."

"I think I finally have you two figured out." He waggled his finger in my face, and I snapped my jaw pretending I was going to bite it. "One second you guys hate each other, the next you're in each other's arms. You like each other. Like... *like* each other." He crossed his arms over his chest. "Go ahead, you can tell me. My heart can take the beating."

"And why would I want my best friend's heart to take any sort of beating?"

"Oh, so we're playing the best friends cards, huh?" He slung an arm around me as we made our way to Mr.

Scott's class.

"I told you, you're my most favorite person who owes me a family with six kids, three dogs and a cat."

"You keep changing the terms on me, and I'm never agreeing to marry you," he teased, but then his expression sobered. "So, you and Roderick?"

Looking at my feet, I whispered, "I like him."

"Don't look so sad." He tapped my chin. "I'm no expert, but I'm pretty sure he likes you too. He'd be dumb or gay not to."

I giggled, and then covered my mouth to hide it.

In the classroom, I sat in front of Roderick's empty desk. My anxiety grew when Roderick never made it to class.

I'D NEVER SKIPPED class before, but that's exactly what I did after lunch came and went, and I still hadn't seen Roderick. It was silly, completely stupid, but I had to go to the cave and see if he was there. Make sure he was okay.

I drove faster than usual, parked and with my book bag on my back I tore out of my car and through the wooded trail that led to the cave. Mud sloshed around me, covered my shoes and ruined my jeans. Not that it mattered.

When I reached the mouth of the cave, I called out Roderick's name before going in. It was as much a warning to him as it was to me.

I was about to out both of us, consequences be damned.

I ran over the puddles and when I didn't see him lying on the ground, I sighed in relief. He wasn't in here. He had to be back with his aunt, safe in her house.

A moan sounded from the other side of the cave and when I turned my flashlight on, I saw him. Huddled on a small ledge, high enough the water couldn't reach him.

He moaned again and I went to him. His eyes were shut. His face pinched.

"Roderick," I said quietly, running my fingers through his hair.

His lids remained closed and when I caressed his sweaty face, I gasped. His skin was hot, too hot, and his cheeks a rosy pink from his fever.

"Roderick," I said again, shaking his shoulder roughly.

His eyes opened, and he smiled at me. "Brinley," he whispered my name.

"I need you to get up."

He shook his head and shut his eyes.

"Roderick, I need you to get up. Please," I pleaded with him.

When I tried to sit him upright, he followed my lead. His head fell forward, and he braced the sides of his face with his hands.

"My car's just a few miles from here. You think you can make it?"

"Anything for you." He leaned down to kiss my

cheek. "First sleep."

I let him lie back down while I tried to figure out what to do next. I sat beside him combing my fingers through his silky hair and across his stubbled cheek. God, he was warm. I needed to break his fever.

Bending down to my knees, I rummaged through my book bag until I found the Tylenol I always kept in the front pocket. When I stood back up, I reached Roderick and forced him to sit up again. I handed him a bottle of water and two pills but he simply stared at his hands with his eyes glazed over.

"Open your mouth," I said, placing the two pills against his lips. When he took them in his mouth, I brought my bottle of water to his lips and urged him to drink.

"Can I sleep now?" Already, his eyes were closing.

I got up on the ledge and together I laid us down. He rested his head on the crook of my arm and fell back to sleep with my hand in his hair.

CHAPTER 18

RODERICK

Tʜᴇ ᴘᴏᴜɴᴅɪɴɢ ʙᴇʜɪɴᴅ my head had gotten better. It wasn't gone, but definitely better. Soft murmurs carried me out of my sleep. When I opened my eyes to find Brinley beside me humming softly while her fingers toyed with my hair, I inched myself closer to her. To the warmth of her body and away from the cold that surrounded me.

This was a dream. It had to be. And it wasn't one I was ready to wake up from.

The smooth skin on the back of her hand stroked my cheek. Although, I didn't want to open my eyes again, didn't want to wake up, I had to look at her. To see the bright green of her eyes, the pretty plumpness of her lips, drink her in, make her part of me so she'd never leave me again.

"You're awake," she whispered.

"No," I argued, pressing my fingers in to her waist as I drew myself even closer to her. "Pretty sure I'm still dreaming." I smiled. "Best dream ever."

"Nope." She kissed my forehead. "You're awake and your fever's better."

That got my attention. Slowly, I sat up, taking her with me. She pressed her small form against my chest and although I didn't push her away, it hurt. My whole chest hurt, felt too tight. I coughed to loosen it to no avail.

"We have to get you out of here," she said as she got off the ledge that was my bed.

"This is the weirdest dream ever." I shook my head, trying to rid myself of the fog.

"Not a dream, Roderick." She smiled. "I can grab one of your bags of clothes. Think you can walk to my car? It's a long hike, but it stopped raining. If you're okay with it, I can call Danny. I know he'll help us."

"Wait, what?"

Brinley was here, in the cave. And she was going to call Danny?

"Danny knows I'm here too?" The pain in my head worsened, and I put my hands against either side of my head and groaned.

She ran her fingers through my hair again. Softly, gently. Barely a whisper. But I felt it. Straight to my heart.

I looked back at her, my vision pained from the growing ache in my head, but I couldn't take my eyes off her.

"What are you doing here?" I asked.

"It's me," she whispered, her mouth pressed against

my forehead. "I'm the one who's been leaving you messages on the wall."

Dropping my hands from my head, I wrapped them around her waist and pulled her to me. I rested my head against her chest where her heart beat wildly, erratically.

"Of course it was you," I murmured. "It's always been you."

Her hands touched my face, and she kissed my nose. And damn, I loved her kisses. Whether they were on my forehead, my nose, my lips. I wanted them all. All of her kisses.

"We have to get out of here," she reminded me.

I took her hand in mine and followed her back to level ground where she picked up one of my bags.

Fear gripped me and I stopped moving. "I'm not going back to my aunt's house."

"No," she agreed with a smile.

I followed her through the woods and tried to get a grip on my thoughts, of what she'd said. She was the one who'd been writing poems with me. The one who'd been leaving me food every day. The one who'd cleaned my clothes and sheets twice last week and had left me a pillow that wasn't soaked.

Fire flickered against my chest, warming me from the inside out. Brinley had taken care of me.

She'd mentioned Danny though.

"What about Danny?"

"If you want, I can drop you off with Danny, but that might be awkward." She swallowed, her slender throat moving up and down with the motion "I was thinking you'd stay with me."

Tugging her to me, I dipped my head down and

slanted my lips over hers. The kiss was soft, tender, giving. She whimpered against my lips and when I pulled away, she touched her fingertips to my face.

"No one knows you've been staying in the cave. Only me." She kissed my jaw. "I wouldn't tell anyone your secret," she promised.

We took another few steps – maybe half a dozen or over a million, but I couldn't walk anymore. My legs were leaden. My chest thick while my vision blurred in front of me. Reaching out, I leaned a hand on a nearby tree and dropped my face as I coughed. Brinley was beside me, rubbing my back while she kissed my shoulder.

"I need to sit," I said.

She helped me down with her face drawn in worry. I hated the concern in her eyes, hated the memory of the hurt I put in her eyes just last week.

"I don't hate you," I said, rubbing my chest. "Last week you said I hated you. I don't."

She sat beside me, wetting her butt when she sat in the same puddle as me. I took her hand and rested it on my lap while I leaned my head on her slender shoulder. Her thumb ran circles over the back of my hand. It was soft and sweet and I felt it everywhere. Like a brushfire over my skin and into my soul. It warmed me, made the frigidity go away.

"You said you did." Her voice was low, pained. "You said you hated me but not as much as you hated seeing me hurt."

I said that. The words rushed out of my lungs to both soothe and hurt. Because in my destructive little world, I clung to the hurt and spread it. Just like she did.

"I didn't mean it," I breathed. My breath caught,

the ache in my chest and head growing, and I coughed again. "I've never hated you. I wanted to."

"It's okay." She pressed her lips against my shoulder and through the layers of clothes I wore, I could feel the warmth. Her warmth. "I hate myself enough for the both of us."

As if her words hurt me more than it hurt her, I leaned over, gripped my stomach where the pain throbbed the most. Letting go of Brinley's hand, I opened my mouth and vomited. Bile rose, my stomach convulsed, and I hurled even more while coughs racked my body.

Bringing my head between my knees, I waited to see if more would come. I spit on the ground, hating everything but the girl next to me. The girl who brought me food, words and peace even when she thought I hated her. The girl who sat beside me, hugging my trembling body to hers.

When I looked back at her, rested my head on my bent knee, she touched my forehead with the back of her hand.

"Your fever's coming back." She looked up, past the tree branches and to the sky. "It's gonna start raining pretty soon. Think you can start walking again?"

I dipped my head in a nod. Taking her hand, she helped me up. My legs were still shaking while my body pulsed in pain. With her arm around my waist, we walked to her car. It was slow and each step hurt, but I had the girl— my girl— tucked beside me.

And this time, I wouldn't let her down.

CHAPTER 19

Brinley

As soon as Roderick sat in my car, I buckled him in, and by the time I quickly changed out of my wet pants and got to the driver's seat, he was asleep with his head resting against my window.

His fever had gone down some, but never left him fully. He was sick, so sick, and I didn't know what to do.

If I took him to my dad, I knew he'd take care of him. But the questions would come and he'd learn Roderick had been living in a cave. He'd have to involve the police and before you knew it, he'd end up back at his aunt's house. The one place Roderick told me he didn't want to go to.

He trusted me. I couldn't betray him. I wouldn't.

At my house, I stirred him awake enough to get him inside and in my room.

Our feet were wet and muddy and so were his pants. After taking off my socks and shoes, I cleaned up the mess we left on the floor. When I went back to my room, I found him sitting on my bed with a forlorn look on his face. In front of him, I sank to my knees and took off his shoes and socks and replaced them with a pair of my socks. They were pink, but warm. I helped him lie down and with nerves quaking, I moved to unbutton his jeans.

He sucked in a deep breath, and then turned his head away from me to cough. I waited for him to finish. When he did, he unfastened his jeans and with my help, and we took them off. I rummaged through his bag and pulled out a pair of shorts. I slid them up his legs and he lifted his butt so I could pull them the rest of the way up. He quivered when I ran my hands over his damp shirt.

"We need to get you out of this too."

Sitting up he took his shirt off and I handed him a clean one from his bag. I quickly changed into one of his shirts but kept my yoga pants on. When he lied back down, I covered him with my comforter. I touched his forehead, feeling his fevered skin even warmer than before.

Sighing, I picked up my phone and called my dad.

"Hey, kid," he greeted me after four rings.

"Hey, Dad." I forced my voice to sound gravely.

From the bed, Roderick's eyes popped open. I leaned in to him, kissed his cheek and hoped he'd continue to trust me.

"Uh-oh," he said. "You don't sound too great."

"I'm sick. Fever, nasty cough." I gave an unconvincing cough that made Roderick's lips spread in a tired smile.

"Body aches?" he asked.

"Body aches?" I parroted.

Roderick nodded. "My chest hurts," he whispered. "Feels really tight."

I rested my hand on his chest, ran my fingers over his shirt.

"Yeah, my body hurts. My chest is really tight." I sniffled and then coughed again. "My head's pounding too," I added, remembering how he gripped the sides of his head as if he were bracing against something he couldn't fight.

"Do you still have the antibiotics I left you last week?"

I jumped off the bed and went to my dresser where the pill bottle sat unused. Shaking it, I said, "Yeah, but I vomited earlier. Won't the pills make it worse?"

"Oh, kid." He covered the phone to say something to someone else. "You sound miserable. Tell you what, I'll come home and take care of you."

Already expecting that response, I said, "Leave your cape on, Dad. I'm fine, just need you to tell me what to do."

"Brinley," he warned.

"Dad," I used the same tone. "If I get you sick, then you'll miss work and not be able to save lives," I teased. "I'm gonna stay in bed, stay away from Mom and the nurse…" I searched for her name, "Bridgette, so no one else gets sick. Stay at the hospital, okay? Just tell me what I need to do?"

He huffed. "If you get worse, you'll call me?"

"Yeah, of course. And Bridgette will be here soon. My very own certified nurse."

"Okay." He sighed.

I knew he hated staying away, not taking care of his

little girl, but he respected my independence. He had to when he and my mom were the ones who forced it on me. Not that it was his fault. Or my mom's. It just was.

"I brought home some Jell-O last week when you started feeling bad," he said. "See if you can eat that without throwing up, and then take the antibiotics with it. I'll ask Lindsey to bring you some chicken soup."

"What about my fever?"

"A cool bath and some Tylenol should help. How high of a fever do you have?"

I touched Roderick's forehead again, and he leaned in to my hand.

"I don't know. I haven't checked, but I'm really hot."

Roderick waggled his eyebrows at me, and I pressed my lips in to a thin line, so I wouldn't laugh.

"Have you taken anything for it today?"

"Yeah," I answered, "about three or four hours ago."

"Take two more pills now, grab the Jell-O. There's also crackers and Sprite in the kitchen."

"Geez, Dad," I joked. "It's like you were expecting the flu apocalypse."

My dad chuckled into the phone while Roderick smiled.

"My daughter never stays home from school. I had to be prepared."

"Keep a stake ready, just in case I turn into a zombie."

"Stakes are for vampires," he replied, his tone serious. "It's like you don't even listen to me when I speak."

Shaking my head, I laughed. And then remembered to cough to keep up the ruse. "Sorry, old man."

"You sure you're okay without me there? We can watch movies in the living room. I already got my yellow nail polish."

"I love you, Dad." My heart squeezed in my chest. "I'm good. Promise."

"Text me to let me know how you are after eating and taking your medicine."

"Got it."

After I hung up the phone, I left Roderick on my bed to grab crackers, Jell-O and a glass of Sprite like my dad instructed. Carrying it back to my room, I flinched when I heard my mom scream. Something crashed against the wall and I raced the rest of the way, without stopping or checking to see if she was going to leave her room.

"What was that?" Roderick asked when I sat on the bed beside him.

I helped him to a sitting position and propped some pillows behind him to lean on.

"Hmm?" I asked, not meeting his eyes. "Neighborhood cat, maybe?"

Blue eyes bore into me so I turned my attention away from him. As far away from his face and his questioning gaze.

"Here." I held out two pills for his fever and the glass of Sprite.

Watching me, he took it from me and swallowed. After opening it, I handed him the Jell-O and a spoon. He ate slowly, as if each swallow hurt more than the other. When he gave it back to me, he tried to lie back down, but I stopped him.

"More medicine," I reminded him.

I took an antibiotic from my dresser and placed it against his lips. When he took it in his parted lips, his mouth brushed against my fingertips. The sensation shot through my body, making my limbs shiver.

"My dad said you should take a cool bath," I said.

He groaned, closing his eyes as he lied back on my bed.

"Maybe later?" I offered.

"Yeah, later," he said.

His eyes suddenly flew open, and he jolted from my bed. Kneeling on the floor, he rummaged through his bag and then held his toothbrush up like it was some sort of victory.

"I'll be right back." He gave me a sheepish smile that I returned.

A few minutes later, he crawled back into my bed a bit more sluggish than when he'd darted to my bathroom to brush his teeth.

"Lie down with me," he said but it came out sounding like a question.

"Yeah, okay."

After locking my bedroom door, I slid into bed beside him. He reached for me, draped a heavy arm over my waist as he drew himself closer. Heat radiated from his body, and his warm breath fell on my face when he rested his head on my arm. He tipped his head down to cough, covering his mouth with a closed fist.

"Everyone knows a good nurse sleeps with her patient," I said when he looked back at me.

He grinned, and it was the same smile I remembered from so many years ago. Before his parents died and tragedy had clawed her cruel fingers through his life.

I ran my hands over his heated arm, smoothing out the goosebumps with each pass. When he looked back at me, I took my fingers to his hair. Closing his eyes, he moaned. God, I loved that moan.

It wasn't one of pain, but of pleasure. Pleasure I'd brought him.

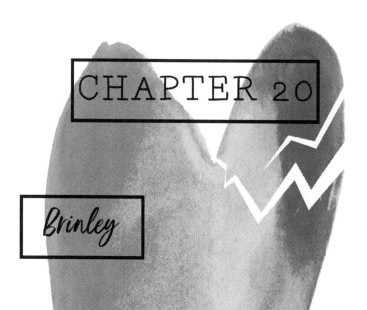

CHAPTER 20

Brinley

Two brisk knocks on my door startled both Roderick and me awake.

"Brinley," the now familiar voice of Bridgette called out.

"Shit, your mom," Roderick whispered, trying to scurry out of bed.

"It's not my mom," I eased, touching his arm, which I was happy to find no longer hot to the touch. "Yeah," I called out.

"You dad said you're not feeling well," she answered through the close door. "He asked me to check on you and remind you Lindsey brought you soup."

"I'm fine. Better," I spluttered out. "Thank you."

"You've been coughing for hours. It sounds pretty bad," she continued. "There's some cough medicine in the pantry I can bring you."

"No," I rushed out. "Don't want to get you or my mom sick. I'll get it myself and the soup. Thank you, Bridgette," I said again, hoping she'd take the hint and leave.

When I heard her footsteps fade away, I asked Roderick if I should grab him some cough medicine. "Your cough is pretty bad. Kinda sounds like an elephant dying."

"Have you heard many elephants die?" he asked, raising a single brow.

"One or two at the most," I replied with a smirk.

He touched his stomach. "I don't think I can handle anymore medicine."

"Lindsey brought chicken soup. That might help."

"Yeah, okay." He took my hand and pressed it against his face. I ran my thumb over his cheek. "Who's Lindsey?"

I jolted, an electric shock ran down my spine to my toes. "My dad's girlfriend. My parents are divorcing." I said it as if it didn't matter. As if dads had girlfriends before getting a divorce.

He trailed his hand over my arm, and when he touched my wrist he brought my hand to his lips where he placed a kiss on my open palm. I melted a little inside, wanted to lie back down next to him, where I was safe. Where nothing else mattered but us.

"Who's Bridgette?" he asked.

"My mom's new nurse."

"Was your mom the one who screamed earlier?"

I jutted out my chin, forced my bottom lip not to tremble. In the past four years, I'd been so careful not to let anyone in. Not to let anyone see. Now with Roderick staying with me for who knew how long, he'd hear everything. Know everything.

"Yeah," I replied, my eyes staring hard at his face as if I could look straight through him. "And the screaming will get worse at night. If you can't handle it, you can go back to the cave."

He sat up, put his arms around me, and held me in a tight embrace while he kissed the side of my head. One kiss, another, and then another.

When he brushed his lips over my ear, he whispered, "I'm here. I'm not going anywhere."

Except he'd eventually have to leave. I couldn't hide him away forever. He'd go back to the cave or his aunt's. And again, I'd have no one to hold me together while my life continued to fall apart.

CHAPTER 21

RODERICK

THE SCREAMING GOT louder. Shrieks that made the walls tremble, and Brinley's large room feel small.

I held Brinley close to me, ran my hands over her arm and back. Her breathing was loud, and her eyes closed while her face pinched in pain.

Loud pounding sounded at the door. Brinley flinched, wrapped her arms around her body, all while keeping her eyes painfully shut.

"Mrs. Crassus," a voice soothed on the other side, "let's get you back to bed."

Her mom wailed. Her tormented screams made the air thick. It lasted minutes, hours. Her hand slapped against the door, demanded to come in.

"It's locked," Brinley whispered, her voice shaky. "Locked. Locked." She repeated the words to herself, to me while I held her.

"I've got you, baby," I said.

I held her, while she held onto herself. When it stopped, when the nurse finally convinced her mom to go back to her room, I felt Brinley shake beside me.

"Baby," I whispered against her temple.

But it was as if she couldn't hear me. Feel me. See me.

I urged her body on top of mine where she curled against me with her head buried against the crevice of my neck. Holding her, I spoke softly in her ear. Words of hope, of encouragement. A reminder that we were together. Fighting our demons, our battles together. Desperately together.

"Come back to me, Brinley." I brushed her hair back, ran my fingers through the long strands over her back.

She continued to shake. I continued to talk, to touch her. To make sure she was still here, with me.

"Roderick?" It came out small. Uncertain.

Her rapid breaths floated across my neck. When her body suddenly stiffened, she moved to edge away, but I held on tighter.

"Stay with me," I said.

I felt her nod and held her impossibly closer to me.

When my eyes fluttered open, I immediately missed

the warmth of Brinley draped over my chest, her head resting by my throat, and her breath hitting my skin. Instead, all I had to hold onto was the raging ache in my head and body.

Wearing my shirt and yoga pants that clung to her slight curves, she stepped out of her bathroom looking fresh and beautiful. I sat up, reached for her, and she went into my arms without question, resting her chin on top of my head while I pressed the side of my face to her chest. My fingers trailed beneath her shirt, over the smooth surface of her back. She shuddered.

"You look good in my shirt," I said.

"And you look like hell."

"That's my girl," I replied, enjoying the way her heart fluttered against my ear. "Always bringing me down a notch, back to reality."

She inched away, so I traced my hands over her waist where I left them.

"Am I your girl?" she asked.

"I don't know." I swallowed and grimaced when it hurt. "Maybe. Yeah?"

Holding my face in her hands, she leaned down and kissed my lips. I wanted to linger there, keep our mouths fused against one another, but she broke the kiss quickly.

"I want to be your girl," she said a little breathless.

"Okay," I breathed out but turned away when I had to cough.

She rubbed a hand over my chest. I took her hand, pressed it where it hurt the most, knowing she'd make it hurt less.

"How are you feeling?" she asked.

"Better." I ran a hand over my throat when I

swallowed again. "Thanks for getting me yesterday. For bringing me here and taking care of me."

"You took care of me too."

"Because you're my girl." My hand trembled, but I forced back the fear. I was tired of being scared, of being alone, of waiting for the earth to split apart and take me, the way it forgot to take me when my parents died. I wanted to be happy. I wanted this life with this girl.

I clenched my jaw, fought back the tears that threatened to spill.

"You're my girl in this ugly world. You make everything better." I ran my hands over her waist, brushed the sides of her breasts and snaked my hands around her neck. "You make the hurt worth going through. You make me feel whole, which is something I haven't felt in years, so I'm gonna hold on tight to you, take care of you."

She tilted her head to the side. "Because I'm your girl?"

"Yeah."

She smiled. It wasn't one of the fake ones, but a real smile that touched her eyes and somehow made them look greener. My insides clenched, but when she rested a hand to my forehead she stepped back. Too far for me to touch her.

"You're still warm." She grabbed two more pills from her dresser and gave them to me.

"Thought you said I was hot?" I corrected her, loving the way her cheeks flushed at my words.

She rolled her eyes to the ceiling and shook her head. A knock came from her door and she covered her mouth as her eyes darted from the door to me.

"Brinley?" A gruff voice said from behind the door.

"It's my dad." She pushed me from the bed and to the bathroom. "Coming," she called.

Leaving me sitting on the toilet, she went back to her room, leaving the door slightly open.

"How you feeling, kid?"

She murmured something, probably pressed against him for a hug.

"Bridgette said you were coughing all night."

"Yeah," she said. "I was able to get some sleep though."

"You're staying home from school today. Why don't you sit on the bed for me?"

"Really?" I imagined her crossing her arms over her chest. "Why?"

"Just want to listen to my daughter's lungs. Not sure if you've heard, but I'm a doctor of sorts."

She snorted and then coughed. It sounded forced, and I shook my head at her. She was an awful actress, I wondered why I couldn't see through her façade before. Why I hadn't noticed she needed me as much as I needed her. Why I hadn't seen our shared fear.

"Your lungs sound clear. I'll let Bridgette know. She was worried about you. Keep taking the antibiotics. How's the fever?"

"Comes and goes," she said.

"And you were able to eat the soup Lindsey made?"

"Yeah, tell her thank you for me."

"I will." He paused, drew in a sharp breath. "How come you locked your door last night?"

Silence followed and all I could hear was the hammering in my head.

"Mom came to my door."

"Oh baby." He murmured something I couldn't hear. "Come live with me, Brinley. Get away from all of this," he pleaded. "It's what Mom wants. It's what I want."

"Dad," she warned.

I heard him kiss her. "Think about it. Please. Can you do that for me?"

"Sure."

"Love you, kid."

"Love you too. Why don't you crash at Lindsey's, so you can get some rest before going back to work tonight?"

"What about you?" he asked.

"You said it yourself, my lungs are clear. I have soup, medicine and a bed. Now I need my dad to get some sleep before he throws on his cape, so I don't have to worry about him."

Again silence.

"I'll ask Bridgette to stay, so she can be with your mom and you can rest." His voice sounded pained, like he wanted to do anything but what she was asking of him. And I hated him for listening to her, for turning away from her when she was supposedly so sick, but was also relieved he was leaving.

"She helped a lot last night," Brinley said. "I'm glad you hired her."

"Yeah." Heavy footsteps sounded on the wood floor, away from the bathroom and toward her bedroom door.

I waited for her to come get me, to let me know it was safe to come out, when I heard the door click shut. When she didn't, I went to her. Her shoulders slumped forward. Her face torn in agony, but damn she made broken look beautiful.

Sitting next to her, I put my arms around her and

eased her on my lap. She went willingly, wrapping her arms around my neck while she rested her head on my shoulder. Her fingers traced over the back of my neck to my head where she started playing with my hair.

"I like your hair," she said.

"I like you playing with my hair."

We stayed like that for a good while. Eventually her tense body relaxed on top of mine, molded against me, and I knew this was it. Where she belonged. Where I belonged.

She eased off of me when I started to cough again. Rubbing my chest, I leaned against one of her pillows that smelled like her. Like the pillow she'd left me in the cave. I couldn't believe I hadn't figured out she was the one writing with me when she was written all over the cave.

The sandwiches she made, the scent she left behind, the pretty handwriting and the sadness I was beginning to see.

Needing to touch her, I took her hand when she sat on the bed beside me. She rested her head on my shoulder and I ran my fingers through her hair.

She felt like peace, like happiness.

She felt as if she'd been created just for me. Mine.

"What's wrong with your mom?" I asked.

She straightened, shot up from the bed quickly and rushed the few steps to the door. Although my body protested, I followed her.

With her hand on the knob, she looked back at me and asked, "What do you want for breakfast?"

I placed my hand over hers, not letting her open the door. "Talk to me."

Her face fell, her head bowed. I tucked her in my arms, held onto her when her body started to shake. Tears fell, wetting my shirt where she rested her head. She clung to me, her fingers wrapped against the back of my shirt, and I held onto her. Held her upright. Held her together.

"She's sick," she whispered against my throat. "Her brain is sick and I think mine is too."

CHAPTER 22

Brinley

THERE, I SAID it. The words that I feared most.

My mom was sick, and there was a good chance I would be too. She'd told me herself countless times. The disease in her brain was genetic. It was relentless in its pursuit to take away my mom. To take away all the good she once was.

One day, it might come after me, and there was nothing I could do to fend myself from it.

"She was fine when I was younger. There were no signs that her brain was sick and getting worse." I nestled to his chest. He rubbed my back with long strokes as if he were creating some sort of masterpiece on my back. As if he could paint over the ugly and make me pretty. It felt good to be held, felt good to finally say the little bit I had, so I continued. "It was like a light switch went off. We went to bed a happy, normal family and when I woke up, my parents were missing." I heaved in a sigh. "During the night my mom had her first of many episodes. I hadn't heard her screaming that night, and my dad played it down so he wouldn't worry me, but you heard her last night. She screams, she hurts herself, she throws things. It's like something inside her is broken, so she lashes out at us to lessen it. It doesn't help, nothing does."

He brushed his lips over my ear, kissed the tip. "Is she taking anything for it? Talking to someone?"

I pushed away from him, splayed my hands on my hips and stared. What did he think? That my dad hadn't tried everything to bring back the woman he married?

He held his palms out to me. "I'm sorry," he said. "I'm just trying to understand."

"Understand what?" I spit out.

"Brinley," he sighed out my name, his eyes red and tired. "I don't want to fight you. I want to fight with you. Remember? Desperately together."

I wanted that, for us to be in this together. But words on a cave's wall were different when you tried to actually bring them to fruition. I could try though. At least I could say I tried, even if Roderick didn't end up sticking by me when he knew everything.

"She takes pills, goes to doctors, and I dunno... maybe it helps. Maybe things would be worse if she wasn't doing those things. But there's really nothing they can do for her except maybe hospitalize her." I looked at my unpainted toe nails. "My dad doesn't want to do that yet. It'll eventually come, but she still has good days, and they both want her to enjoy those good days freely, not stuck in a hospital." When I looked up at him, it wasn't fear or disgust that marred his features, but sorrow and worry.

"She's up all night screaming and crying and banging on your door." He sounded angry. "You're terrified of her. What happens if she gets in?"

I steadied myself, took in a deep breath. "When I don't lock my door, which I'd never done before last night, she comes in. Sometimes she yells at me." It came out defiant. "Sometimes she throws things at me." My tone lowered. "Sometimes she hits me." My voice wobbled.

Horror streaked across his face. There it was, the blow that would drive him away.

"What about you?" he asked.

I blinked back the tears, but still a few fell. "I take it. Whatever she does, I take it."

"What?" His lips pressed together, his fists trembled by his sides. "Why? Why doesn't your dad stop it?"

"He can't stop it!" I yelled, my own anger taking over. "He works and…"

"…And he leaves you by yourself to defend yourself?" His voice rose with mine, both of us battling each other.

Not together. Never together. We were still enemies, unable to form the truce we said we wanted, so we could fight together.

"What else is he supposed to do?" I pushed passed him to sit on my bed. Hugging my pillow to my stomach, I said, "Tell me, Roderick. What else is my dad supposed to do?"

"Protect you," he whispered.

Protect me. From the woman who once told me

she loved me more than anyone else in the world. The woman who said the day she was chosen to be my mom was the best day of her life.

"He doesn't know she hits me. Besides, I protect myself."

"No," he countered, "you don't. You just said you take whatever she does to you."

He sat beside me, brushed his thigh against mine. I turned from him, not much but he noticed and edged away from me.

"Why do you take it?" he asked. "Lock your door like you did last night, or better yet, go live with your dad when he moves out."

"I can't defend myself when she can't defend herself, and I can't fight her when she's fighting herself. I won't leave her, at least not until I go to college in L.A."

"Why?"

"I'm her daughter."

He stared at me, waited for me to continue.

"Don't you get it? That could be me one day, completely lost in my own mind. That could be me, Roderick. I need to know what I'm up against."

That terror I saw before? It was nothing compared to his expression now.

"It's genetic," I pressed. "My mom can pass it down to me the way my dad gave me his green eyes."

His mouth hung up, the pulse on his neck quickened. He'd leave soon, run from the real freak. The one who hid from the world. I pushed harder.

"I get tested every year," I said. "My dad and the doctors talk alone in the office, but he'd tell me if anything was wrong. So for now, it's safe to say everything looks normal, but my mom told me they don't really know what they're looking for. It could come without warning, just like it did to my mom."

"It could." He took my limp hand in his. "It doesn't mean it will."

I gave him half a smile. "You gonna take a gamble and find out?"

"Yeah."

I jerked my hand from his grip, but it only made him hold on tighter.

"I told you, you're my girl, and we're in this together."

"There is no together in this." I looked at our joined hands. It was crazy how well our broken pieces fit. "It's just me. Not you, not my dad, or my mom. When…"

"If," he corrected. "There's no when, only if. It might not happen."

"And I'll live the rest of my life in fear, thinking it might."

He scowled. "You can't live like that, baby." He kissed my hand. "You have to live, just live. Whatever's gonna happen will happen whether or not you spend your life worrying about it."

I scoffed. "Live, huh? You've done a lot of that since your parents died?"

He flinched.

"No," I continued, ignoring the pained expression he wore. "You isolated yourself, so no one else could reach you and hurt you. That's why you like being alone, isn't it?"

"You said I didn't have to be alone anymore."

Hurt. Pain. That was what I was good at. What I knew how to deliver.

"You lost your parents and it sucks. There's no coming back from that but maybe you like that kind of pain. So now you're gonna chase after a girl that'll leave you too? That's what I'll do, Roderick." This time he let me take my hand from his hold. "When my brain takes over, when I get sick too, there'll only be short flashes where I'm better, where I'm me again. Between those times, I'll be gone to you. To everyone."

"That's why you did it, then?" He rubbed his hands over his knees. "That's why you pushed your friends away? Why you made new ones with people you don't like?"

"I didn't want anyone to know anything that was going on," I replied.

"So, that's it. You're just going to wait for something that might not come? You're gonna give up before you even try to fight?"

I grunted. Didn't he get it? I couldn't fight something I couldn't see, couldn't hear, couldn't sense.

"What is there left to fight for?" I asked.

"Me. Us."

He stood from the bed on a cough and walked around to the other side of the bed. After pushing back the comforter, he got in and rested his head on the pillow. He patted the empty space next to him.

I shouldn't have gone to him. I knew it even as I lay down facing him.

His cheeks were red and his lips were cracking. After putting his hand on my waist, he closed his lids where dark lashes kissed his skin.

I traced a finger over the sharp planes on his face.

He hadn't given up on me.

Inching his body closer to mine, he wrapped an arm over my waist, and rested his palm against my back.

"Let me fight with you," he whispered.

He wanted to fight with me. For me. For us. *Desperately together.*

I pressed a kiss against the side of his lips. His eyes fluttered open.

"I'm not ready to give up," I whispered back. "I'll fight with you, but if I lose, you have to promise me…"

"I'll never leave you," he interrupted.

"That's not what I was going to say."

He chuckled when I narrowed my eyes at him and then turned his face to cough. "I know," he said, when he faced me again. "But leaving you isn't an option."

"What if I leave you first?"

Fear gripped my heart, twisted it until it hurt.

"I'll find you and bring you back."

CHAPTER 23

Brinley

Roderick's fever had finally broke, but his cough only seemed to get worse. By Thursday, I was worried, but he wouldn't listen to reason and outright refused to call his aunt so she could take him to a doctor.

She knew he was sick because he texted her on Tuesday to let her know he had to miss school. She'd messaged him back right away and then called him. He ignored both.

I pressed him for answers. When I wouldn't relent, he closed his eyes, drew himself close to me and fell asleep with my fingers in his hair. I hated that he wouldn't talk to me, hated that he didn't trust me, but for now I let him go until he was feeling better. Then, I'd make him talk to me, tell me why he no longer lived with his aunt.

He could stay with me for as long as he needed,

that wasn't why I asked the questions he didn't want to answer, I just wanted him to know I was there for him the same way he showed me I could trust him.

On my bed, which now smelled like him, I rested my head on his chest while he looked at our group assignment. We'd worked on it throughout the week and finally had our poem that I would turn in when I returned to school tomorrow.

I wasn't crazy about going back without him. Wasn't crazy about leaving him here by himself.

But he wanted me to go, so I could go to the Fall Ball on Saturday without any of the teachers asking why I'd missed school but was able to go to the dance. He didn't get that I no longer had any desire to go to the dance. Not without him.

Danny could find someone else. I'd already warned him he would probably have to.

Although Roderick said we were in this together, he had a way of hiding where I couldn't reach him. I tried and would continue to try, but he made it difficult. Nearly impossible.

Turning the paper around, he showed me his artwork on our assignment.

Instead of blacking out the words we didn't use, Roderick drew swirls across the page. Thick purple designs that looked like waves crashing onto the beach's shore. Together, we had circled the words to make out our poem, but the words didn't relate to him. They were mine, another gift from Roderick to help me.

Afraid to show my depth
I use my shallow
as a shield

I was scared to turn in something so honest, but I knew I would since it was one of the things that brought Roderick and me back together. It was special, something I would keep and treasure forever.

"Looks good," I said, planting a kiss on his chest.

"You look better."

I lifted my head when he turned to cough. When he finished, he drew in a few breaths as he angled his body back toward me.

He reached to me, rubbed his thumb over the bridge of my nose. "You're giving yourself early wrinkles," he said. "Stop looking at me like that."

"Your cough sounds awful."

He rubbed his chest but smiled. "I'm fine."

After grabbing some cough medicine and forcing him to take some, I lied down beside him, curled myself to his form. His fingers found my waist and he pulled himself closer to me. I loved the way he did that. The way it seemed he could never feel close enough to me.

"When I go back to school, I'm going to see the counselor so I can apply to go to UCLA," he said.

"That's where I'm going!" I shrieked.

He chuckled as he brushed a strand of hair behind my ear. His fingers lingered, made a few sweet passes across my cheek.

"I know," he said. "That's why I'm applying there."

I sucked in my bottom lip as heat slammed through my veins and spread across my chest.

"How'd you know I was going there?"

"You only told the entire school last year when you got your acceptance letter," he replied.

I giggled. "I did, didn't I? Did you apply anywhere

last year?"

"A few universities."

"Where'd you get in?" I asked, knowing he would've been accepted anywhere he applied. His grades had always been better than mine, and mine were pretty great.

"I got a full scholarship at the Art School of San Diego." He shrugged.

My eyes widened. "A full scholarship? Roderick, you can't give that up to go to UCLA. That's... that's a full scholarship! At an art school. You'd do amazing there."

"I'd do better close to you."

"Can you just stop being sweet for a second and think this through," I scolded.

He grinned and despite what I said, I melted a little more inside.

"You're not gonna get a full ride to UCLA so late in the game."

"So I'll apply for financial aid the first year and a scholarship the next year," he argued.

"I want to be with you." I ran my fingers through his hair. "I want to be with you so bad, but it doesn't make sense to throw away your scholarship."

"It makes even less sense to throw us away."

God, this boy. His words. He slayed me. Tore straight through my heart. I never stood a chance against him.

"We wouldn't be throwing us away," I retorted. "I'd visit San Diego all the time and you could visit me in L.A. until you can go to UCLA."

"We could do that." He kissed my nose. "Or we could move in together, rent an apartment in L.A. and go to the same school."

"Yeah." I huffed. "Your idea sounds way better."

"Of course it does," he agreed. "Now go to sleep. You have school tomorrow."

"So bossy."

I yawned. This time it was his fingers that played with my hair. And when I fell asleep, I didn't hear my mom's screams. I didn't hear the echo of a future I was afraid of.

All I heard were the soft sounds of Roderick's breath in my ear.

CHAPTER 24

RODERICK

BRINLEY'S ROOM WAS pretty. Simple and warm, a lot like her handwriting, but mostly like Brinley herself.

She had her reasons to push people away. While I didn't understand why she hurt people when it never made her feel better, I supposed that was the point. That was her punishment. She ridiculed others and it was she who suffered the most.

She hated herself. I remembered her telling me that when we were walking to her car from the cave. I couldn't let her hate herself though, not when there was so much to love about her.

Love. Yeah, I loved her. I always had. She'd been my best friend at one point and although she let me go, I didn't think I ever truly had accepted it. Instead, I tried to hate her as a way to keep her in my life.

Ridiculous, wasn't it? How we pushed away the very people who could help us.

I knew she would try to push me away when things got dirty again, when I made her talk about things she didn't want to talk about. I'd be there to push back because that's what you did when you loved someone. You didn't give up on them. You didn't let them give up on themselves.

You pushed back until they learned the comfort of leaning on someone they could trust. You pushed back until they saw themselves for who they really were. Worthy of love from others and from themselves.

Resting on her bed, I surrounded myself with her smell as I wrote in a notebook she gave me. Writing wasn't just an obsession for me but a purge of sorts. It was the only way I could give voice to everything I'd hidden.

Brinley and I had that in common. We hid well. So well in fact, I didn't realize how much I didn't want to be alone until she gave me someone to talk to. Just as she didn't realize how much she hated herself until she found her passion in writing. At least, that's what she told me. That through putting emotions on paper, she found out how much she disliked the person she'd become. That feeling grew and grew until she felt she couldn't live in her own skin.

We didn't write words. We bled them. It was those words that coursed through our veins and brought us back to life. Brought us back into each other's lives. And now that I had her, I couldn't let her go. Despite her warnings of what the future may hold. That didn't mean I wasn't terrified. I was beyond terrified. The idea of losing her, whether it was to herself or to someone else, paralyzed me.

For now, I had her. For now, she was mine and I would keep it that way forever if I could.

I wondered how different school would be when I went back. Would she walk with me down the hall, hold my hand and nestle against my chest? Would she let me kiss her in front of everyone? Would I have someone to sit with during lunch?

A smile played on the corner of my lips, and I imagined being the one walking her into the Fall Ball tomorrow. I imagined her soft figure pressed against me as we danced beneath the twinkling lights of whatever hall the school had rented. Her face pressed close to mine with my hands running across her back as her fingers played with my hair.

It would be the perfect night, except it would never happen. I was still sick and didn't have a suit. Although we clung to each other in the privacy of her room, I wasn't sure she'd want to be seen with me like that in public. I was still the school's outcast, the freak and despite all the changes she'd made, she was still the school's princess.

A few coughs shook my body, and I tried to suppress them so Brinley's mom couldn't hear me. She'd been pretty active today, walking across the hall to Brinley's door several times, and I didn't want to give her a reason to come inside. Despite my best efforts, the coughs sputtered out, so I pushed my face into a pillow to soften the sound.

When I came up for air, pain radiated while fire licked against my chest. My lungs seemed to fold into themselves, war with each other rather than grant me the oxygen I so desperately needed.

I coughed to ease the tightness, then closed my eyes on a groan. Even with my eyes shut, the world seemed to spin. Gripping onto Brinley's sheets, I took slow breaths. But each inhale seemed to set my lungs on fire.

Nausea rose with every cough. With my vision blurred, I lowered myself to the floor and crawled to the bathroom. Saliva dripped from my mouth and when I raised the lid to the toilet, I vomited. More came up and I choked on it when I continued to cough.

Beads of sweat collected on my forehead and my back. Everything in me shook.

Suddenly, a hand rested on my shoulder, and I jumped at the contact. Looking back, I saw Brinley's mom peering back at me. Her features were soft, her lips pulled down in a frown. She looked so much like Brinley, which shouldn't have shocked me, but it did. The woman who screamed and cursed to the high heavens had the beautiful face of an angel.

"You're not Brinley," she said, her voice small.

I shook my head, unable to speak, and then leaned back over the toilet to vomit again. Water ran behind me, and I nearly groaned in relief when she put a cool cloth over the back of my neck. She rubbed my back, spoke words of comfort and when I leaned back, she took me in her arms while I tried to breathe.

Each inhale hurt more than the other.

Behind me, she stood up and went to the sink where she turned the water on again. I tried to control the coughs, control my breathing while I watched her touch the water every so often. She didn't speak again, but would look down at me through concerned eyes.

Leaning against the wall, I closed my eyes.

Brinley would be home soon. She couldn't see me like this. Already, she worried too much about me.

"There we go," her mom said.

She reached an open palm to me. I hesitated but took it and she helped me to my feet.

"Lean over the sink and take deep breaths," she said.

I did as she instructed and when I leaned over the sink, she put a towel over my head. I stilled, but she pushed my head down further and I followed suit.

Steam stung my face and when I tried to straighten back up, she held me to the sink with a firm hand.

"Breathe in the vapor," she said. "It'll help open your bronchial tubes."

Closing my eyes, I took in a deep breath and coughed out a release. Again, I inhaled and exhaled. Each time I coughed until tears stung behind my eyes.

"You're doing good," she said, rubbing my back.

Long moments passed before I could finally breathe again. This time, when I stepped away from the sink, her hands fell from my back.

"Thank you." I turned to face her and saw Brinley standing behind her mom.

"Close your mouth before you catch flies," her mom teased her.

Brinley snapped her jaw shut, but her eyes continued to jump from her mom to me. Extending my arm, I reached for her and she stepped into my embrace.

"Hi, Mom." She leaned her head against my shoulder. "I guess you met my boyfriend, Roderick?"

Her mom smiled back at her. "I guess I did. Any idea what he's doing in your bedroom while you were at school?"

She nibbled on her bottom lip as her cheeks turned a pretty pink.

"His aunt's out of town for work, and I didn't want him staying at home by himself when he got sick," she finally said.

I sagged in relief when her mom nodded in understanding.

"You have a nasty cough, Roderick," her mom said. "When your aunt gets back you should have an X-ray done of your lungs. Do you mind if I have a listen?"

"A listen of what?" I asked.

Brinley laughed. "Of your lungs with her stethoscope."

"I used to be a doctor before…" she trailed off, her eyes looking passed us. She snapped her attention back to me. "I'm Rosie by the way."

"Yeah." I coughed. "Sure, Rosie, I'd appreciate it if you listened to my lungs."

Brinley kissed my cheek, and then took my hand to lead me back to her bed. I let her help me in and thanked her when she covered me with blankets.

"You know, Brinley." I winked. "Your mom's kind of hot."

Red spread across her cheeks and she covered her face. "Ohmygosh! Don't say that."

"She totally is." I nodded.

She smacked my shoulder lightly and then kissed where she'd hit me. "Are you okay?" Her voice trembled. "When I got home, you sounded awful. Worse than…"

"I'm okay," I interrupted her. "Your mom helped me. I guess being awesome runs in your family."

She didn't reply. She didn't have to.

Seeing the notebook that I must've let fall to the floor, she picked it up and tilted her head. I nodded and she opened to the first page. Her hand found mine as she read my words. Expressions crossed her features.

"Beautiful," I said, running my thumb over the back of her hand. "You're so beautiful."

She peeked up at me from behind the notebook but put it down when her mom came back in.

"Okay, Roderick, sit up for me."

Rosie took Brinley's place beside me and after warming the bell of her stethoscope, she placed it on my back beneath my shirt.

"Take a deep breath for me."

I did and God, it hurt. A cough tore through my lungs, but I continued to breathe as she listened. After moving the stethoscope to my chest, she patted my shoulder.

"You'll need a chest X-ray but I'd say you have bronchitis."

"And will these antibiotics," Brinley reached for the medicine I'd been taking, "help him?"

Rosie raised a single brow in question when she examined the pill bottle. Turning it around, she pointed to Brinley's name.

"Please don't tell Dad." Brinley looked down at her shoes.

"It's my fault," I blurted out. "My aunt left and instead of telling her to come back home, I called Brinley. She was trying to help me. I don't want her getting in trouble because of me."

Turning the bottle back to face her, Rosie said, "That'll help but you also need steroids. When does your aunt get back?"

"Today." I swallowed hard. "She should be home any minute."

"Good." She patted my knee. "Have her take you to an urgent care. The one close to your school has an X-ray machine, but don't take these pills with you." She shot a disapproving look to Brinley who squirmed under her scrutiny. "You can get in a lot of trouble for giving someone your pills. What if he'd been allergic to them?"

Brinley nodded, letting her hair spill in front of her face.

"It's okay," I said. "I'm not allergic to anything. Brin helped me, she took care of me."

Rosie placed a hand to her forehead. "I'm going to lie down for a bit." She smiled, but it wasn't like the other smiles I'd seen. This one was forced.

"Mom?" Brinley stood beside her, put her hand on her mom's elbow.

"Take your boyfriend home. Maybe you should stay at Nicole's tonight." She squeezed her eyes, holding a closed fist by her chest.

"I'm staying with you," Brinley argued.

"Call the nurse before you leave. It was nice meeting you, Roderick. I hope you're feeling well soon."

"Thank you for taking care of me, Rosie," I said to her departing back. "I'm glad I finally got the chance to meet the woman behind Brinley's gorgeous looks."

She angled her head to the side and gave me a smile. A real one.

"Take care of my girl when I can't," she said, her smile falling.

"Always." Standing, I wrapped my fingers around

Brinley's waist and held her to me as her mom went back to her room.

We heard her door shut, and Brinley leaned her back against me with a sigh. "You need a chest X-ray."

Something in my chest squeezed, but this time it wasn't my lungs. I dropped my head to her shoulder.

"Do you think you can take me to my aunt's house?"

CHAPTER 25

Brinley

Tucking a pillow beneath my arm pit, I made my way to the front door where Roderick waited for me. I'd already put his bag in my trunk but I ran back in to grab this.

His call to his aunt was tense, and I knew going back weighed heavily on him. I couldn't save him from that. He had to go back and see a doctor, but I hoped the pillow might offer him a little bit of comfort.

"What's that?" he asked.

I widened my eyes in mock shock. "A pillow."

He shook his head. "Why are you bringing it with us?"

"So you can sleep with it."

He took the pillow from my grasp and pressed his face against it.

"It smells like you." He smiled.

"And the pillow I'm keeping for myself smells like you." I closed the door behind me and locked it.

"Seeing as you've told me a couple times I smell bad, I think you're getting a pretty bad deal out of this." He nudged me with his shoulder.

"Shut up."

The drive to his aunt's house was silent. Not uncomfortable, even though I knew Roderick was nervous. I could feel his anxiety crawling on my skin, but he kept to himself and I let him. He kept the pillow I gave him on his lap, his fingers touching the soft fabric and playing with the ends while his knees bounced in anticipation.

"Are you going to be okay at your aunt's house?"

"Yeah." He leaned over and kissed my cheek. "You don't have to worry about me."

Drumming my fingers on the steering wheel, I turned in to his neighborhood. "Of course I'm gonna worry about you. You wound up living in a cave to get away from her."

"It'll be fine, baby."

Baby. I loved it when he called me that. As if I wasn't already falling head over feet for him.

"I wish you'd talk to me," I muttered.

Long moments passed where he stared out the window. Finally, he spoke. It came out heavy, sad. "You know I've been living with my aunt since my parents died." He rubbed a hand over his chest. "She's not bad or anything, we just don't get along. We fight a lot." He hesitated. "Maybe it's my fault. I'm not easy with her. I pick fights just because I can. But it's also her fault. I've lived with her for five years." He stammered out a breath. "And I still feel like a visitor. Our last fight she told me I'd overstayed my visit so I left. Didn't really want to go back to her house, but I don't have a choice."

"You can stay with me," I offered.

His eyes warmed, and the affection I saw on his face made my heart soar. "You can't hide me away forever. It's better if I stay with her until we move to L.A."

We were quiet again.

"Will you call me when you get back from the urgent care?"

"Yeah, and if I'm not hacking up a lung I'll talk to you all night." He winked.

"All night's a really long time," I teased. "They cancelled the football game tonight." I looked up at the black sky. "I could stay with you if you wanted me to. My mom said for me to stay at Nicole's anyway." I lifted a single shoulder in a shrug.

"I want you with me every night," he said, his tone serious.

I couldn't fight back my grin. "I'll go to your place after you get back from the urgent care then. What about your aunt?" I paused. "Am I going to have to sneak in through a window or something?"

He wheezed out a laugh and put a hand to his stomach. "You can come in through the front door. I'll let her know you're staying with me."

"And she'll be okay with that?"

"Yes." His word was final, and I didn't bother arguing with him.

Roderick messed with the radio, turning the knob until he found a song he liked. Beside me, my phone vibrated and Danny's name lit up on the screen. I let it ring until it went to voicemail. I'd call him later, after I left Roderick's place.

When I got to his house, his aunt ran out of the front door. Roderick grunted before opening the door and when he stepped out, she embraced him in a long hug that he eventually returned.

While they talked, I grabbed his belongings from the trunk and gave them to his aunt. She eyed me suspiciously.

"This is my aunt, Victoria," Roderick said. "And this is my girlfriend, Brinley."

I shook his aunt's hand, vaguely remembering her face from when we were younger.

"Nice to meet you," I muttered.

"I'm sure Roderick's told you all sorts of wonderful things about me," Victoria teased. It didn't sound mean or anything, just curious.

I stayed quiet.

"You'll be coming by when we get back from the doctor?" she asked.

"Yes," Roderick answered for me. It came out stiff.

"Do your parents know you're staying the night here?"

"No," I answered honestly before Roderick could say anything. "They think I'm staying at another friend's house."

"I can't let you stay then."

Roderick worked his jaw back and forth.

"But you can let your nephew stay outside for three weeks, so he winds up with bronchitis?" I asked. "That doesn't bother you?"

Red spilled across her cheeks. I could see her pulse hammer against her throat as she narrowed her eyes at me. "I didn't let Roderick stay outside. That was his decision. I asked him to come back here. He didn't listen."

"You asked him to come back?" I snorted. It was ugly and disrespectful, but I was angry. "Tell me, did you say please when you asked?"

"Brin." Roderick rested his hand on my shoulder. A warning for me to stop, but I kept going.

"It's been raining for weeks. How many times did you go out looking for him? How many people did you call to see if he was with them? What did you do to get him back?" My heart shook with my anger. "I'm staying the night to make sure someone takes care of him."

Roderick followed me to my car where he opened the door for me. Before I could get in, he took me in his arms and rested his face against mine. My hands snaked around his back and I held onto him.

"I'll see you later," he brushed over my ear.

Just below the surface
she crept and
stole the ground beneath me.
Now I'm falling
In to her.

I purposely kept Roderick's notebook, so I could read his poem again.

My phone vibrated, and I picked it up to see a selfie of Roderick wearing a nebulizer mask. His thumbs up made my heart clench.

Rather than taking him to an urgent care, his aunt had taken him to the Emergency Room where they confirmed he had bronchitis and had given him two breathing treatments and no timeframe as to when he'd be able to go back home.

It was already after ten and with the rain coming down harder than before, I wouldn't be going to his house.

I huffed in disappointment and sent him a quick text.

Me: The mask looks great on you. Very Bane-like

Roderick: Bane? Like from Batman? Pls tell me my girl knows her Superhero movies

I shook my head. He was ridiculous, but God, I liked him.

Me: Yeah

At the same time I sent my next text, his reply came in

Roderick: That is the hottest thing ever. Don't say anything else

Me: My dad forces me to watch them

Roderick: Moment ruined. Thks

I sent him a heart emoji and then went to Danny's name to text him since I never replied to his earlier call.

Me: Hey, I'm not gonna make it to the dance tomorrow. Please don't hate me

I wasn't surprised when I saw his name flashing with an incoming call. Danny would rather talk than text.

"Do you hate me?" I asked in way of greeting.

"Never," he answered. "Everything okay?"

"Yeah, I just haven't been feeling well."

"You're not sick, Brin." He said it with such confidence that I couldn't deny it.

"No, I'm not."

"Talk to me."

"My mom's sick," I whispered into the phone.

He stayed quiet. Tears welled in my eyes and I didn't know why I wanted so badly to tell him. Why the words beat against my tongue, desperate to come out and confide in someone else. Cleanse myself of everything I'd held onto.

I told him everything. The same I'd told Roderick, but this time without the sickening feeling that I would be left alone.

"Do you want me to stay with you tomorrow?" he asked when I finished. "We don't have to go to the dance."

"No." I blushed. "Actually, the reason I'm not going to the dance is because I'm going to Roderick's. He's at the ER right now, has bronchitis and although he wasn't going to go to the dance anyway, I want to take the dance to him."

"Oh I see." It came out amused and I felt my blush deepen.

"Shut up," I muttered.

He barked out a loud laugh.

"Are you angry with me?" I asked.

"Not even a little bit," he answered. "Is Roderick okay?"

"Yeah, they're giving him some breathing treatments and medicine. I'm hoping he'll be home soon."

"Don't you think it's weird that you and him were sick on the same week?" His voice was nothing but a tease.

A loud wail echoed from the other side of my door. I held my breath, waited for my mom to stop, for Bridgette to take her back to her room. Her fingers squeaked against the door as I imagined her falling to the floor.

"Mrs. Crassus," Bridgette's soothing voice said, "why don't we go back to bed, dear? I'll make you some tea and we can paint together."

"Yes." Her voice was shaky. "I'd like that very much."

My heart stalled and then swelled. My mom had gone back to her room without a fight.

"Was that your mom?" Danny asked.

The lies, the secrets were gone and even though nothing had changed, I had. I felt better in sharing my burden with the best guys in my life – my boyfriend and my best friend. Neither would desert me.

"Yeah. She had a good day today. When I got home, she was back to her regular self." I paused, left out anything that would reveal Roderick had been staying with me. "It always hits her the hardest after a good day."

My mom had broken through the fog enough to help Roderick. When I got home, I was shocked to see her taking care of him in my bathroom. Even more shocked when she offered to bring out her stethoscope.

She'd met my boyfriend today and liked him. The memory of her smiling at him warmed me.

"Do you want me to come over?" he asked. "I can sleep on your floor to keep you company."

"I love you, Danny," I breathed into the phone. "So much. You know that, right?"

"Yeah." He cleared his throat. "Why else would you want to marry me, have eight kids, four dogs, and a porcupine?"

I grinned. "Yeah, you're definitely my favorite person in the world."

"So is your favorite person in the world coming over with chocolate bars?"

"Another night. It's late and raining."

"This rain's never gonna stop is it?"

"It'll stop," I answered.

"Holy crap, maybe you are sick!" he shouted into the phone. "Were you just… optimistic?"

"Temporary lapse. Won't happen again."

An incoming text made my phone vibrate. After telling Danny to hold on, I clicked on Roderick's name.

> Roderick: Heading home... still want me to call you when I get in?
>
> Me: Yep
>
> Roderick: K

"Roderick's heading home now," I told Danny.

"I'll talk to you tomorrow then?" he asked. "You know, when you're not busy playing nurse."

"Yeah, tomorrow."

"Love you, Brin. Thanks for trusting me today," he whispered.

"I always trusted you," I rushed out. "It was me I didn't trust."

After hanging up the phone, I went back to Roderick's journal and re-read his poem for the hundredth time. He was falling for me, and I was falling for him.

Grabbing my pencil, I wrote him back. It wasn't on a cave's wall, but each word spilled from my heart. Still genuine, still raw, still me.

"Hey," I said into the phone when Roderick called.

"Hey, baby."

"You sound tired."

He was quiet for a bit. "I am. I wish you were with me."

"So do I."

"The doctor said I should stay in bed for a few days." I heard him shuffle on his bed, and I imagined him lying on his side, his eyes looking back at me. "Will you come by tomorrow before going to the dance?"

I smiled. He had no idea I'd be going to him for the dance. "Sure. Are you feeling any better?"

"Jittery, but the doctor said that's normal with all the breathing treatments they gave me. He wrote a script for enough treatments to last two weeks. Gave me antibiotics and steroids."

He coughed.

"I kept your notebook," I said.

"I know. I was looking for it so I could take it to the hospital."

Running my hands over his poem, I said, "I'll give it back to you tomorrow."

"Did you write back to me?" His voice sounded sleepy.

"I did. Want me to read it to you?"

"Yeah," he breathed into the phone.

"Do you have the pillow I gave you?"

"Yeah."

"I have your stinky pillow too."

He laughed.

"Close your eyes," I whispered.

"Okay."

"Pretend I'm playing with your hair."

He sighed. It sounded content and filled me with longing.

"Can you feel my fingers through your hair?"

"Yeah, baby."

"He took my heart,
held it in his secure hands.
And I fell for him.
It wasn't slow this descent,
but all consuming."

"Brin…"

"I'm falling so hard for you, Roderick," I said before he could say anything else. "And I'm terrified."

"Don't be, baby," he whispered. "By the time you finish the fall, I'll be there to catch you."

CHAPTER 26

RODERICK

ANGER MADE MY fingers itch and I sucked in a breath that I exhaled on a cough. Just once I'd like my aunt to see things my way, but she was trapped in her own thinking.

"I don't want your girlfriend coming over," she repeated for the third time. "I don't like her, don't like the way she talked to me."

"She was defending me," I argued, trying and failing to keep my voice calm.

"Defending you from me?" She shook her head.

"Yeah." Dragging my hands over my face, I said, "She cares about me, okay?"

"And you don't think I do?" Her voice rose. "I didn't want you to leave, that was your choice! And I did what I could to protect you, so you could be happy and go to

179

school and not get in trouble for running away."

Running away. It sounded so juvenile, but I guessed that's exactly what I'd done. I ran away three weeks ago, wandered through the woods and slept against the trees, until I found the cave. Until I got sick and Brinley took me in.

"Was not renewing my lunch card part of you protecting me?" I choked on a dry laugh. "I had nothing to eat when my job cut my hours. If it weren't for Brinley, I wouldn't have had anything to eat."

Her face fell, her lips curled down. She blinked a few times, and it was gone. "I forgot about the lunch card." It came out grave. "I'm sorry about that, but you had your phone. You could've called me. You could've come back here."

"For what? So we can keep doing this?" I gestured to her and me. "Because we get so much accomplished with our talks," I spat out.

Grinding her teeth, she said, "She's a disrespectful brat, Roderick, and I won't have her in my house."

"Your house," I huffed out. "That's what it always comes down to. This is your house, not mine."

"Roderick…"

"I get it," I interrupted. "You have less than six months before I'm gone, and my girlfriend's coming to hang out with me whenever she wants. Let me have that." I didn't mean for it to come out so desperate, but it did.

Her features softened for a fraction of a second before she set her mouth in a thin line. "If she's rude to me again…"

"I'll talk to her." Again, I interrupted her. She hated when I did it, so I did it often. Her temper was one of the few things I could control in her house. She always rose to it, always reminded me of the burden I was to her.

"This is your house too," she said to me when I turned to leave.

I tightened my hands into fists and forced myself to relax. First my neck, then my shoulders and back. "It isn't," I countered. "This place will never be mine."

She let out an agitated breath.

When I got back to my room, I put on my headphones and turned on the music on my phone. Brinley had texted me earlier this morning, and we talked in the afternoon before she headed to the mall to get her nails and hair done.

I was glad she was going to the dance and hoped she'd have enough time to swing by for a few minutes before she left. These dances were important to her, they'd always been. I'd never gone to one, but I got to see her smiling face in the pictures she'd post on Instagram. At the time, I'd tell myself her happiness angered me, but it never did.

How could it when her happiness brought out mine?

Danny had also texted me in the late morning. He didn't seem to know anything other than I was sick and had spent a few hours in the hospital. I texted him back a thank you to his get better message and asked him to take care of Brinley tonight and make sure she had a good time. He agreed, and although this was what I wanted, I felt a twist in my gut that I wouldn't be the one making her smile. That I wouldn't be there to catch her laughter and hold it to me as we danced.

While I wasn't the type to go to school events, I'd make an effort this year. I'd go to the games to watch

Brinley cheer, go to dances, and whatever else she wanted. Even go to every one of Danny's games, so I could be with her as she watched him play.

This girl, she was making me crazy in the best possible way and every second I spent away from her hurt.

When the doorbell rang, I turned the music up louder and leaned on my side, away from the new nebulizer that sat on my night stand. While the machine and the medicine I put in there helped with the tightness in my chest, I dreaded the moment when I'd have to do another treatment. The after effects of the medicine made me shaky, not in a way that my limbs shook but in an I'm-going-to-crawl-out-of-my-skin-way.

Digging out my phone, I clicked on the picture Brinley had sent me of the poem she wrote for me. The memory of her soft voice reading it to me last night filled my heart, my soul.

Brinley was falling for me. I'd already fallen. Which meant I'd be there to catch her when she made her final descent.

A loud knock came from my door. I angled my head to it, but turned back away. Another knock, this one louder.

Taking my headphones off, I called out, "Yeah?"

This time the knock was more tentative.

On a grunt, I swung my feet over the bed and opened my door. And there on the other side was the most beautiful girl. *My girl.*

I inhaled a sharp breath, and this time the dizziness didn't come from my lungs, but from the girl standing in front of me.

A silver dress sculpted her pretty figure, clung to her

like second skin. Strappy heels made her taller, almost my height. I tugged one of the curls that framed her face and then palmed her cheek. She leaned into my touch with a sweet smile on her face.

"Hi," I said.

"Hi," she replied.

"You look beautiful." I couldn't take my eyes off her, couldn't move from my spot in front of my door. This girl, she took my breath away, gave it back with new meaning. "You always look beautiful."

She tilted her head to the side. "Can I come in?"

"Yeah, sure." I scrambled inside, tripped over my feet.

Carrying a large tote bag, she stepped into my room. I picked up a few pieces of dirty clothes from the floor and threw them into a nearby hamper.

I was nervous. We'd spent the past week together, but being here in my room scared me.

She stepped toward me, it was a small step and I met her the rest of the way. Pressing my face against her neck, I touched her arm with a feather light graze. She shivered and wrapped her arms around my neck. My fingers followed the small curves of her body. When I touched her back where her dress dipped low, I pressed my palm against her warm skin.

"You're here," I said, nipping her ear.

"And I brought food."

My stomach rumbled in response.

"Are you going to be late to the dance?"

She edged her head back, kissed my nose, and shook her head.

"We probably shouldn't kiss," I said. "The doctor last night said I was contagious."

She pressed her lips to mine, ran her tongue against the seams, and I took her in. Our tongues tumbled, her taste invaded me. It wasn't enough. Holding her closer to me, I deepened the kiss.

It wasn't just a kiss, but a breath of life. Every part of me, she filled with fire, with want and need, and with love.

It was like a dream, an embrace. It was poetry. The kiss I'd been waiting for my whole life. It was mine.

When we parted, her eyes remained closed, her cheeks flushed. I touched her cheek and her eyes fluttered open.

"I missed you," she said

"I missed you too."

She took a step back, put her tote bag on the bed, and started taking food out. I helped her and after getting her the chair that sat by the computer, we opened the lids of the containers. There was plenty of food, enough to feed Danny's football team

"I wasn't sure if you'd be able to eat, so I got you soup and spaghetti. You don't have to eat both."

Sitting on the bed, I leaned into her and kissed her cheek. "A thousand thank yous will never be enough."

Her eyes snapped back to me, and the sides of her mouth crinkled when she smiled. "I love that. You left me two notes saying that."

I lifted a single shoulder, not meeting her gaze. "It was something my mom used to say to me when I did something that made her feel special."

"She was special." Her tone was light but when I looked back at her, she seemed nervous, shy. "I remember having her as a teacher in first grade. She had the best smile. Actually, I think you have her smile."

My heart stammered to a stop, and when it started again, it bumped hard and fast.

"Do you remember when she dressed up as a princess for my birthday party at school?" Brinley asked.

Reaching for the memory, I grinned. There was no sorrow or anger, just my mom dressed up because one of her students was sad.

"My dad was working at the hospital, and my mom got called in to an emergency." She dug in to her food and after a few bites, she twined her hands with mine as we sat across from each other palm to palm. "Neither of them could make it, but my mom had already left everything for the party at school, so your mom said we'd still celebrate my birthday. I was so happy." She chewed on bottom lip. "But then the princess cancelled, and I burst into tears."

"So my mom got another teacher to watch her class, drove home, and made a princess outfit out of what she had in the closet."

I brought our joined hands to my chest, and damn, it hurt, but it also didn't. Somewhere between the pain, was joy.

"She was pretty great," I said.

"She made me feel special that day."

My mom had a way of making everyone feel special. Like they were the most important part of her day. Without her, I disappeared.

"You made me feel special when you took care of me," I said.

"You are special."

Putting the soup to the side, I reached for Brinley. She came to me after placing her own food on the floor.

We sat together, her nestled on my lap, for a long time.

"I miss her." It came out broken.

Touching my face, she kissed my jaw. "I'm sure she misses you too."

I took in a shaky breath, it stalled on my tongue.

"It's crazy, all those times we took them for granted," she said with a shake of her head. She was thinking about her mom. I was thinking about my parents. "We didn't know, couldn't know they'd be ripped from us. But I believe," she touched my face, framed it with her hands, "I believe your parents are still here. Whether they're watching us right now, or alive inside of you, they're here. You're their son and not even death can take that away from them. They're here." A tear fell down her cheek, and I wiped it away with a trembling finger. "Right here, right now, they're here."

I rested my head on her temple, took in another shaky breath. She pressed a hand to my chest, right over my heart, and I covered her hand with mine.

"Do you feel them?"

I did. I felt them inside me, around me. Everywhere all at once.

"Do you hear them?"

My mom's laughter floated in the air. My dad's booming voice called to me.

Inside, my heart quaked.

"Yeah," I sighed. "They're here. I feel them."

My mom's eyes lit up in the back of my mind, and I imagined my dad putting his arm around her.

"I see them."

She tapped a finger to my chest, and I brought it to my lips.

"They're here."

A tear ran down my cheek. And then another. With her thumb, she wiped them away and I laughed, uncomfortable sharing my sadness. But she wanted it, had taken it from me, and turned it into something incredible.

For the first time since my parents' death, I felt peace.

She held me, let me cry in her arms, helped me rebuild stronger.

When I eased her back, her cheeks were wet from her own tears. I kissed them, stunned she'd cried for me. Cried with me.

It was no wonder I was helpless in my fall.

"Are you done eating?" she asked.

"Yeah." My carton of soup sat by my foot, most of it still there. "Sorry I couldn't eat more."

On her feet, she took my soup and grabbed her half-eaten plate. Her dress moved with her, and I fought a groan when she bent over to put the food on the floor by my door.

"I'm so happy you stopped by, but you should probably head out before you're late," I said.

She tucked a curl behind her ear, her lips tipped up in a soft smile.

"You're so cute." Picking up my phone, she handed it to me. "You think I got all dressed up for some dance at school?"

I nodded. That's exactly what I thought.

"The dance is here." She stepped closer to me. "In your bedroom." Another step and this time she cusped her hands behind my neck. "You're the DJ, pick something good."

I smiled. I couldn't have stopped my lips from spreading even if I wanted to.

Brinley came to me. She chose to share her last Fall Ball with me. Her nomination in the court would be nulled and while I'd never been nominated for anything in our school, that night I felt like the king to her queen.

CHAPTER 27

Brinley

I swayed in his arms, my heart soaring, seeming to float outside of my chest and dance to the rhythm of his heart beat.

Song after song, he chose them. All of them slow. All of them about finding love.

And I'd found it, hadn't I? In a cave, with words that exposed our deepest pain, our greatest fear.

I found him. Heck, I was pretty sure I found heaven.

Gray clouds hid outside the house as rain tapped against his window. The soft sound of his breath rang in my ear, shivered down my spine and vibrated in my limbs. Dreams of our future rose with the howling wind, all the worries I'd held onto fell away.

He pushed his lips down to mine. A fire sizzled in my chest, burned through my veins. An ache built deep in my belly. I whimpered against his lips. With a tender touch, he slid his hand up my spine to the back of my neck where he cradled my head. His fingers dug into my hair.

I ran my hands over his arms, to his back where I snaked my hands beneath his shirt. When I touched his bare skin, he inhaled a sharp breath.

"Brinley." The way he said my name made it sound like a plea.

I nipped his jaw, and he groaned. Feeling brave, I skimmed my hands to his stomach. He jumped at the contact, and his muscles quivered when I drew small circles over his chest. The pulse in his neck quickened, and I pressed my lips to it. His heart raced against me, mine keeping tune with his.

His hands went to my back again, he drew me to him. I inched my body closer, needed to mold our bodies together.

Another groan, this one more raw, more needy. He took a step back, dropped his hands to his side. I kept my hands on his shoulders, and when I touched his face he tipped it down on a pained expression.

"Roderick?" I stepped in to him and he retreated. My brows furrowed, confusion and rejection warring for space in my heart.

Without saying anything, he cupped my face in his hands and crushed his lips to mine. He stole my breath or I gave it willingly. It didn't matter. Everything I had was his anyway.

On a curse he pulled away, his breaths fell quickly from his parted lips. He pushed his tongue out to wet his lips, and I mimicked him.

"Are you okay?" I asked, breathless as well.

My heart galloped at his silence, and I wondered what I'd done wrong.

"I just…" he dragged in a breath through clenched teeth, "need to calm down."

Not sure what he needed from me, I watched him with my hands crossed over my chest. He raked his hands over his face, and when he looked back at me he laughed.

"Come here." He held his arms out. "Don't look so scared."

I went to him, rested a hand over his chest where his heart raced against my palm. "Do you need to do a breathing treatment?"

He smacked a kiss on the side of my head and tucked his chin to my shoulder. "My breathing isn't the problem."

"What is it then?"

I pressed my chest to his, wrapped my arms around his neck. Then I felt it, something hard pushed against my pelvis.

"Oh." I edged back and looked down at him.

He fixed his pants and when I peered back at his face, he blushed.

"Can't help that." He laughed uncomfortably. "It's just something you do to me."

I touched my face, felt my cheeks inflame. He laughed again and kissed my temple.

"Just ignore it and dance with me."

"Are you sure?" I looked down, didn't mean to stare at the bulge in his pants, but that's exactly what I did. God, this was awkward. "Maybe we should just talk?" I asked.

"Dance with me." He said it with such tenderness, with such delicacy, it made me feel precious. "I'd never do anything to hurt you, baby. I just want to dance with you."

So we did. He took me back in his arms and we danced for hours, long after the school's Fall Ball had finished.

CHAPTER 28

Brinley

Just because nobody saw him, didn't mean he wasn't there. Roderick was a part of the school's thread. He was in every yearbook, attended all of his classes, played some sort of role in everyone's life whether they realized it or not, but it was like they finally noticed him on Tuesday when we walked hand in hand through the hallways.

They smiled at him, talked to him, and while he smiled back, he was reserved. Not at all like the Roderick I'd come to know the past week.

I nudged his shoulder with mine after we got our food from the lunch line. He was carrying my food on his tray and, his thoughtfulness, the way he looked out for me made my heart skip a beat.

"Where do you want to sit?" I asked.

He pointed toward Danny, who was waving in our

direction. Danny's smile was wide, but different. Since I met up with him in homeroom yesterday he'd been acting weird, but he'd dodged every one of my questions. I wondered if something had happened at the dance, after he'd won the title of King. Tonight, I'd call him, make him see he could trust me.

Most of the guys from the football team were sitting at Seth's table. It was the loudest group on the outdoor patio, and while that's where I'd been sitting since the day I called my friends assholes, I wasn't sure how Roderick would feel being around so many people after years of separating himself from the world.

"I think Danny wants us to sit with him." He kept his tone light.

"I didn't ask where Danny wanted us to sit," I said. "We can sit by ourselves if you want to."

With his free hand, he urged me forward, toward Danny and the group at the table. "You're not ditching Danny for me," he said under his breath.

I drew my brows together. Was that what I was doing? Ditching my best friend for my boyfriend? I shook my head. No. I just didn't want Roderick uncomfortable on his first day back. Already so much had changed since he was last at school. Danny would understand that.

After taking a seat between Danny and Roderick, I picked up Danny's soda and took a sip. He narrowed his eyes at me, pointed at my water, and I shrugged in response. Soda wasn't really my favorite drink but sometimes a girl needed a little fizz in her life. I tilted it to Roderick, but he was too busy staring at his food to notice.

When I leaned against Roderick, he put an arm

around me, and I placed a hand on his bobbing knee. The corner of his lips twisted up. The smile, sitting with my friends, talking to others when he was most comfortable with his silence, had to be nerve wracking for him, but he did it for me.

"I never would've thought of you two together," Seth said, his eyes jumping from Roderick to me.

Seth was more at ease around me, around everyone really. After we'd talked on the picnic table after cheer practice, we'd become friends. Had even exchanged numbers. Every day, I asked him what he was working on. Every day, he showed me pictures of his progress.

Roderick stiffened, but didn't say anything. Instead he took a bite of the sandwich he'd bought with his aunt's money. Apparently, she'd forgotten to renew his lunch card that month, and that was why he hadn't been eating lunch before I started making him sandwiches. She promised him she'd have it fixed by next month, before winter break started.

"Why not?" Ari grabbed a fry from Danny's plate.

Danny glared back at Ari. It wasn't a tease, but a look of annoyance.

Seth pushed his glasses back. "I don't know. Brinley's Brinley and Roderick's Roderick."

My heart felt weightless. Like it did when we were dancing in his room, as if I were floating.

I was me and Roderick was Roderick. Together we were an *us* unlike any other.

"We're good together," I said.

Beside me, Roderick shifted to his side. Eyes wide he looked back at me, and I felt a hot blush spread over my cheeks. But I didn't want to take back the words. They were true.

Emotions twisted in my gut, fought to spill out, and I wanted to tell the world – tell Roderick – how much he meant to me.

I settled for half the truth. "I like him."

Roderick's breath caught in his throat, relief was raw on his features, but he kept his grin playful. "I like her too."

My spirits lifted even higher.

We weren't hiding. We were together for the school to see.

Jacob and Nicole passed us, wearing similar sneers on their faces. I glared back, daring them to say something. But they continued to walk and if I hadn't been staring, I would've missed the hurt that flashed behind Nicole's eyes.

"Yeah," Ari said, his eyes flitted to Roderick, me, then he squinted at Danny, "I think we can all tell you like each other."

Squirming, Danny took his soda back and rubbed his neck. Yeah, something was definitely off. When I tugged on his ear, he snapped his attention to me. But immediately, he drew his eyes down to the food he'd barely eaten.

"Let's go for a walk." I kept my voice low.

He gave me a hesitant nod, and I twined my hand with his.

The three of us stood – Roderick, Danny, and me. While Roderick and Danny threw away our trash, I told the table we'd see them later.

"Diner tonight," Ari called out. His focus wasn't on me though, but on Danny who had already started walking to the football field.

"I'm gonna hang out here," Roderick said when I went to his side.

I angled my head to the side, kept my eyes on Danny's departing back. "You don't want to go to the field with us?"

"Go talk to him, see what's going on." He smiled, kissed my nose, and man I loved his kisses. "I'll be here when you get back."

"You'll be okay on your own?"

This time he laughed. "I've been alone for years. I think I can manage for a few minutes."

"Yeah," I hugged him. "But I told you, you don't have to be alone anymore."

Tipping his forehead down to my shoulder, he said, "I'm not alone." The way he said it with such conviction sent butterflies dancing in my belly.

"No, you're not," I agreed.

From a distance, I saw Danny's figure stop before stepping on the football field. He turned toward me, his arms crossed over his chest, and his shoulders slumped forward. My heart ached for him, for whatever was hurting him.

Roderick urged me away so after a quick peck to his cheek, I ran toward the field. The ground was still sticky from the rain, but mud puddles had started to dry up after two days of sporadic drizzles. It was as if Mother Nature had finally avenged her anger and was reining it in.

"Ari kissed me," Danny said when I reached him.

I smiled, but it quickly fell when he let out an agitated huff.

"Why is that bad?" I asked, scrunching up my nose. "Was he a bad kisser?"

Dirt billowed in front of us when he kicked the ground. "No."

"Then what's wrong?"

"Ari kissed me." He threw his hands in the air. "He kissed me, and I liked it." Panic caught in his throat, made his voice crack.

"Oh, Danny." I turned to him, put my arms around his waist, and rested my head on his chest where his heart thumped hard. "There's nothing wrong with you liking Ari or the way he kissed you."

He stayed quiet, so I tilted my head up to look at him. Grief flared in his eyes and stung my heart.

"There's nothing wrong with me liking a boy?" A bitter laugh fell from his lips. "C'mon, Brin, you know better than that."

"There isn't," I insisted. "Ari's a good guy, and from the way he kept looking at you, I'd guess he likes you as much as you like him."

"It doesn't matter." He dropped his forehead to my shoulder. "It's not like we can go around and kiss in public or do any of the normal things people do when they like each other."

"Yes, you can. Of course, you can. And if anyone gives you any crap about it, they'll have to deal with me."

"Yeah?" I felt his cheeks lift up when he grinned. "You gonna throw your pom-poms at them?"

"Or run them over with my car." I shrugged.

He laughed, but it held none of the enthusiasm Danny embodied.

"No one that matters is gonna care," I said, running

a hand over his back. "People love you because of who you are, not in spite of it. You have friends in this school that'll stand by you. Give them a chance to show you."

He nodded, gripping the back of my shirt in a closed fist. "What if Ari doesn't want that? What if he wants to keep us behind closed doors?"

"Talk to him." I paused. "But from the looks he was giving you during lunch, I'm pretty sure he's waiting for you to say you're okay with everyone knowing about you guys."

He peered back, hope flickered in his eyes and when he smiled, I was the one left grasping onto hope that I wouldn't later be tasting the twinge of regret. But we had hope and it had to be real.

"I'll talk to him," he said.

"Good." I kissed his cheek. "I want you to be happy. Do what makes you happy, okay? Screw everyone else."

"Yeah," he breathed out.

The school bell rang, alerting us that lunch was over. We made our way back with our hands clasped together. The walk back was lighter, and I felt even happier than I had before. I had a boyfriend I was crazy about, and my best friend would soon have one too.

"I need details on this kiss, Danny." I couldn't help the tease in my voice. "As your best friend, you owe it to me."

"I don't think I do."

I pushed my bottom lip out. "Please."

"Tell me about your dance."

My face reddened. That seemed to be its new complexion since Roderick and I got together.

"I asked first," I countered.

"Lies." He tugged my ponytail. "I asked you on Sunday and then again yesterday."

"We danced, we kissed." I was sure my cheeks would catch fire any minute. It would almost be a mercy if it started raining again so I could cool down. "It was the best night of my life."

Grasping my wrist, Danny stopped us midstride. He looked around, and when his eyes met mine, there was real joy in them.

"A group of us went to the dance together in Ari's car." He kept his voice low. "Ari and I talked a lot, but it wasn't anything major. We're friends, we hang out all the time, but something felt different." He looked over his shoulder, and I hated how nervous he was about someone listening in on our conversation. "After the dance, he dropped everyone off and left me for last. Instead of taking me straight home, we went to the playground by his house. We didn't get out or anything, just talked. And then, I kissed him."

"Wait." I held out my palms and then smacked him. "You said he kissed you. But you…" I waggled my finger in front of his face. "It was all you."

"Yeah, but I ended it quickly and apologized." He dug his toe into the sand. "Then he kissed me."

"Danny!" Excitement vibrated off every cell in my body. "Was this your first kiss?"

A sheepish smile took over his face. "Yeah."

"And it was good? Not just good for your first time, but good."

"It was amazing," he breathed.

And that's exactly how it should be. That's how you knew you found someone special. Their kisses were amazing. Their touch made you feel everything. The right person could make you soar.

CHAPTER 29

THE DINER WAS crowded with football players and cheerleaders.

Everyone I once avoided.

I hated it. Felt like I was suffocating, like all the bodies in the room were taking up too much space, sucking in all the air and leaving nothing for me.

It made eating the food I'd ordered hard, so eventually I gave up and pushed it to the side.

Brinley was in her element though. Girls from her team surrounded her, asked her questions, kept her mind busy. Her smile was unreserved. Completely breathtaking. And I knew I'd do whatever I had to, to keep it there.

Even though most of the guys had become friends with Seth, I understood why he didn't show tonight. It was hard going from seeing everyone as your enemy to having more friends than you cared to have. While we had our differences, we weren't that dissimilar. Where I was invisible, he was a target. It was the same people who'd ignored me, that had made his school life impossible. Now, those same people wanted to be our friends, as if they were some holy grail we should clasp onto.

Although weary, Seth welcomed them. I tolerated them for Brinley.

Funny how I went from wanting to hate her to realizing I never stopped loving her. The love had evolved over time, from something innocent in our younger days to something ugly up until only a few weeks ago to something more than I could've hoped for.

I loved her selfishly. I loved her selflessly. I loved her completely.

"Hey." Danny rapped his knuckles on the table before sliding into the booth in front of me.

He scooted over to make room for Ari, and I hoped the rest of the guys wouldn't join them. I purposely sat at an unoccupied table so I wouldn't be forced to talk any more than I already had to. Keeping up with all of Brinley's friends— a mixture of some old friends and a lot of new ones – throughout the day was exhausting, and I was relieved when the last bell sounded, only to find out we were coming here later. At least I got a few hours at my aunt's house to myself and my writing before she picked me up for dinner.

"Mind if we join you?" Danny asked.

"Looks like you already did," I said.

He ignored my dig and pointed at a napkin I'd been writing on. While Brinley and I hadn't written much together, I wrote every chance I had. Sometimes, like now, I was so lost in thought I didn't even realize I was writing.

Crumbling up the paper, I put it in my pocket and said, "It's nothing."

This time, he arched a brow but didn't say anything.

Silence grew and just when I was going to stand up and find another booth, Jacob came over. He waited for me to make room for him, but I glared at him, unmoving. Turning, he grabbed a chair from a nearby table and sat on it backwards.

"Brinley and the freak, huh?" His smile was wide, disconcerting.

Anger flared, and I fisted my hands beside me.

"She always had a bit of drama in her," Jacob continued. "Not even surprised she stooped so low to get attention."

"Leave it alone," Danny warned.

"Does our Brin taste as good as she looks?" Jacob directed that question to me. "I bet she does. I'd give anything to have her sweet, tight body wrapped around me. Have her beneath me, screaming my name." He chuckled while red spots tainted my vision. "She's what dreams are made of, am I right?"

Gripping the table, I leaned toward Jacob. "Don't speak her name." I shuddered out a breath, braced myself so I wouldn't pummel through this guy and embarrass Brinley. "Don't think about my girl, don't talk to her or about her."

He lifted his chin, narrowing his eyes in challenge. "What are you going to do about it?"

"Get you kicked off the team," Ari said before I had

a chance to respond.

I turned my anger to him, not wanting anyone to speak for me when it was my job to defend Brinley.

"Keep your mouth shut, and your head out of your ass," Ari continued. "One call to coach, that's all I have to do. He gave you one last chance. Don't blow it." He waved his phone in front of him.

Jacob slapped an open palm on the table, the irritating sound of his laughter rang loudly in my ear. "Roderick knows I'm joking. Right, man?"

Hot rage pumped through my veins, settled in my chest. Slowly, I stood up and leaned in to him. "Say my girl's name again, and it won't matter what your coach knows or says. I'll make sure you can't play. Got it, *man*?"

As I sat back down, Jacob cursed under his breath. Said something too low for me to hear before he jumped out of his chair and rushed to the door, leaving the diner without saying a word to anyone. Even without him looking back, I'm sure he felt the heat of my tempered glare on his back.

Danny leaned back, his gaze seeming to assess me.

"I didn't need a save." I leveled Ari with a heavy stare.

"I didn't do it for you," Ari said, his tone bored. "I did it for Brinley."

"And because Jacob's an asshole," Danny added.

Ari grinned. "That too."

Suffocating. I was suffocating with the noise, and the two guys sitting in front of me.

I searched the diner for the bathroom, but there were too many people standing by it. Five minutes, that's all I needed by myself. Outside would be better. Fresh air, no crowd. I inched toward the edge of the booth and as if she sensed me, she turned around. I met Brinley's gaze from a table down. She smiled and I stopped moving. After a few words passed those lips I dreamt about, she got up from her table to sit beside me. And I felt the world right itself. The space was no longer too small, too loud, too anything.

It was perfect with my girl beside me.

"What are we talking about?" Brinley asked.

I put my arm around her and scooted closer to her. She squirmed in to my side until she found her favorite spot where her head rested on my shoulder.

"We weren't," I answered.

"You weren't, what?" She peeked up at me, her pretty green eyes seeming lighter behind the dark lashes framing them. "Talking?"

"Just sitting here," Danny said. "Not saying anything."

"That's... nice?" She scrunched up her nose.

Ari laughed. "It was uncomfortable."

"No one made you sit here." I chewed on my inner cheek to keep from saying anything else. Something that would hurt Brinley if she knew how much I didn't want to be here.

Ari angled his face to the side. "Danny didn't want you sitting by yourself."

The confusion and hurt that marred Brinley's features reached inside of me, tore into my chest.

"You were alone?" she asked.

I twisted her in my arm to kiss her neck, trail my nose to her ear. I let my lips linger there and whispered, "I told you, I'm not alone. Not anymore."

Weaving her fingers through mine, she tugged on my hand. "We're gonna head out," she said to Danny and

Ari.

Danny slid out of the booth, and Brinley let go of my hand to hug him. When she whispered something in his ear, he nodded.

From over her head, Danny looked at me, repeated the same words from two weeks ago. "If you hurt her…"

"You'll hurt me," I interrupted. "Got it."

He smiled and I felt my own lips twitch in response. Yeah, Danny wasn't a bad guy. Maybe Ari wasn't either. It was me who had to get used to hanging around so many people.

When she turned back to me, her hand reaching for mine, I took it, let her lead us out of the diner. It wasn't until we were in her car that I could finally breathe. Away from the noise. Just me and my girl.

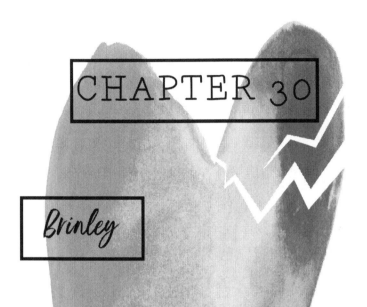

CHAPTER 30

Brinley

WE SAT NEXT to each other, cross-legged with our knees touching. With both our phone flashlights on, our cave was bright. The stuff I hadn't taken with us when I brought Roderick home with me was still here. Cold and wet.

"Nicole wasn't there tonight," I said.

Up until two weeks ago, I'd never gone to the diner with the guys. It was just them, some sort of bonding the coach urged them to do outside of football. But since Ari had invited me, I'd told the girls in my cheerleading team in the hopes Nicole would go so we could finally speak.

"Have you talked to her?" he asked.

"At practice, but other than that, no." It saddened me how easily she gave me up. "She won't return my texts or answer my calls."

"I'm sorry, baby."

I knew he was, just like I knew he didn't understand why losing her made me sad when we were never as close as we pretended to be. This proved it. I was replaceable, forgettable.

On limber legs, Roderick stood up and went to our wall. Read our poetry. And I wondered what he thought now that he knew the girl writing with him was me.

"You don't hate being alone," Roderick said, breaking the silence. "You hate the silence that comes with it."

When I went to him, he put an arm around my shoulder and held me close to him. Safe, I was safe. "When you surround yourself with people, you kinda force yourself to listen to what they have to say, and it drowns out your own thoughts."

"But your thoughts…" He turned me in his arms, so we faced each other and pointed at the wall. "I love your thoughts."

My eyes shifted down. "I hate them. When I'm alone, they're all I hear and I hate them."

"Why?"

"Because they yell at me about my mom, about what she's become, about what…" My voice broke, and I cleared my throat. "About what I might become."

He took me in his arms, as if he could shield me from my fears. I wished he could. Except all he was doing was exposing them when they should stay where no one could see them.

"What about you?" It came out harsh, but I kept going. "Alone isn't a tragedy?" I scoffed, taking a step back, away from him while I peered up to see the hurt cross his face. "You hate it."

"I don't hate it," he countered. "I prefer it over being in a roomful of people I don't like."

"The only reason you isolated yourself was to protect yourself," I barreled through. "If no one got close, they couldn't hurt you if they left. Tell me I'm wrong," I challenged.

He sighed. It was heavy and sad. "You're not wrong, and I'm not fighting with you tonight." He roughed a hand through his hair and stared at the wall. "I see you. I know you. That's all I was trying to say, not start a fight."

Biting my bottom lip, I watched him pick up the discarded black marker from the ground. I fought back tears when he pressed it to the wall to write. He shook it a few times when it didn't work and then threw it against the wall on a grunt. The top popped off while the marker rolled away.

"Here," I said, digging into my jeans and taking out a marker I'd taken from the diner after seeing how panicked Roderick looked sitting with Ari and Danny. He'd gone to the diner for me, so I wanted to bring him to our cave for him.

He took it without looking at me and started to write.

Of all the places
he sought to hide
the only safe place

I put a hand to his shoulder, stopping him from continuing.

"Can I finish?" I asked.

His Adam's apple bobbed when he handed the marker to me.

I changed the *he* to *they* and continued.

Of all the places
they sought to hide
the only safe place
they found was
in each other

I bowed my head, regret making my skin tingle. "I'm sorry," I said. "I'm good at being mean to keep anyone from seeing too much. I don't know how to stop. But you're my safe place."

"Groups of people are your safe place," he countered.

"I use people." I accepted that about myself. People were nothing more than a means to an end, very few of them were actual friends. "I surround myself with them to quiet my thoughts, but my mind is most silent, most at peace, when I'm with you. You're my safe place," I repeated.

He shook his head, and I readied myself for the blow. For his rejection. It was something I deserved after I deliberately tried to hurt him.

"At school, at the diner, that's when I see you the happiest, the most comfortable. Not here with me. Not when I was sick in your room."

Confusion twisted in my gut, made bile rise to my throat. "Why do you think that?"

"Your laughter, your smile, your voice – you're the most animated when you're around everyone. When it's just us, you're quieter, more reserved."

I wanted to laugh, to shake him for seeing so much while seeing so little. "In a group of people, I'm the center of attention, but still I somehow feel completely alone. I circle around everyone so that they notice me, but no one really sees or hears me, just what they want to see and hear. But you... you listen for what I don't say, you look for what I don't show you." I steadied my gaze on him, blinking back the frustration and hoped he heard what I was trying to say. "When we were younger, I felt like you were minutes away from finding what I was trying so hard to hide. That's why I stayed away from you. I knew if anyone could've figure me out, it'd be you."

Grief flared behind his eyes. He clenched his jaw as if he were bracing himself against an attack. As if he were bracing himself against me.

"Sometimes I think I know you." His voice was like gravel. "Most of the time I know I don't. You've gotten so good at hiding, do you even know who you are anymore?"

"No." It was the most honest answer I had. "But I'm trying to find out."

"Tell me one truth about yourself. Something you don't hide from the world."

My bottom lip trembled, so I caught it between my teeth. "I'm not a good person."

He threw his hands in the air. "Lie!" The word echoed in the cave, reverberated in my chest. "You hide the good. I don't know why, but you do." Silence fell between us. "You can't do it, can you? One true thing that everyone knows. Just one, Brinley."

I sucked in a breath and let it go on a sob. Wrapping my arms across my chest, I held myself together. Panic throbbed in my veins, seized my lungs until breathing became painful.

I wore masks, played roles. The girl everyone at school thought they knew didn't exist. Like Roderick said, I was good at hiding. I was fake. If only I could find a way to hide from the hope he awoke in me, from the sharp pieces that sliced through my defenses and left me open to him.

He wanted one truth. That's all I had anyway.

"I like you," I whispered, meeting his shock with tears tracking down my face. "Yesterday, when everyone asked me why I didn't go to the dance, I told them I was with you." Using the back of my hand, I wiped my nose on a sniffle. "And after today, I think everyone knows we're together. You're the only truth I have, the only part of myself I'm not ashamed of."

Another sob wrenched from my body at his silence. I stood there, shaking and crying, waiting for the boy to love me back.

"Are we…" A strangled cry ripped from my throat. I took in a shaky breath, steadied my heart. "Are we still together?"

"God, Brinley."

He fisted a hand in my hair and crushed his lips over mine. His kiss was hard. It tasted like hurt. It was rough. It felt like a promise.

His head fell to rest against mine. I breathed in his exhales.

"Of course, we're still together."

The hands that moved to brace my face shook, and I wrapped my fingers around his wrists. The corners of my lips turned up, but it hurt to smile.

"You're my only truth." My voice shook with every word. "Is it enough?"

He brought me in for a hug, pressed me close to his chest.

"No." The word brushed against my ear. "But we're gonna find all your truths, and when we do, you're gonna share them with the world. You have nothing to hide from."

I nodded.

He was wrong though. I had everything to hide.

CHAPTER 31

Brinley

WE DIDN'T GET much commotion in our sleepy, little beach town. The occasional traveling surfer most of the girls congregated to. And a few teenage pregnancies because of those surfers.

Bonfires on the beach, that's really as crazy as we got.

Our local police didn't bother us when we threw those parties as long as we didn't cause trouble. According to my dad, it was a passage of right. So I went to them, nursed a bottle of beer and spun circles around everyone I knew.

The only difference between tonight's party and the others was that it was the start of our spring break, and the day before Roderick's birthday. Three months had passed since Roderick and I got together.

He still hated being around a crowd. He still went

215

out to make me happy.

I was selfish and took what he so willingly offered.

In the months we'd shared together, we'd come up with a good compromise. While we went out with my friends a couple times a week, we spent a lot of time in our cave or in my room talking, writing, or kissing.

Kissing was my favorite.

And we spent holidays together, even Christmas where my mom came back to me for a few hours.

Our only holiday rule: no big crowds.

New Year's Eve was one I would remember forever. We hung out on the roof of my house eating grapes and watching the fireworks go off from the beach. My dad spent it with my mom instead of Lindsey. Loud noises made my mom's episodes worse and although Bridgette was there and knew how to handle my mom better than my dad or I ever did, he wanted to be there too. Just in case.

We had a double date on Valentine's Day with Danny and Ari, who were together but not as open about their relationship as we were. Since neither of them wanted to go to a restaurant and couldn't take the other to their house and risk their parents finding out about them, we brought them to our cave. At first I was nervous about them reading our poems, but Roderick made me feel like I could do anything. Be anything.

The picnic I packed us was fun. When they read our poems, and we told them exactly how we wound up together. They gushed over our story, and then demanded to write their own poem. Roderick handed them a marker, and they left the mark of their love on our wall.

I had plans for tomorrow for Roderick's birthday, and with Danny and Ari's help, I was going to turn our cave into the most romantic spot.

I just had to get him through tonight.

"That's like your third beer," I told Roderick when he came up from behind me and circled his hands around my waist.

He kissed me neck, flicked his tongue against my quickening pulse. Warmth pooled in the pit of my belly. I twisted in his arms to face him, and when he kissed my lips, I pulled away.

"Did you do shots too?" I asked.

He hung his head. His dark hair fell across his face. The gesture reminded me of a little boy in trouble. It was cute. He was cute.

"No more, okay?" I framed his face with my hands.

He pulled his bottom lip in with his teeth and nodded. I couldn't help but stare at him. This guy was beautiful. And he was mine.

"I can't take you to your aunt's house drunk."

He grinned. It was lopsided and lazy. "If my aunt and I have another fight, I can always stay at your place again. I miss sleeping with you."

I ran my hand over his neck where his pulse beat wildly as if it were racing my own heartbeat. We hadn't slept together since he moved back in with his aunt. She wasn't my biggest fan and although Roderick insisted me sleeping over wouldn't be a problem, I didn't want to overstay my welcome and not be allowed back in.

"I miss sleeping with you too. Maybe you should text your aunt and tell her you're not going home tonight."

"Home." The word sounded bitter.

"Your aunt's house," I amended. "I'm your home."

Big blue eyes snapped back at me, and this time when he smiled it reached my heart.

"Yeah," he agreed. "You're my home."

"Brinley!"

I turned at the sound of my name and forced a practiced smile on my face when Nicole sauntered to us with Mariah by her side. They balanced two trays of shots as they weaved around our classmates.

Nicole held out a shot for me, but I shook my head.

"Oh c'mon, Brin!" Mariah whined. Her voice, the tone grated on my nerves. "Have fun with us."

"I'm good, thanks." I tipped the end of my beer bottle at them.

"Just stop, for one night, stop being perfect," Mariah said.

I bristled at her words. She didn't get how badly I needed perfection, to maintain that image. If I drank, if I let go of those inhibitions, I was scared of what I might say. Because what if I let down my guard, let everyone see me for who I was and no one liked what they saw?

Roderick stumbled to my side, dropped a heavy arm on my shoulder and kissed the side of my head. "She is perfect."

"Says the freak." Nicole snorted.

"Grow up." I scoffed. "Just grow the hell up already."

"Oh." Nicole's eyes lit up, a slow smile stretched across her face.

It made my stomach drop, and I twined my hands with Roderick's to get away from them.

"What's this?" she called out, taking out a folded piece of paper from her pocket. "What do you think your perfect Brinley wrote about you not even a month before you got together?"

Fear cloaked over me, but it didn't hide me. Only made me more visible. I didn't remember what I'd written, but knew it wouldn't be good.

She stretched out her hand, holding the paper between two fingers. I went to take it from her, but she pulled it away with a laugh.

"It doesn't matter," I said to Roderick. "Whatever I wrote was never true."

Turning his attention to me, he ran his hands through the long strands of his hair, making the muscles on his arm flex. "Read it to me," he said. "I want to know what you said."

"No." I shook my head. "Whatever it says doesn't matter."

He dropped his head and rested it on my forehead. "It matters to me."

"Don't do this, Roderick." It came out rushed, urgent, scared. "You know who I was, why I did and said things I didn't mean. You know me now. Don't make me read something that'll hurt you. Hurt us."

On a laugh, Mariah took the paper from Nicole and started to unfold it. We watched her, my limbs shaking, my heart shattering.

"You already know then," Roderick said, pulling away with a quick jerk. Hurt glistened in his eyes. "You may not know exactly what you wrote, but it's what you thought about me."

"No," I stammered out.

He turned away, stared at Mariah, as if he were waiting for her to read aloud words that would end us.

"I love you," I said. Taking his face in my hands, I forced him to look at me. "I love you, Roderick. Every poem I've ever written, every scribbled line on our wall, they're all for you. They were written with the image of you in my mind, in my heart. Can't you see?" I rushed on. "I always knew it was you reading them. I wanted you to know me, when I hid from everyone else." My voice wobbled, each word trembling with conviction. "Every song we've danced to, every poem we've written together, every kiss we've shared, they're because of you. Everything good I have to offer, it's for you. You're my truth, my whole world. Whatever that piece of paper says, doesn't fucking matter. The only truth you need to know is that I love you."

He touched my lips with his forefinger, grazed it across my cheek. "You cussed." His lips twitched.

I laughed, but it held no humor. "That's what you heard? I told you I love you and all you hear is me dropping the F-bomb?"

"I heard that too." This time he smiled. "I love you too."

He tipped his head down, his lips almost touching mine. I wanted this kiss, wanted his breath dancing with mine.

Mariah cleared her throat, and we broke away before we made contact. Nicole came from behind her, snatched the paper from her hand. Mariah protested but to my relief, Nicole threw it into the nearby fire. Sparks crackled and flew to the night sky.

"Brin's right," Nicole said, flipping her hair over her shoulder. "Whatever it says doesn't matter. Seems like the freak found his princess. How fitting." She scoffed.

I skimmed a hand over the back of his neck, ignoring Mariah and Nicole when they left. When I brought my lips to his, my pulse quickened like it always did. Thousands of emotions I never knew I would feel, clenched in my stomach. Like it always did.

Kissing Roderick wasn't as simple as kissing. It was poetry he orchestrated with the rhythm of his lips against mine; his tongue dancing with mine as his hands roamed over my back and arms, neck and face. I was his greatest prose, composed by a moment that was anything but simple.

"Drink some water, sober up a bit, so I can take you home."

He traced the outline of my face with his long fingers. "You're my home." He said the words as if he couldn't believe they were true, as if he were afraid they weren't.

Gripping onto his wrists, I squeezed. "You're my home," I whispered back.

His lips touched mine, moved them against mine. Soft yet consuming. Intimate, yet a burning flame of passion that immersed my soul.

"I love you, Roderick," I said against our kiss.

His fingers dove into my hair where he dug and pulled my head to the side to deepen the kiss. It was as if with this kiss, he could delve past my shredded heart, take away all the wrong I'd done. It was as if he wanted to burrow himself inside me, fix the broken, and latch on while he lost himself in me. And I lost myself in him.

I clung onto him, my breaths falling quickly when we parted. I reached for his face, touched his cheeks, his lips, his nose. Memorized everything about his features in this moment. The moment I almost crushed us. The moment he forgave me. The moment he knew the depth of my love.

Dropping my hands, I held his and guided us through the crowd. After picking up two bottles of water, I led us to the lifeguard post. We climbed the ramp and when we reached the top, we sat with our backs leaned against the frame of the small house.

I crawled into his lap, held myself tight against his chest.

I could've lost him, almost did, because I was stupid. Because I pretended to be someone I wasn't in order to keep my spot on the top.

On a cry, I buried my face in to his neck. Breathed him in.

"Baby." Concern made his voice shake. "What's wrong?"

I shook my head, wiggled my body closer to his.

Hands that had shown me how beautiful love felt, smoothed my hair back. "Don't cry, baby." His voice, I could listen to his voice forever, and it wouldn't be enough. "Please don't cry."

"I can't lose you." I hiccupped in to his neck.

"I'm right here." He pressed a kiss into my hair. "I'm not going anywhere. Desperately together, remember?"

"That note... whatever I wrote... Roderick." I hugged him tighter when his hand stilled in my hair. "I hate myself. I..."

"Don't say that," he interrupted. "Don't say that to me, Brinley." He pulled me back, braced his hands on my shoulders and squeezed. "You can't hate yourself. You can't. Do you hear me?"

With the back of my hand, I wiped my nose. "I hurt

you. I…"

"You did," he interrupted again. He did that often, like he didn't want people to finish their thoughts. "You hurt me, but it's okay."

"It's not okay. Me hurting you is never going to be okay." I paused, not wanting to keep going, knowing I had to. "I could've destroyed this. Us. When you're my favorite part of every day. Why would I do that?"

He shrugged his shoulders and when they fell, they slumped forward. "Nicole said you wrote the note a month before we started dating." Dropping his hands from my shoulders, he brought them to his side and gripped the wood boards we sat on.

"You never deserved whatever I wrote." More tears spilled. "No one deserved the things I said, least of all you. I'm sorry." I tilted my head down when I climbed out of his lap. I hugged my knees to my chest. "I'm so sorry."

No matter how hard I tried, I couldn't outrun my mistakes. They were always there, waiting to strike and remind me of the person that waited just beneath the surface.

Beside me, Roderick stood up and went to the railing where he stared out into the ocean. I waited for him to leave me. For everything I'd put him through to finally be too much.

When he turned back to me, he held out a hand. I took it. I'd always take his hand.

Music started to play from his phone. He placed one hand on my waist, used the other to bring my hand to his chest where I felt his heart thump hard.

"Dance with me," he said.

He didn't tug me to him, but waited for me to reply. I went to him, rested my chest against his, brought my unused hand to the nape of his neck where I played with his hair.

We swayed slowly, had barely completed a circle when the first song ended and the second one began. He didn't let go and neither did I.

"I'm the one who's sorry," he whispered, his head bent down with the side of his face pressed against mine.

I tried to pull back, but his hand on my back kept me in place.

"I never saw past my problems to see yours."

"Roderick, I never wanted you to see them."

He sighed softly, his warm breath tickling my cheek. "I was supposed to be your best friend. I should've seen how much you needed me."

My bottom lip trembled at his words. The truth was in all my pushing and manipulation, I kept hoping someone would see. Would care enough to look.

"We both know how cruel I can be." It came out angry and I had to stop myself from lashing out when all I wanted was to be held. To be forgiven.

"You're only mean when you feel cornered."

I dropped my head to his chest. "That's the thing, isn't it? I always felt cornered. You-you noticed something was wrong when I went back to school after my mom's first episode. You asked questions, do you remember?"

I needed him to remember. I hoped he didn't.

"It was the first time I lashed out at anyone. The last time we hung out," I continued, gripping the fingers that held mine. "Do you remember what I said to you after you asked me if I was okay?"

"You…" He blew out a breath. "You told me my parents were never coming back."

The memory of his broken expression, of the pain in his eyes twisted in my gut. I held onto it. The way his eyes rimmed with unshed tears. The way he wrapped his arms around his body. The way he waited for me to finish.

"I told you…" The words shook in my chest, made my heart beat with so much pain I didn't know how I'd survive it.

"If I hadn't begged them to get ice cream for me, they wouldn't have been in a car accident and would still be alive," he said.

Air whooshed from my lungs. Dizzy, I let go of Roderick. Rather than let me fall, he held on tighter.

"You were right."

"I wasn't," I argued, but my voice, my strength was gone. "I was wrong."

"I let you go after that." He hesitated, but his hold on me remained firm. "Watched you push away everyone but Danny while you made new friends. I wondered…" He cleared his throat. "I wondered why you still wanted Danny, but not me."

"I tried to push Danny away too." It came out so low I barely heard the words.

"He didn't let you. I shouldn't have let you. Fuck, I'm sorry, Brin." His voice broke, and he brought me closer to him.

I kept my hands to the side, fisted the empty air around us.

"I'm so sorry, Brin." He kissed my cheek. "I shouldn't have let you go."

"Of course, you should have."

He shuddered when I brushed my hands over his arms.

"Anyone would have after the things I said."

He bowed his head when I brought my fingers to his neck and ran them through his hair. As he rested his head on my shoulder, I pressed my cheek to his.

"I should've been in the car with them, not in my neighbor's living room waiting for them." Still, he sounded so broken. My broken and sad boy. "I should've died with them."

"No." The fear of losing him made me want to scream. "I know I pushed you away, I know I made you feel like you didn't matter," I gripped the back of his shirt. "I'm glad you weren't with your parents. I'm glad you didn't die. I'm glad you're here with me. I know it isn't enough but…"

"It's enough," he interrupted. "It's more than I knew was possible to dream for."

"I'm sorry for what I said that day, for pushing you away and not being there for you." I sucked in a long breath. "I'm sorry for every bad thing I said about you through the years, for making fun of you with Nicole, when the truth is I never thought anything bad about you. I saw you disappear into yourself and I let you. I'm sorry, Roderick. So sorry."

"It's over," he whispered. "No more sorrys for tonight."

"Your birthday present is in my room," I continued speaking. "It's a bunch of poems and short stories I wrote, a couple of my favorite books, a playlist of my favorite songs. Do you know what they have in common? Why

I'm giving them to you?"

"No."

"Every time I write, listen to a song, read a book or dream, I see you. The boy I ran off. The boy I couldn't turn away from. The boy I disappointed. The boy I've loved since we were little kids. Every love poem I've written, every poem about hope or despair I've written has you in it and I didn't realize it until I was reading over them a couple weeks ago."

He didn't reply but kissed my shoulder.

"You're all I've ever seen, all I've ever wanted. You're every love song, every love story. You're my heart."

"These are the words that matter," he whispered. "Not what was on that paper, not what you said four years ago."

My heart soared. I didn't deserve him. This love, so fragile and tender. So hopeless and messy. So beautiful. This love that made me feel alive, made me feel like living without fear of the future.

CHAPTER 32

RODERICK

Eyes the deepest of blue
so much like the endless sea.
Now they remind me of the sweeping current,
fierce but beautiful.
They remind me of stormy seas
with thunder rumbling from his irises.
He's the oncoming storm,
fierce but beautiful,
but he only destroys himself.
If only I could be his safe haven
But I let him go,
and he never came back.

Poem after poem, I read Brinley's words, immersed myself in her heart. Like she said, they were all about me. A boy with inky black hair, lips that no longer smiled, but she dreamt of that smile, of making me smile again.

I hadn't gotten to the short stories she'd written yet, but had already downloaded the songs on her playlist even though she said she had them on her phone. But I wanted them, wanted to find myself in them and see how she saw me.

"Roderick," she whispered from the bed beside me, "it's almost midnight."

"Yeah?" I didn't look up from the next poem.

He saw me today,
saw past the words
I use like a harsh cord,
past the ugly exterior
I hide behind.
He saw me today
I was his princess,
not the vain one,
but a beautiful queen
to his noble king.
And he loved me.

I looked up to the top of the page at the date, saw it was written a few months into our freshmen year, around the same time I started calling her princess. The turmoil that settled in my gut twisted my insides. I hurt her, the same way she hurt me.

After putting the folder she gave me on her night stand, I turned back to face her. Ran a finger over her sleek cheek.

"I hurt you a lot," I said, my heart bleeding with the words.

"We're not doing anymore sorrys, remember?" she asked. "Those were your rules back at the beach – no more sorrys."

"Okay." That didn't mean I wasn't and that I wouldn't do everything to make it up to her.

"Besides, I didn't give you those poems to make you sad, but so you could see I never let you go. Not really."

I leaned in a bit closer so that my lips barely grazed hers. Her hands found my hair, and I closed my eyes at how perfect it felt. How perfect she felt.

We'd hurt each other, but I was done hurting her. Never again. And I hoped she was done hurting me.

"One minute before you turn eighteen," she said with an excited lilt to her voice.

"And I'm spending it with my favorite person."

She smiled. "The only thing that would make this moment even better is if we had a cake." Her eyes lit up when she jumped out of bed.

I sat up. "Do you have a cake hiding in here somewhere?"

"Not a whole cake." She made a dash to her closet.

"So like half a cake? A slice of cake?" I teased.

"Close your eyes."

I did. When I felt her sit down beside me, I reached for her, and she took my hand in hers.

"You can open now," she said.

My eyes fluttered open, and I felt my lips spread in a big smile when I saw her holding a cupcake with white icing and a carrot on top.

"Carrot cake?" I asked.

"Your favorite." Her face changed, uncertainty crossing her features. "Is it still your favorite?"

Dipping my finger in the icing, I brought it to my lips and smiled. "Still my favorite."

"You cheated!" She batted my hand away. "You're not

supposed to have any until I sing happy birthday."

Bringing my hands to the back of my head, I leaned against a pillow and waited. "You better start singing then."

She did. She lit a candle and sang to me. It was the sweetest sound I'd heard. I was the happiest I'd ever been. When she finished, I blew out my candle and for the first time in five years I didn't wish for a past I couldn't outrun, but for a future I could look forward to.

When I dug a finger into the icing again, she placed one hand on my chest and the other around my wrist where she guided my finger to her mouth. I moaned, a deep ache built when she licked the tip of my finger. Her fingers moved against my shirt over the collar until she touched my neck, and I loved the feel of her soft hand on my heated flesh. I leaned up, set my cupcake on her nightstand and crushed my lips to hers.

She closed her eyes and I followed suit. My tongue met hers. She trembled.

Her fingers roamed to my hair while she used her other hand to slide it under my shirt. She splayed her palm over my chest where she caressed me with a feather light touch.

A groan rumbled from my throat but I kept the kiss soft. Slow.

The air in the room felt heavy. As if the room itself felt my desperation. My need for this girl. My girl.

Her fingers dug into my scalp. I only left her lips to move mine over her neck. My hands reached for her shoulder. With a single finger, I shifted the strap of her tank top down and grazed my lips over where the strap had rested.

Trailing over her shirt, I traced the bottom of it and let my fingers touch her stomach. Heaven. I'd found heaven.

Her breath became ragged. I edged away to look at her face. Her lips were parted, her eyes wide with the same raw desire pulsing in my veins.

She clasped the bottom of her shirt and lifted it over her head.

"Brinley," I rasped out. "You don't have to…"

"Touch me, Roderick." With both hands, she pushed my hair back, out of my face. "Kiss me."

I kissed her forehead, her nose, her cheeks and lips. My fingers followed, memorizing everything. I needed to take in everything about her, all the details. Everything she hid, everything she gave me.

With soft movements, I moved her so that her back rested against the pillow, and I hovered over her. Her chest rose and fell rapidly.

Cupping her bra, I moved a hand over the soft fabric. The ache that had been building surged in the pit of my stomach. I held it back, or tried to, but a moan fell from my lips when she arched her back.

"Touch me," she all but pleaded.

I skimmed a thumb under her bra and inhaled a sharp breath when I made contact with her breast. Closing my eyes, I brought my lips to her chest. I kissed her. From her neck to her stomach, I covered her with everything I had to give.

This crazy, intense love swam through me. I loved this girl. Forever.

CHAPTER 33

Brinley

Ecstasy. Euphoria. Total bliss.

I slipped my hand under his shirt, over the lean muscles that rippled at my touch. Needing to see him, I edged his shirt up, hating the absence of his lips on me when he pulled the shirt over his head. But his bare chest was beautiful. He was beautiful.

Roderick gripped my waist when I leaned up to kneel in front of him.

It didn't make sense, how much I needed him. Needed everything he could give me. Needed to give him everything I had to give.

With my hands splayed on his shoulders, I brushed a kiss over his chest, swept my tongue every now and then to sate my desire to taste him. As I explored him, he cradled the back of my head. He tugged my face closer to his and weakened me when I felt his lips back on my neck, trailing down to my shoulder and across my chest.

Long, beautiful fingers dug into my hips. When I traced my lips to his neck, he leaned his head back on a guttural moan. My own hands reached for his waist, brought his body closer to mine and when his pelvis met mine, I felt his excitement.

Lust. Love. They blurred together.

I leaned back, rested my back on the bed, while bringing Roderick down with me. With his weight on top of me, he pressed his body pressed between my legs where I throbbed the most. My hips pushed up on their own accord, and I sucked in a breath when I felt how badly he wanted me.

Friction. I wanted friction.

He inched his face down, our lips touching again. This kiss was wilder. Rawer. More desperate. I moved my hips against his again.

It was my turn to moan. Maybe he did too.

"Roderick," I breathed his name.

A tremor shook my body. I wanted more. Needed more.

He ran a hand over my thigh, across the side of my stomach to my breast, where he lingered.

"Take it off," I begged.

He fumbled with the back of my bra when I sat up. Breaths heaved loudly in my ear where he continued to tease me with his lips and tongue.

"Take it off," I repeated, my tone on the verge of breaking.

He laughed, but it sounded more frustrated than amused. "I'm trying."

Twisting in his arms, I reached behind my back where I unhooked my bra. It dawned on me so quickly, it hit me in my gut. I'd taken off my bra. I was mostly naked in front of Roderick.

I didn't have time to feel shy or insecure. Not when Roderick's heated stare took in every inch of me with appreciation.

"Beautiful." His voice was like gravel, and it sent an electric shock down my spine.

He filled both his hands with my breasts. The corners of his lips curled in a smile that made my stomach twist.

Heat flashed in his eyes before he kissed me.

And love, love settled in my chest.

I PLANNED ON having sex with Roderick last night. It was one of his birthday presents. But we never got to the part where our pants came off before we reached a sense of pleasure that was new to both of us.

He was embarrassed, made all sorts of apologies only for me to reassure him the same thing had happened to me. After a quick peck on his lips, I rushed to the shower and kept it running after I finished so he could clean up.

His stare raked over me while I fumbled into clean clothes after I dried myself. I would've felt self-conscious if he didn't make me feel so beautiful.

Sleep came to us quickly after that. If my mom had an episode that night, I didn't hear her. And when I woke up this morning, I felt more refreshed than ever before.

"What's this?" Roderick asked when I handed him another present.

I grinned, my heart hammered in my ear. "Open it and find out."

He gently tore through the wrapping paper. He held the envelope in his hand, flipped it from one side to the other. Anticipation weighed in my belly, and I had to fight myself from tearing it out of his hands and ripping the envelope open. Years might as well have passed by the time he finally opened it and unfolded the letter. While he read, his eyes bounced from the letter to me.

"Is this real?" he asked, holding the paper up. His eyes were huge, merriment spilling from behind them.

My smile widened and I nodded.

He threw himself at me, locked his arms around me. "You're serious?" Disbelief and awe washed over his words. "You got accepted in to the Art School of San Diego?"

I hugged him back, inched onto the tip of my toes to kiss his neck. "Yeah."

"And you're going?"

"Yeah."

"What about UCLA?" He stopped, ran a hand over my back and into my hair. "You were so excited when you were accepted. You can't throw that away. I told you, Brin, I got into UCLA and should be approved for financial aid." He paused again, blew out an agitated breath. "You can't give up UCLA. It's too important."

"I'm not giving up anything. UCLA is…" I kissed

his cheek. "I dunno. I thought I wanted to go there, but I looked up the school in San Diego. They have so many classes I can take for writing. I can be an editor, journalist or even write the next great novel." I giggled. I seemed to do that a lot lately. "I looked into it for you, so we could stay together without you giving up your scholarship," I said softly. "I'm doing it for both of us – you and me. I want this. I wanna see if writing takes me anywhere, and I want to do it with you right beside me."

He sighed. It sounded content, like I'd said the right thing. It was one of my truths he'd helped me unbury, one I wouldn't keep hidden now that I'd told him my plan. I wanted to write. I wanted to be a writer.

"I spoke to my dad, and we're actually going to drive up there to look at apartments on Wednesday. He took three days off from work, so we'd have plenty of time to look around. And," I dug my face in to his neck to hide my blush, "I asked your aunt, and she said you could come with us if my dad was okay with it and if… if you wanted to."

He stepped back, his brows reaching his hairline. "Yeah, of course I wanna go with you. Is your dad okay with me going?"

"Yeah." I giggled. "I ran the idea by him before I called your aunt. They talked – my dad and your aunt, and we're all set."

"We're going to San Diego in five days?"

"We're going to San Diego in five days," I repeated.

Strong arms wrapped around me again. He bent his head down, rested it on my shoulder and breathed. He felt relaxed in my arms. At ease, as if everything in life was right. And maybe it was. Maybe we were doing more than fighting desperately together. Maybe we were healing.

"I have one more present for you," I said.

He chuckled. "Pretty sure you've already given me enough."

"You'll like this one."

He laughed harder. "Pretty sure I liked them all."

"Yeah." I ran my hands under his shirt and across his back. "Which was your favorite?"

"Was us making out on your bed one of my presents?"

My cheeks heated.

"Then that was my favorite."

Mine too, but I didn't say anything. Pretty sure the blush on my cheeks spoke enough for me.

"You coming to San Diego with me… Brin, do you know what that means to me?"

"You giving up your scholarship to be with me… do you know what that meant to me?"

He grinned. It made him look like the sweet boy I grew up with. "You love me." The way he said it, made it sound like he was accusing me.

"You love me back," I threw at him.

"I do."

"Me too." I rested my head against his chest. It was my favorite place to be, where I could listen to his heart thump against my ear. "My dad wants to take us out to breakfast." I tilted my head up to look at him. "Is that okay?"

"Yeah." He kissed my nose.

"After that, I'm yours until three-ish. We can do whatever you want."

"What happens after three-ish?"

I tsked. "It's a surprise which means I'm dropping you off at your aunt's house, and you can't sneak out to try to find out what I'm planning."

"Bossy."

I stuck out my tongue.

"It's cute," he said.

"You're cute." The blush that had crept over my cheeks before? It was nothing compared to the way my cheeks lit up in flames at that moment.

"Yeah?" He stroked my face with his knuckles.

Jutting out my chin, I narrowed my eyes. "Yeah."

He braced a hand to the small of my back and brought me closer to him. When he tipped his head down and traced his lips over my throat, a breath trembled from my lips.

"You're beautiful," he said between kisses. "And you're mine."

It was an exhilarating declaration that left me breathless.

I was his. His girl.

"You're mine," I replied.

My guy, my heart, my world, and my truth.

CHAPTER 34

Brinley

Wɪᴛʜ ᴍʏ sᴛᴏᴍᴀᴄʜ full of pancakes, eggs and bacon, I practically crawled back to my car with my dad on one side of me and Roderick on the other.

"What are you kids up to the rest of the day?" my dad asked.

"I dunno," I answered. "Birthday boy gets to choose what we're doing today."

"I shall remember this day as the day Ms. Brinley Crassus relinquished command of her schedule and let another rule for the day," my dad teased.

"Ohmygosh," I groaned. "You're such a dork."

"A monumental day indeed, Mr. Crassus," Roderick joked with him.

I loved seeing them together, how easily they formed

a bond. Even if it was a bond built on teasing me.

"I told you, Roderick, call me Phil."

"Right, sorry… Phil," Roderick said.

"But Phil is such a dumb name," I said.

My dad grabbed me in a headlock. I laughed while I tried to wiggle away.

"Dr. Crassus, now that has a ring to it," I said once I escaped his clutches.

"So, um, Phil." Roderick shoved his hands into the front pockets of his shorts. "Thanks for letting me go to San Diego with you guys."

"I'm not going to lie to you." My dad's voice rang with authority and Roderick straightened at his tone. "I don't like the idea of my little girl living with a guy, but if she's going to do it anyway, I'm glad it's you."

My heart, that crazy little organ that thrived when I was closest to Roderick, beat hard against its cage.

"I'll take care of her." Roderick put an arm over my shoulders, took a step closer to my side. "I'll never hurt her."

"That's an impossible promise to make," my dad said. "If you're in someone's life long enough, you're bound to hurt them. Even if you don't mean to."

Roderick nodded in understanding. "Then I'm already sorry for the times I'll hurt her, but I swear it'll never be done purposely."

"I know, son," my dad said and then cleared his throat. "I trust you with her, but more," he turned his attention to me, "I trust Brinley with herself. If she says you're good for her, then you're good for her."

Stepping into my dad, I put my arms around his waist. Even though I didn't have to, I stood on the tips of my toes to plant a kiss on his cheek. I loved the way my dad trusted me, the way he accepted Roderick from the first time they met, the way their relationship grew in such a short period of time.

"I gotta talk to you for a second, kid," he said to me.

Without saying a word, Roderick walked back to the restaurant to give my dad and me some privacy. I watched him go and felt my stomach plummet when I saw Nicole's car park in front of him. She waved at me when she stepped out. It was timid, and I raised my hand in a quick wave in return.

Worry crashed into me. Worry of what she'd say to Roderick. Worry of what he'd believe. But I had hope that everything we'd talked about, everything we'd become to each other in the past few months would make any doubt he had disappear.

Turning my attention to my dad, I forced my lips in a smile. "What's up?" I asked.

"Lindsey and I aren't working out," he said, his words coming out quickly.

"Dad." I touched his shoulder. "I'm sorry. I know you really liked her."

He cupped my face with an open palm and shook his head. "I didn't tell you so you'd feel sorry for me." He laughed. "I'm telling you because I'm moving back home."

"Wait." I held up my hands. "You can't just move back in. Moving out was hard enough on Mom. Her screams when you first left… they were worse than ever. I love you, Dad, I really do, but you can't move back in only to move out in a couple weeks or months. That's not fair to Mom."

He huffed. "I love your mom. I've never stopped loving your mom. She's the one that wanted me to move out. For years, she's been pushing me out, telling me to find someone else because she doesn't love me anymore. I…" His voice cracked, his expression broke. "I didn't want anyone else, Brinley. I wanted her. I still want her."

"Her episodes… I thought… Dad, I thought you couldn't take it anymore."

"I'll take whatever I have to so that I can have her on her good days. I love your mom. So, so much. I should never have dated Lindsey." He raked a hand over his face. "I did it…" He cleared his throat. "I did it so I could tell your mom, I tried. And I tried, Brinley. I tried for her and for you, so I could give you the normal life she wants you to have. The normal family she says you deserve. I did it so I could show her she's the only woman for me."

Despair caught in my throat. I forced it down with a hard swallow.

"You love her that much?" I asked.

"More than anything."

Pain flared from his eyes. It hit me how much he had given up, how much he was willing to give up.

Would that be Roderick one day? Lost in love while I pushed him away, into another woman's arms.

"What are you thinking?"

I shook my head, tried to keep the tears away. A sob broke free, made my body tremble.

Arms that have loved me through everything, been there for me since before I can even remember, held me. My dad kissed the top of my head as he smoothed my hair back.

"Talk to me, kid," he said. "I need to know what

you're thinking."

"I can't," I choked out.

"Brinley." It came out stern. "You're stronger than this. Talk to me," he repeated.

I gripped his shoulders, felt my knees weaken beneath me.

"Is this going to be Roderick and me?" My voice quaked, each word harder to get out.

"What?" He jerked back as if I'd slapped him.

I fell to my knees, hit the ground hard enough to scrape my exposed knees. Roderick was by my side in seconds.

"Baby." He ushered me into his arms, held me close to his chest. "Shhh, it's okay."

I looked up at my dad, his figure blurry from the tears.

"Tell me," I demanded.

His face pale, his hands shaking, my dad dropped to his knees and took my trembling hands in his. "Why? Why would you ask me that?"

"The doctors," I managed to say.

"The doctors?" he asked, his booming voice loud in my ears. "What doctors?"

"The doctors!" I yelled back. "The ones you and Mom take me to. The ones that run all those damn tests on my brain."

Shock registered behind his eyes. My dad bowed his head, sucked in a few breaths before he looked at me.

"I thought you knew." He shook his head. "I thought you knew. God, I'm sorry, Brin. I thought you knew."

"Knew what?" Roderick asked from behind me.

"The doctors, the tests, they're for her mom," he

answered Roderick but looked only at me. "To placate her fears. But you… Brin, kid, you're okay. Your brain is fine. It's always been fine."

"She said…" My head hurt, felt like a storm was thrashing inside trying to find a way through my skull. "She said it was genetic." I sniffled. "She… she said… I had to do the tests to look for changes but… but there was no way to know for sure. One day I'd be fine, the next I'd be like her."

"No, baby girl, no." Distress tumbled from my dad's lips, crashed in to me. "She can't give you what she has. It's not genetic. It's not one day to the next. Hell, kid, it's not even a disease, but trauma from an accident when she was young, about your age."

"No." I shook my head, denying his words.

She'd been well. I remembered…

"Remember the skiing accident I told you she had?"

I tilted my head, vaguely remembering him mentioning a skiing accident. But it hadn't seemed important at the time, not when my mom's episodes were getting worse.

"She had extensive damage to her brain. The doctors put her in a medically induced coma for almost two weeks to help with the swelling. When she finally came back to school she was…" his voice broke. "She was supposed to be fine. Then she started having these outbursts. They weren't often, but when she had them, she always came looking for me." Red rimmed his eyes, but he was no longer looking at me, but at something I couldn't see. "She said I made them better. I think I did, or maybe I fooled myself into believing I was some sort of hero." He scoffed at himself.

"You're my hero." I reached for him. He opened up his arms, and I went from Roderick to him. "You've always been my hero."

"That's why I wear a cape to work," he joked. "But your mom, kid, the doctors don't know why her brain is getting progressively worse or how to stop the deterioration, but it's not something you can get from her. You understand me? She suffered major brain trauma, and this," he shrugged, the vision of defeat on his face, "this is the outcome."

"You knew when you started dating her? You knew she was sick."

"Yeah." He exhaled a sharp breath against my hair. "She told me everything after I helped her through an episode at school. She was fifteen."

I let the thought linger, pictured my dad at seventeen helping my mom. "Why would you date her knowing she was sick?"

He sat quietly for a moment. His hand stilled in my hair. "Roderick," he said, "you thought there was a possibility my daughter might have what her mom has, right? You thought there was a possibility you might lose her?"

"Yes." His voice sounded behind me, and I looked back at him to see him.

He watched me with a careful expression.

"Believing that, why did you date her?" my dad asked.

"Because I love her," Roderick answered. His eyes flashed to mine, and a small smile crept across his lips. "I've loved her forever."

"Weren't you scared of losing her?" my dad questioned

him further.

Grief passed momentarily across his face. "I was more scared of not having her at all."

"There you go, kid," my dad said to me. "That's your answer. I love your mom. I've loved her forever. I knew I'd eventually lose her, but the fear of not having her at all was bigger than the fear of eventually losing her."

"I'm sorry, Dad. I'm sorry you're hurting so much because of her."

"It's okay, sweet girl. I'm okay."

"You're a real life super hero." I smiled at him. "Better than Thor."

"Better than Thor?" A brow quirked up. "Looks like we're gonna have to do a movie night and watch every movie he's in to see if you still feel that way at the end of it."

Closing my eyes, I pretended to snore. I then jerked my head up and said, "Wha?"

"Ha ha," he mused. "Now help your old man up. My ass hurts."

"Dad!" I slapped his shoulder. "You just said a bad word."

"What?" He looked up at Roderick while I helped him to his feet after I stood up. "Is ass a bad word?"

"Nah, I don't think it is," Roderick answered.

"Are you two ever going to not gang up on me?" I crossed my arms over my chest.

"Probably not," my dad said. "Are you okay, Brin? You know you're not sick. You're not going to be sick. You know that, right?"

I breathed, filled my lungs to their capacity and then drew out a long string of air. My heart, it hurt for my mom, for what she suffered through since she was just a kid. For my dad, for what he'd gone through so that he could be with her.

I hurt for myself. For the lies I'd been told, the fears that had swallowed me whole. For the life I'd led because of what I believed.

But it wasn't true. I was okay. And I had the boy who'd never faltered; who'd never ran away from me.

"I'm okay. But why didn't you tell me the truth sooner?"

He dropped his hands, his shoulders slumping forward. "I thought you knew, Brinley. I talked to you, I thought you understood. I swear, I thought you knew we did it for her. I went along with it for her, not because I thought you might be sick."

He had talked to me. I hadn't listened, hadn't been able to focus on his words.

"Mom told me though… four years ago after her first episode, she said…" I stopped, collected myself, but so much was still broken. "Why'd she lie to me? Why'd she say it would sneak up on me the way it did to her when none of it was true? Why would she scare me like that?"

"She was sick." He looked sad, disappointed at himself, at my mom.

"She was sick," I repeated.

"I'm sorry, kid. I didn't know. It's not a good excuse, but it's the truth. I didn't know you thought the tests were real. I didn't know you thought you might get sick."

"You didn't know."

"I'm sorry," he repeated.

"No more sorrys," I said, stealing a quick glance at Roderick. "It's over. I know the truth now, and I'm okay."

It was over. The fear I'd built my life on crumbled to the ground. The truth I had now, the truth I held onto, the truth I couldn't let go, put his arms around me. He kissed the side of my head. He held me together when I thought my world was falling apart.

CHAPTER 35

RODERICK

I DROVE BRINLEY's car back to her house. She tried to urge me to take us to the beach, or to the park so we could go hiking. The weather was great for either, and I probably would've jumped at the chance for a quiet hike with my girl, but she was hurting. She hid it well, but I knew her better now.

A smirk graced her pretty lips when I opened the car door for her. "Are you trying to get me back in bed with you?" She arched a single brow in my direction.

"Always," I said.

We made our way to her room with her hand tucked in mine. She stopped in front of her mom's closed door, where we heard Rosie speak loudly with her nurse. They were talking about a painting, about the colors and what Rosie used to paint. She sounded happy. Excited.

"She's an artist now," Brinley said, her lips tipped up in a small smile. "Bridgette gave her some paint supplies and canvas, and that's what they do during her episodes. It helps her, I think, to focus that energy on something else."

"Have you seen her work?"

"Yeah, she's really good." It came out wistful, hopeful.

"Next time she's having a good day, tell her I want to see it too."

"She'd love that."

Brinley tugged me the rest of the way to her room. I eased her on her bed, took off her sandals before I took my shoes off. She lied down, rested her head on a pillow and closed her eyes.

"Now what?" she asked.

I crawled into her bed, brought her to me so that she tucked her head against my chest. Toying with her hair, I watched the back of her head rise and fall with my breaths.

"Do you need anything?" I asked. "Water?"

"This," she answered. "I need this."

Turning her phone in her hand, she started a song from her playlist. It was one of the songs she said reminded her of me. I listened to the lyrics, to the piano and guitar, to the melancholy mood of the song. The words played in my head as I continued to comb my fingers through her hair.

It wasn't about love found, but love lost when you were too blind to see the person you once had was your everything. It was too late for the singer.

It hadn't been too late for us.

"Is this really what you want to do for your birthday?"

She inclined her head to look at me.

Her eyes were puffy, red rims along the outer edges. Although she smiled, I didn't feel it the way I felt her other smiles. The ones that were real and genuine.

"We can watch Avengers," I said.

She rubbed her temple on a groan. "I just had to mention Thor, didn't I?" The corner of her lips twitched, and I loved how she teased me. How she wanted to see me smile. But the pain was there, lingering just behind her eyes.

"Does your head hurt?" I cradled the back of her head, and she rested against my palm.

"I'm fine." She closed her eyes when I took my hand to touch her cheek.

"I want your truths."

Her eyes popped open. She nodded. "A little."

I sat up, scooting her to the side so that she lied fully on her bed. "I'll grab you water and some pain pills."

"Thanks," she murmured into her pillow.

After a search through her kitchen, I found the miniature Hershey bars I bought her last week in the pantry and went back to her room with the whole bag along with water and two pills. She took the pills and water and swallowed while I unwrapped a bar. I held the chocolate to her mouth and suppressed a moan when her lips covered my fingers.

"Mmm, perfect," she said.

She was perfect. She'd made my birthday perfect. Kissing her, exploring and touching her was the only way I would ever start all my future birthdays. It didn't matter how far we went. Although everything we'd done last night felt better than amazing, it wasn't the physical

I was after. What I so desperately craved.

It was Brinley.

The way she made me feel whole with a single look. How she undid me with her sweet caress. How she brought me back to life with a kiss.

"Avengers?" she asked.

"We can sleep so your headache goes away," I suggested.

"Avengers it is." Her eyes narrowed in response. "We're not sleeping your birthday away."

With a few clicks, she turned on the movie. I settled next to her. She curled into me, her phone in her hand.

"The other present I have for you," she murmured in to my chest. "Do you mind if we do it tomorrow?"

"That's fine," I replied.

It's not like I needed anything else. She'd already given me everything.

I couldn't believe we were going to San Diego together. Couldn't believe we were going to look at apartments this week with her dad.

It was happening. Our future was taking shape and it looked amazing.

After unlocking her phone, she sent a text to someone and then placed a kiss on my chest, over my shirt. I felt it as it she'd brushed her lips over my bare skin. It made me crazy for her, or crazier than I already was.

"Will you take off your shirt?" It came out shy, quiet.

While I stripped off my shirt, she undid her bra from beneath her shirt. My pulse raced, my stomach clenched. I lied back down and when she placed her head on my chest, I swept a hand through her hair. Her fingers trailed over my skin, leaving me fevered. She sighed. Such a sweet sound that somehow tempered that growing need, so I could give her a few hours of peace until she was ready to talk.

DANNY'S NAME FLASHED on my screen with an incoming text. With Brinley sleeping next to me, I opened his message.

Danny: Nicole called me. Is Brin ok?

Nicole and I had been talking in front of the restaurant while Brinley spoke to her dad. I forgot all about her when Brinley fell to the ground. All I saw was her – my girl crumbling, and me not being there to catch her.

Me: She's ok. Sleeping now.

With her lips parted, she nestled in closer to me. Beautiful, always beautiful. Asleep or awake, angry, laughing or at peace.

Danny: wht happened?

Brinley had told Danny about her mom, about

the disease she thought she'd one day inherit. It wasn't the first time Danny and I had worried about Brinley together. He loved her. She trusted him.

> Me: Long story, man. But her mom lied to her. Brinley isn't sick, she can't get sick. What her mom has isn't genetic. Hell, her mom was in a skiing accident that caused everything. She didn't get it all of a sudden like she told Brin she had but her brain progressively gets worse.

His response came immediately.

> Danny: thts good tho....our girls fine.
>
> Me: Yeah, she's fine. Or she will be. She just needs to get through this.
>
> Danny: u've got her, rt?
>
> Me: Always.
>
> Danny: grab her some chocolate... always makes her feel better.

I laughed.

> Me: Already done.

Rather than finish watching the movie, I grabbed the folder Brinley gave me with her poems tucked inside. I reached for another paper and smiled when I saw it was a blackout poem. Words were circled with purple swirly designs blacking out the words she didn't use. It was dated almost a month ago.

a smile turns into A blush gentle fingers Caress Happiness overtakes love Found

Flipping the paper over, I grabbed a pencil from her nightstand and wrote out the poem the way I would if I'd written it. I added deep swirls and other doodles. When I finished, I stared at it. Read it over.

A smile
turns into a blush.
Gentle fingers
caress.
Happiness overtakes.
Love found.

Love found. She'd written this three, almost four weeks ago. Had she loved me for so long? And kept it a secret? My fingers clenched at the thought. But I had kept my love for her silent too.

Hearing her say those words, saying she loved me… I didn't know how badly I needed to hear them. How badly I needed to say them back. Fear, though, fear had kept me from revealing my greatest truth. I loved her. I'd loved her for so long, I knew I'd never stop.

I went to the next poem. This one was two years old.

If solitude is bliss
then he has found Heaven.
But in his world of happiness,
why does he always frown?

I turn to yet another one, this one a little over a week old.

For the beautiful boy
who makes me smile without trying.
For the beautiful boy
whose kiss makes me forget everything.

For the beautiful boy
who writes with his heart.
For the beautiful boy
who makes my heart beat out of its cage.
For the beautiful boy
I love you.
You said you'd catch me when I fall.
Are you ready?

That one made me smile. Made me feel special in only the way Brinley could.

After reading a few more, I stopped when I got to one she wrote two days ago.

Fake
Vulnerable
Weak
Powerless
Shallow
I am none of those things
and all of them
I am strong
because no one but you
knows my truths

I rubbed my chest, hating and loving her words. She molded herself into someone she wasn't, to keep anyone from seeing her. I fed in to her ploy and fueled her insecurities.

Turning over the page, I wrote her back. When I finished, I rested the paper between us and closed my eyes. I reached for her, edged myself closer to her, and she responded by tucking her body closer to mine.

Even while asleep, she came to me. Never shied from me the way I feared she might when we first started dating.

We were together. A truth we both showed the world.

We'd be together forever. A great love story without an ending.

CHAPTER 36

Brinley

Soft laughter,
that floats deep into my chest.
Pretty blonde hair,
that I run through my fingers.
A smile,
that outshines us all.
Precious and cherished,
beautiful and good.
Her soul
I treasure.
Her heart
I keep.

Blinking back the sleep, I read Roderick's words again. And then again.

Her soul
I treasure.

Her heart
I keep.

As usual, his words filled me, left me empty of nothing but him. It was amazing to me how much he loved me, how he could make me feel special and alive with his words. I needed his words, as much as I needed him.

I stroked his cheek, loving the way he edged closer to me at the contact. Loving the way he always reached for me, always seemed to need to touch me. A hand in my hand, on my waist, or around my shoulders. He was always touching me. And it felt amazing.

Being loved by Roderick was amazing.

I dipped down, brushing my lips over his. When he didn't respond, I let my hand roam over his chest. He moved closer, but his eyes remained closed.

My heart pounded in my ear, anticipation growing in my chest.

I needed him. Needed to taste him.

Slipping my tongue over his lips, I brushed it gently across the seams. His lips parted, and he sucked in a breath while he wrapped his arms around my back. He pulled me to him, and I landed on his chest with a hard thud.

We didn't break the kiss though. His tongue met mine in a slow caress while his hands trailed under my shirt. My stomach, my back. I arched in to his touch, took his hand in mine and placed it over my breast.

I ground down, and he jerked his hips up.

"Brinley," he hissed.

When I kissed him this time, it was with fervor. With

hunger and need building too high, too fast. I broke the kiss to sit up. When I moved my trembling fingers to my shorts, Roderick covered my hand with his.

His face looked pained and when he spoke it was with restrained control. "We don't have to do this." He swallowed hard. "We can just kiss."

"We're a forever thing, right?" I asked.

He cupped my face with his hands and kissed me hard on the lips. When he drew back, all I saw was love. The insurmountable love he had for me. "Of course," he said. His chest heaved and he licked his lips. "We're forever."

I took his hands to my shorts, led him beneath the fabric of my panties. He panted harder.

"I want this," I whispered. "I want all of you."

Light blue eyes darkened. The storm behind them grew. "Forever."

Somewhere between the passionate kisses and hurried touches, Roderick had the forethought to protect himself. I watched in equal parts fascination and nerves. We were doing this. I was going to give myself entirely to Roderick, in a way no one else would ever have me. When he leaned over me, pressed himself into me, his body bare but the thin layer of latex that was between us, I knew I'd been waiting for him forever. Knew I'd need him forever.

Because us? The magic we created, was a forever thing.

CHAPTER 37

Brinley

AFTER THE THIRD ring, I answered Danny's call, yawning a hello into the phone.

"Morning, Sleeping Beauty," he chimed, sounding cheerful when I was the one who'd reached her peak of happiness. "Come outside!"

"Outside?" I asked. "Like outside my house?"

"Uh, yeah." His tone was dry. "Ari and I are waiting for you and Roderick."

"Right now?"

"Geez, Brin, you're not this slow." He laughed.

"Danny and Ari are outside," I told Roderick.

He arched a brow.

"He wants us to meet them."

"Tell him to go away," Roderick groaned, a teasing smile playing across his lips.

"No way," Danny replied, having heard Roderick. "Not after we put in so many hours getting his final birthday present ready."

I shot up from the bed. "What?"

Danny's laughter echoed in my ear.

"You're serious?"

A slow smirk built on my face. Taking Roderick's hand in mine, I tugged. "We have to get dressed."

"Dressed!" Danny shouted. "Details I don't need to know, best friend."

Roderick sat up on a laugh. I looked down, hiding my blush behind the hair that fell in front of my face. Brushing my hair back, he rubbed his knuckles over my cheek.

"I love it when you blush," he said. "It's sweet."

"Shut up," I grumbled.

After hanging up with Danny, I threw Roderick's shirt and shorts at him. I dressed quickly, excitement taking over. I couldn't believe Danny and Ari had prepared the cave for us.

"Where are we going?" he asked, putting on his socks and shoes while I put on mine.

"Remember your other present?" I grinned. "Danny and Ari got everything ready for us. When we got back from breakfast, I texted Danny I wasn't feeling great and wouldn't need his help until tomorrow. Guess he and Ari wanted it to happen today anyway."

"You have good friends."

"*We* have good friends," I corrected.

Holding his hand, I ran out the door. When I saw Danny leaning against Ari's car, I launched myself at him in a strong embrace. Then I threw my arms around Ari.

"You guys are the best. You know that, right?" I asked.

"Obviously." Danny tugged on my hair.

"Meet you there?" I asked them.

"No," Ari replied on a chuckle, "this is your night."

"And you guys made it happen," I retorted. "Roderick, you don't mind if they go with us, do you?"

"Considering I don't know where we're going…" he trailed off.

I playfully smacked his shoulder, but then kissed him, not wanting my last contact to be anything but full of love.

"I don't mind." He brought my hand to his lips.

"It's settled." I clapped my hands. "You guys go in Ari's car and meet us there."

"Where is there?" Roderick asked.

"To the moon!" Danny shouted.

"Your friend is weird," Roderick said when we got in my car. He sat in the driver's seat while I took the passenger seat.

"Our friend," I amended.

"Whatever." He shrugged. "As long as you admit he's weird."

"He is." I giggled. "But I love him."

He playfully stuck his bottom lip out, and I tugged on it.

"I love you more," I added.

He bit down on my finger. Not hard, just a small nip. It did nothing but make me want to crawl back in bed with him.

"Liar," he said. "But I guess you can have us both."

Roderick and Danny. They were my guys, my favorite people. Where Danny was my best friend, Roderick was my soul mate.

He followed Ari's car to the parking lot that led to our cave. After he parked, he arched a brow in my direction. I shrugged. When we met in front of the car, he took my hand where we hiked the two miles to our cave. Danny talked the whole way. I interjected when needed while Roderick and Ari laughed at our banter.

It was fun having the four of us together. While not exactly how I originally planned tonight to go, it felt right. We were a unit.

When we stepped into the cave, white lights adorned the walls, hung to the lowest parts of the ceiling. Roderick and I took it in in silence. It was better than I imagined and was grateful I'd found the solar lights that would last for at least eight hours after the sun had fallen.

Roderick's hand rested on the back of my neck where he massaged. It was soft, I wasn't sure he was even aware his fingers moved. But his eyes, they danced across the cave, took everything in. His breath stalled when he looked at our wall. I followed his gaze and after blinking a few times, I went to it.

Resting on the floor, against our wall were framed poems. Our poems. Roderick's and my words.

On a gasp, I turned to Danny and Ari.

"You guys did this?" I asked.

"Or some Poetry Fairies." Danny grinned. "They're kind of like the Tooth Fairy, but they leave poetry, instead of taking teeth."

"Roderick's right. You are weird."

At the same time Danny said, "I'm hurt", Roderick shouted, "I never said that!"

Ari tugged Danny to him, splaying his hand on

Danny's waist. "You are weird," he said.

"Yeah?" Danny arched a brow. "You're dating me. Who's the weird one now?"

"You," Ari and I said together.

I walked deeper into the cave, closed my eyes when the smell of pizza invaded my nostrils. Following the scent, I went to the ledge Roderick once slept on and opened up the box.

All meat, no pepperoni. Exactly how Roderick liked it.

After grabbing a plate, I started serving us. Together we sat in the middle of the cave.

"It's not homemade pasta," I said between mouthfuls. "But it'll do."

Danny pointed a finger at me. "You're the one that's supposed to make the homemade pasta, not me. I order pizza. That's the rules."

"Fine." I huffed. "But only if you agree to four kids, a dog, two leopards, and a shark."

"Where would we keep the shark?" he asked.

"The bathtub," I answered.

"Or if your house has a pool in the backyard, you can keep it there," Roderick suggested, biting back a grin.

"Don't encourage her."

"Or you could live on the beach and keep the shark in a large steel cage," Ari added.

"That's animal cruelty," I protested.

"Worse than keeping it in a bathtub?" he asked.

"Whatever," I griped. "Don't be logical."

"Spock!" Danny shouted. "Logic doesn't make sense in our world, young Spock."

"Who's Spock?" I asked.

Roderick and Danny groaned.

"What?" I asked. "Is he another dumb superhero?"

"So much to learn," Danny sighed into his hands.

"Tomorrow," Roderick said. "We're having a movie night to teach our Brinley the important things in life."

Danny raised his soda bottle. "Here, here."

Roderick clinked his water bottle against it.

"Do you know who Spock is?" I asked Ari.

"Sadly, yes," he replied. "I've already been educated."

"You're still coming to movie night," I said. "You can't leave me alone with these two lunatics."

He winked. "You're on."

Once we finished, after Danny went back for like a thousand more slices, he called me to him. He opened a box to show me the cake I'd ordered. A collage of all the Marvel superheroes stared back at me.

Danny helped me ease it out of the box and with our backs turned to Roderick and Ari, we lit eighteen candles. He helped me balance it on my hand, and I walked carefully to Roderick, who Ari was distracting.

"Happy birthday…" I started to sing when I was just a couple steps away from him.

His head swung to me, his smile growing as I neared him. Eyes I'd taken to memory flashed with surprise when I placed the cake in front of him.

Sitting on the floor, he stretched out his hands to me. I went to him, nestled in to his chest as Danny, Ari and I finished singing.

"Smile!" Danny called out.

We looked back at him, our smiles matching the others when he took our picture.

Roderick cupped my face, turned me back to him.

Soft lips touched mine. He kept the kiss gentle, stroked my lips with his. Still, I whimpered against him. Because kissing Roderick was everything. Fast or slow, gentle or frantic.

"Make a wish," I whispered, trailing my nose across his cheek to his ear.

"I have everything I want."

With me still in his arms, he leaned over and after closing his eyes for a few seconds, he blew out his candle. He then snuggled his face in to the side my throat, breathed me in.

"Birthday boy gets the first slice," Danny announced as he sank a knife in the cake.

I reached for the offered plate, cut a small bite with my fork and took it to Roderick's mouth. His lips parted and he smiled.

"Never knew superheroes could taste so good," he said.

I giggled, loving it when he was relaxed and silly.

We shared bites of his slice, him letting me eat more than him.

When we finished, Roderick reached for his phone, went to his playlists and turned on the list he'd made for me.

We stood.

I went into his arms. Wrapped myself in him, his scent, his warmth, and his love.

Danny and Ari went to each other.

Love found us. Or we found it.

The proof of its existence hung from every part of our cave. It bared the weight of the universe. It was comfort, warm. It was home. It was an everlasting flame.

And finally, life made sense.

CHAPTER 38

RODERICK

Dark waves crashed into the sandy beach. Brinley sat between my legs with her back pressed against my chest. My fingers trailed over her thigh in absent sweeps.

Her skin was warm, and a bit darker from the hours we'd spent on the beach. But it felt good to be out here. To play volleyball with a few of her friends. To watch her read a book in her white bikini.

Danny and Ari were a bit more open with their relationship that day. Flirting with each other, passing a few gentle grazes and heated glances.

It sucked they felt they couldn't be more open around others, but I knew the importance of hiding and couldn't fault them. Although Brinley insisted they didn't have to worry, I reminded her how well she hid until she was ready to be seen.

Every day, she showed the world a bit more of herself. Just last night, she, Danny, Ari, Seth, and I went to her house for a movie night. When her mom came out of her room, her eyes lost and a bit wild, she introduced her friends to Rosie. Before the nurse could usher her back in the room, she asked the guys if they wanted to see one of her mom's paintings.

To her mom's confusion and delight, we all celebrated her art. After she retreated back into her room, Brinley told the room about her mom. Didn't leave anything out, including how she was once led to believe her future could look similar to her mom's.

Rather than the silence I expected, Seth offered to make her mom a worktable, so she could sketch and paint on it. That night Brinley's joy, the trust, and loyalty she found in us, reached into my chest and squeezed.

Her dad joined Brinley and me after his shift, after our friends had left for the night. He and I argued over which was better – Star Wars or Star Trek. The obvious answer was Star Trek, but he disagreed until he realized I wasn't letting up. It was good having her dad in my life. A man I was coming to like and respect.

Back at the beach, I waited for Nicole to show up like she said she would when we talked outside the restaurant. It was the main reason I pushed for us to come. I knew how much Brinley missed her friend and although I didn't understand it, I wanted my girl happy.

After making an excuse about talking to Danny, I left Brinley on our towel when Nicole finally showed up. She nodded in my direction, but I could feel her nerves as if they were my own.

Immediately Brinley's spine straightened when

Nicole sat in front of her. I warred with myself, wanting to go back to Brinley, wanting to give her space and privacy to try to mend things over.

"They'll be fine," Danny said, following my track of vision. "Nicole misses her."

"Yeah." That's what Nicole had told me. It was the only reason I wasn't rushing to Brinley's side and putting a protective arm around her. "I don't trust her."

"I do," he said, as if that should be enough.

I guessed it was. It wasn't like Danny would ever do anything to hurt Brinley.

"Did she say anything about what happened in front of the restaurant?" I asked. We hadn't had a chance to talk about it, and I couldn't help but worry Nicole would say something to others.

"Just that she was worried."

I scoffed. "If she was so worried, why didn't she stick around and, I dunno, be a friend? Make sure she was okay?"

"Mariah was meeting her for breakfast," Danny said, his tone even. "She didn't want Mariah to see Brin like that because she knew Mariah would go nuts telling people and starting rumors, so she left and had Mariah meet her somewhere else. That day, she was being a friend."

Relief washed over me. I looked back at the girls. My gut tightened when Brinley threw her arms around Nicole.

"Prom," Ari said, sitting down next to us. Seth followed along with Jeremy. "We need to figure out what we're doing for prom."

Danny stiffened. When Ari gripped his lap and

squeezed, tension grew. Ari removed his hand on a sigh.

"I was thinking we could rent a limo," Ari added.

I nodded. My heart dropped. Although I continued to work at the ice cream store, I didn't earn that much money. The little I was able to save went into my Prom fund, so I could rent a tuxedo. I also needed to get a corsage for Brinley and a boutonniere for myself. At least, my aunt told me I had to make sure to get those things.

A limo, I wasn't sure I could afford that. Not without completely wiping my small savings and leaving me nothing for after graduation. I couldn't do that. Couldn't rely on Brinley's dad to support me, even though he didn't want us paying rent for whatever apartment we found in San Diego. He was a good man, treated me with more kindness and understanding than my aunt. I couldn't take advantage of that.

"My grandpa said he was going to rent a limo for us… or for me," Seth stuttered.

"Why do you need a whole limo for yourself?" Danny teased. "Aren't we good enough to go with you?"

"Yeah, sure." Seth drew his brows together. "Unless I get a bunch of girls to come with me. Then you guys are out."

I laughed. Hard. And when Ari stuck out his fist, Seth tapped it.

"A man with priorities," Ari said. "I like it."

"We can all pitch in for the limo," Danny said.

Red spread across Seth's pale complexion. "My grandpa won't take your money. He's too happy I'm going to a dance at all. I mean, it's not like I've had much of a social life for a few years." He laughed. It sounded tense and nervous.

"You guys thinking about asking anyone?" Ari asked him and Jeremy.

"I won't be here for Prom," Jeremy replied. "I'm starting some college courses after spring break at UCLA." He shrugged. "By then, I'll have all the hours I need to graduate high school, so it didn't make sense to stay here."

"Ah, college girls." Danny nodded his head in approval. As if the four of us didn't know he was with Ari.

"I've been talking to Sammi some," Seth piped in. "I was thinking about asking her."

Sammi. The image of a small girl with pink hair and braces crossed my mind. She was cute, enthusiastic. Maybe the kind of girl that would draw Seth out.

"Drama girl?" Ari asked.

Seth dipped his head down to hide his blush.

"Invite her to the diner tonight," Danny suggested.

"I don't think…" Seth stammered.

"Don't think!" Danny shouted and grabbed Seth's phone. "Invite the girl, get the girl."

Seth took his phone back, fumbled with it a few times, before it landed on his lap. Finally, he unlocked the screen and sent a quick text.

I looked back when I felt Brinley's hand on my shoulder. While I brought her fingers to my lips, she knelt behind me before she sat down and fanned her legs on either side of me. I leaned in to her, she wrapped her arms around me and rested the side of her face against the back of my shoulder. She kissed me.

"Have I told you how much I love you lately?" she whispered too low for anyone else to hear.

"Not in the last five minutes or so," I replied.

My fingers spread over her wrists, held her to me. Refused for her to ever let me go.

Nicole sat beside Danny. She looked happy and when she looked back at me, she mouthed, "Thank you."

I didn't know what she was thanking me for, but I nodded in response.

"What!" Seth scrambled to his knees, thrust his phone in Danny's face. "She said yes. Sammi's coming to the diner tonight."

"You better bathe then," I joked. "I've heard girls don't like it when guys smell."

Danny threw back his head in laughter while Brinley dug her teeth into my shoulder.

I rubbed where she'd nipped me. "Vampire."

"Smelly boy," she shot back.

"Not anymore," I said, my voice low. "I didn't have a home before. Now I do."

There were so many different meanings behind that statement. Sure, when she first accused me of smelling bad I was kinda homeless, but what I said went deeper than that. I knew she got it.

I felt her smile against my shoulder. "Always."

I brought our joined hands to my lips, kept her fingers there while I pressed kisses onto her warm skin. She sighed behind me.

"I gotta run to the bathroom," Seth said.

"Don't forget to wash your hands!" Danny shouted to his departing back. "Anything more than two shakes, and you're just playing with it!"

Seth shook his head, sent his middle finger in the air. Brinley pressed her nose in to my back and giggled. It was such a pretty sound, my favorite sound.

"Volleyball?" Danny asked.

The guy was always moving. Never stopped. As if he thought that by standing still, life would somehow pass him by. When in reality you missed so much more when you didn't take things slow, take them in.

He and Brinley were a lot like that. Exuberant, running circles around others, talking to everyone. Me? I was happy doing exactly what I was doing.

I let go of her hands, when Danny and the others stood. Turned my head back when she didn't move.

"I think I'm gonna stay here." A satisfied smile twisted her lips.

It was the first time she'd chosen me over a group when we were around her friends. I cozied back into her chest when her fingers danced through my hair. It was the first time she chose to be background music rather than take the limelight. But Brinley, she always had my full attention.

Closing my eyes, I soaked in the sun. Soaked in the embrace of the girl who was my forever.

"Seth hasn't come back yet," Brinley said after at least ten minutes went by.

I turned to the building that housed the bathrooms and after a few more seconds went by, I stood up. Taking Brinley's hand, I helped her up. We walked quietly together. It was as if we knew... something bad had happened.

CHAPTER 39

Brinley

From a few feet, I could see Jacob and Joseph saunter to the parking lot. I hadn't even realized they were here, but was grateful they were leaving. They sent equal glares to the door that led to the men's bathroom and then laughed, high fiving each other like the idiots they were.

Fear gripped me. Completely took over. Letting go of Roderick's hand, I sprinted toward the bathroom. Didn't bother pausing before flinging the door open. Roderick was beside me, placed a hand on my elbow when I stopped suddenly.

Two quick strides carried me to Seth, who laid on the floor, his body huddled in a ball. I sank to my knees beside him, whispered his name before I reached for him. When I touched his face, he flinched.

"Seth?" I said his name a little louder this time.

Cuts marred his face. A small puddle of blood rested on floor where his head lay. Urine spread around him and I was sure he had some on him as well.

My heart trembled, but I stood up. Willed the anger back while I took paper towels from the dispenser and wet them under the warm faucet.

When I turned back to him, Roderick had helped him to a sitting position with his back against the bathroom wall. He kept his face turned down, but I could see one eye was already swollen shut.

Back on my knees, I placed the wet towel against his cheek. He flinched again and closed his other eye. I spent the next few minutes trying to clean up the mess two people I once considered friends had done.

Blood trickled from a cut on his forehead, from cuts below his right eye, from a cut on his lips and one beside his mouth.

The urge to cry built in my chest, but that would have to wait, when Seth no longer needed me.

When I finished, I leaned my back against the wall and sat down beside him. Leaning my head on his shoulder, I placed an arm around his waist. His shirt had small wet streaks that had stained his white shirt yellow. He pulled my hand away.

"It's full of piss," he said, his voice quaking.

"Then let's take it off you." I touched the bottom of his shirt and when he leaned forward a bit, I pulled his shirt over his head, careful not to touch him with the wet parts.

Tossing the shirt across the room, I rested my head back on his shoulder as I twined an arm around him.

Danny squatted in front of us and handed me a

towel. I hadn't even seen him come in, hadn't heard the door when he'd opened it.

"You alright, man?" Roderick asked.

With his head leaned against mine, he nodded. It was slow, sluggish.

I covered the towel over the red marks on his chest and stomach and when I put my arms around him, I was careful not to hurt him.

Danny rocked on his feet, from his toes to his heel. "Ari's taking care of Joseph and Jacob," he said.

"I'll see if he needs any help," Roderick said.

"Roderick," I called to him.

But he'd already turned away, already made his decision. I just hoped he wouldn't get hurt or in trouble.

"Brin," Seth said my name slowly. "Sitting with you on a piss infested floor with your arms around me while even more piss covers my body is what dreams are made of," he edged back to give me a slow smile, "but do you think you can take me home?"

I snorted out a laugh. "Yeah, sure."

Outside, Seth stood under the spray of one of the showers. His hands splayed over the concrete wall while he kept his head down. After I finished rinsing off, I looked around the corner to the parking lot.

Sure enough, Roderick and Ari had taken out their fury on Jacob and Joseph. I was happy to see their faces bloody, their shirts torn. They deserved worse. But someone had broken up the fight, and while the twins limped to their car, Roderick paced the parking lot like a caged animal.

"Your boyfriend looks crazy scary right now," Seth said, coming beside me.

I wrapped a towel over his shoulders, enveloped an arm around his back.

"Head high, shoulders back," I instructed. "You ready?"

He nodded. As we neared the parking lot, his hand slinked around my back, and he dug his fingers into my waist. He stammered out a breath, stopped moving entirely when other students from our school turned to watch us. Roderick came to us, waited for us to continue walking to the car.

"Head high, shoulders back," I whispered again when Seth took a tentative step forward. "You have nothing to be ashamed of."

"Not when you've got the prettiest girl, wearing nothing but a tiny bikini with her arms around you." Roderick winked.

I covered my chest with a single hand and Seth laughed. It sounded real. Pained, but also real.

"My bikini is not tiny." I stuck out my tongue.

I led Seth to the front passenger door of my car. When he got in, I stepped back. Danny snapped one of the straps of my bikini, and I shoved his hand away.

"It is pretty tiny," he said.

Roderick's hands skimmed over my waist, grazed the side of my breast. His eyes heated, his lips remained in a frown.

"You okay?" I touched his face.

He turned into it, pressed a kiss to my wrist.

"I am now."

"Diner tonight." Danny smacked the top of my car while he spoke to Seth.

"I don't think I'm gonna make it," Seth answered.

I got it. Understood why he didn't want to go, why he wanted to hide. But hiding didn't solve anything.

"Why don't we go to the cave instead?" I asked.

"Seth's got a hot date tonight," Danny said. "She's supposed to meet us at the diner."

A blush deepened on Seth's cheeks and relief flooded me when his dimples popped out. He was hurt, but not broken. He'd be okay.

"Yeah?" I arched a single brow. "Who's the lucky girl?"

"Sammi," he mumbled. "But it's not a date," he rushed out.

"Okay, so bring your non-date to the cave."

"What cave?" he asked me.

"You'll see."

Roderick and I had gotten to our cave early to stream up the lights I'd left outside the cave so they'd be exposed to the sunlight. Our work didn't come out as nice as Danny and Ari's, but it looked good. The framed poems they'd given us on Roderick's birthday were spread equally in Roderick's room and in mine. I kept his poems, and he kept mine. But he let me keep the one we'd written together.

"Think we can start eating before they get here?" he

asked, sneaking a quick peek at the takeout we'd gotten.

I angled my head to the side. "Maybe some tortilla chips and salsa."

"That's my girl." He grinned.

After a quick rummage through the bag, he pulled out a small bowl and the container with chips. He dipped a chip in the salsa and brought it to my lips. I took a bite and moaned. Not because it was that good, but because I loved the heat that collected in his eyes when I did that.

"What's this?" Danny raced into the cave. Sweat collected on his forehead, but he didn't seem to be the least bit winded. "You guys eating without us?"

"When we were a few feet away, he swore he heard you guys eating," Ari said, an amused expression behind his eyes, "so he took off in a sprint."

Danny shot an accusatory finger in our direction. I pointed at Roderick, who still had part of the chip I hadn't finished in his hand.

"I thought we were friends," Danny said.

"It was all Brin," Roderick defended himself. "She made me feed her a chip."

"Sure," the melodic voice of Sammi reached me. "Blame the girl."

I grinned. "Don't you know we're always to blame?"

With her head tipped up, she spun a few circles. She took in everything with an open smile. When she stopped, she held a hand to Seth's shoulder while he cupped a hand on her elbow. My smile widened, I couldn't help myself.

Seth's eyes narrowed in my direction, and I bit back my smile. Not that it mattered, his attention went back to Sammi as soon as she spoke again.

"This place is amazing," Sammi said.

Roderick held me from behind, trailed his nose over my throat. "Yeah, it is," he replied.

"How'd you find it?" she asked.

Roderick and I laughed. I told her our story, not the whole thing. I left out how Roderick had slept here, how I'd found him here sick and took him back to my house. That part was ours.

Roderick told them about our poems. I didn't feel self-conscious when they read them. Only assured in the boy that had stolen my heart.

"Can I write a poem too?" Sammi asked.

"After dinner, woman," Danny griped.

"You and that endless pit of a stomach," I said.

"A growing boy needs sustenance," he replied.

Ari held out a plate he'd prepared for Danny. He took it but didn't start eating until Ari was by his side. At least his manners extended to his boyfriend, if not to the rest of us.

I swiped a piece of beef fajita from Roderick's plate. He pretended to stab me with his plastic fork while I ate it.

"So good," I murmured.

"Yeah, it's not bad," Seth said. "Thanks for picking this up for us."

"To Brinley, my hero." Danny raised his soda bottle in the air.

I raised my middle finger.

"Does your face hurt?" Sammi touched the side of Seth's mouth where one of the deeper gashes lay and then traced her finger just below the eye that was swollen shut. "When you chew I mean?"

He dipped his head down, but then peered back at her with a small smile. "I'm fine."

"I'm glad you two kicked their asses." She pointed her fork at Roderick and Ari.

"Yeah." Seth coughed. "Thanks for that." He met my gaze. "And thanks, Brin, for, you know, taking care of me."

"It's not every day I get to cuddle with my favorite wood-crafter," I said, keeping my voice gentle.

"Wood crafter?" Sammi asked. "You can make stuff with wood?"

While Seth showed her the pictures on his phone, Roderick leaned in to me, brushed his lips against my ear. "I'm pretty crafty with wood too."

I laughed, hard and long. Tonight, spending time with some of my favorite people, was a memory I wanted to trap in time forever.

CHAPTER 40

Brinley

"I heard this crazy rumor that charities started accepting donations again," I deadpanned.

"You feel that?" my dad asked, and I shook my head. "You ruined the moment with your obnoxious talk of altruism."

Seated behind us, Roderick laughed. It sounded free, no longer like the lonely boy from the cave. Our trip to San Diego was fun. We even found a two bedroom apartment we fell in love with. Although we said we didn't need two rooms, my dad insisted. Absolutely insisted. In fact, he argued he had no other use for his money than to pay the rent on that apartment. Which brought us to the current conversation circling in the car.

"Phil," Roderick spoke up, "I really do appreciate you wanting to pay for my part of the rent, but I can't let

285

you do that. It doesn't feel right."

"You take care of our girl, and I'll take care of both of you," my dad replied. "I want you two to focus on your education, go out and have fun, but not too much fun. And if you do have too much fun, call a cab or me. I don't care how far the drive is," he rambled on, "I'll drive the three hours to San Diego to pick you up. Just no driving drunk."

"Yes, sir," Roderick agreed. "But the rent…"

"Get a job, pay for all your other expenses, leave the rent to me." He turned his head to look back at Roderick. "Paying your side of the rent is cheaper than a home security system anyway."

"Dad!" I smacked his shoulder. "We do not need a home security system."

"Not when you have Roderick living with you." He grinned. "I saw what you and that football kid did to the twins."

My mouth hung open. "How… how did you hear about that?"

"Their parents took them to the ER, and I had the pleasure of working on them. When the cops came, they told them what happened."

"Sir…"

"Don't you sir me, son," my dad interrupted. "It's Phil, or nothing. Besides, those two deserved it. What they did to that poor kid, it's disgusting. They should be expelled from school. And you." My dad gave Roderick a pointed look, and I turned my head in time to see Roderick's face pale. "I'm proud of you, Roderick."

Roderick swallowed hard, making his Adam's apple move.

"You're a good man," my dad continued. "I'm glad Brinley and you are together."

"Th-thank you," Roderick stammered out.

"Now, don't go and screw it up." My dad laughed at his own joke while I shook my head. "And, Brin, I'm proud of you. Of the way you took care of that kid, Seth. Maybe there's a doctor in you yet."

Rolling my eyes, I said, "Not going to happen. Wait, but how'd you hear about all that?"

He gave me a knowing smirk. "Small town, people talk. When Seth heard the twins were pressing charges against Roderick and what's that football kid's name?"

"Ari," I said.

Reaching my hand back, I put it on Roderick's knee. Strain made the sides of his eyes crinkle. He put a hand on top of mine.

"Right, Ari. When Seth heard about that, he came to the hospital and told the police what the twins had done to him. All charges were dropped after that. I had a long talk with Bert, our chief of police after that," my dad continued. "Told him if he ever thinks about pressing charges against Roderick again I'd tell his wife how he comes to the hospital and plays poker with me when I'm not busy rather than going home to her."

This time, I laughed harder. My dad and Bert were longtime friends, sometimes enemies.

"I don't care if Danny or Ari are gay," my dad rushed out. "I don't care…"

"Wait." I placed a hand on my dad's shoulder, a bit dizzy from all the leaps in my dad's conversation. "How do you know Danny and Ari are gay?"

"One of the twins said they were together." His brows

drew together. "Is it a secret?"

My heart drummed loudly in my ear. Roderick squeezed my hand before I took it back so I could text Danny.

"Neither of their parents know," I replied.

"And they'd be upset if they found out?" my dad asked.

"They think so."

"Shit," my dad cussed.

"Yeah."

Turning to my phone, I typed out a quick message to Danny. Although, I had to tell him Jacob and Joseph knew about him and Ari, I didn't want to do it by phone. I just hoped I wasn't too late.

> Me: Heading back home now. Should be back in less than an hour. Wanna come over?
>
> Danny: Can Ari come?

Tension eased from my shoulders. After I replied, I told my dad both Danny and Ari were going to come by later.

"Want me to grab some Thai food for you kids?" he asked.

"What kind of question is that?" I teased. "If we're talking Thai, the answer is always yes."

After getting home, Roderick and I stayed in my bedroom while my dad went to see my mom. Mom had seemed more at ease since dad moved back in with us the day after he and I spoke. She still had her episodes, but painting soothed her. My dad being back with her calmed her further.

By the time Danny and Ari got there, Seth, Roderick

and I were hanging out in the living room. I'd worried about Seth while we were in San Diego, had texted him every day just to chat, so while Roderick and I cuddled on my bed, he suggested I also invite Seth over. I was sure Danny and Ari wouldn't mind Seth being there when I told them about Jacob and Joseph.

Danny kissed the top of my head while Ari tousled my hair.

"Before we say anything," I started, going over what I'd rehearsed, "I need to tell you guys something."

My attention jumped from Danny to Ari. They nodded, the tension on their shoulders matching mine.

"My dad treated Jacob and Joseph when they were in the ER," I said. "They had a lot to say, which whatever, isn't as important." I waved my hand, already floundering what I wanted to tell them. "Anyway, my dad said that one of them, he's not sure who, was telling people you guys are together."

A muscle on Danny's jaw ticked. "Yeah." It came out like gravel. "Seth already told us."

"Oh." I pushed my teeth onto my bottom lip. "Glad I've been worrying about telling you for hours then."

Danny smiled. It wasn't his typical happy smile, but it didn't look sad either. It just was.

"Are you guys okay?" I asked. "Have your parents heard anything?"

"We'll be fine," Ari said, resting a hand on Danny's arm. "We can't stop them from telling people, but we know they're talking so there's that." He shrugged. "I told my parents I was gay a couple nights ago though. They were shocked, I guess, but they're okay with it."

Danny covered Ari's hand with his. "I haven't really

spoken to my mom in a few years, so I guess it doesn't matter if she hears something. But my dad…" His brows drew together, his lips turned down in a scowl. "I'll tell him after I graduate and am in college."

Silence stretched between us. Although my heart bled for Danny, the quiet wasn't altogether uncomfortable.

"Oh!" Danny exclaimed. "Seth has something to tell you." He waggled his eyebrows at Seth twice. "About Sammi?"

Mashing my lips together, I tilted my head to the side and waited.

Seth drew in a sharp breath as he fiddled with his thumb. "We're supposed to go to the movies next weekend."

"My man." Danny extended his hand for a fist bump that Seth tapped.

Beside me, Roderick squirmed on the couch. He roughed a hand through his hair before he let it drop to his lap. He'd been uncomfortable since Seth had arrived. I wasn't sure why, but I'd waited him out. When he squeezed my hand, I knew he was ready.

"Hey, Seth," Roderick started, "Brin's dad also mentioned that you showed up at the hospital when the twins were trying to press charges against me and Ari." He cleared his throat. "He said you told the cops what they did to you."

He scratched the back of his neck, seemed to struggle with his words. Leaning into him, I pushed a hand beneath his shirt and stroked the soft skin of his stomach.

His hand found my knee. "I appreciate you doing that," he continued talking to Seth. "Pretty sure my aunt would've cut me out of her life for good if they'd gone through with it."

Hearing that hurt. Knowing his aunt wasn't there for him. Knowing that at twelve he lost more than his parents, but his home. At least until we found each other again.

Seth tapped a foot against my parents' hardwood floor. "Yeah, of course."

"When we're back at school, we'll be watching your back," Roderick said. "Danny, Ari, and I won't let them get near you."

The tapping got quicker, a bit louder. "I was actually hoping I could learn how to fight." It came out unsure, but he kept his gaze level on the three other guys in the room. "You know, throw a punch, block a punch, not get my ass kicked in the bathroom."

"You know the captain of the wrestling team... Sean?" Danny angled his head to the side and we all nodded, we knew who he was. "Sean texted me a couple days ago and said if you wanted to learn some moves, he'd teach you. I didn't say anything 'cuz I wasn't sure what you'd think."

His foot stilled. "Yeah. That'd be cool I think. It's crazy that a few months ago I didn't have any friends." He breathed out a long string of air. "I mean there's Jeremy, but we're not really friends. We do group assignments together and eat lunch at the same table because no one else would."

Roderick hadn't had any friends either but he stayed quiet, a small smile building on his lips.

"We're the ones that missed out," I said, my hold on Roderick's waist tightening. "I wish... I wish I'd been friends with you since freshmen year. School would've

291

been a lot better."

I wished I'd never lost Roderick. Wished we'd never known how lonely life could be. At least I'd had Danny though. Roderick, he hadn't had anyone.

Roderick smoothed the top of my head, kissing where he touched.

"I don't know if school would've been better for you," Seth scoffed. "But for me, to have had friends…" He started tapping his foot again.

"For me, to have had friends I actually liked being around," I said, "who actually liked me… it would've meant a lot to me."

"Think in twenty years we're gonna look back at high school as the best time of our lives?" Seth asked, his dimples making an appearance.

"That's what it's supposed to be, isn't it?" I laughed. "The best years of our lives."

"The best years of my life started in a cave." Roderick's admission came out low.

"Mine too," I admitted.

"Your cave is pretty special," Danny said, his voice as somber as the rest of us. "I wrote my first poem in there."

"I danced with a boy I love in there," Ari added.

Danny stilled, brought his lips to Ari's for a tender kiss. Angling his head down, he rested his forehead on Ari's. "I love you too," he said.

I wasn't sure, but I thought we witnessed the first time they spoke openly of their love. It made me almost as happy as Roderick's and my first kiss made me feel.

"I had my first date in there," Seth said.

I found myself in that cave. Found Roderick. Found love.

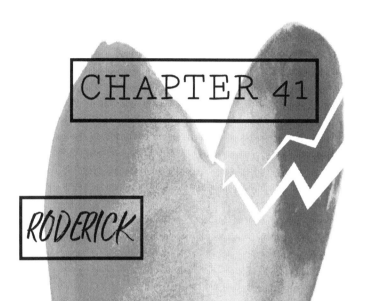

CHAPTER 41

RODERICK

A KNOCK ON my bedroom door woke me. Looking at my phone, I groaned. It was still another hour before I had to get up to go to school. On a muffled swear, I got out of bed and put on my shorts before answering the door.

My aunt's tear filled gaze met mine. "Roderick." Her voice cracked. "The police need to speak to you." She angled her head to the side. "Why don't you put on a shirt and meet us in the living room?"

I nodded. What else could I do when emotions choked me?

Grabbing my phone from the bed, I sent a text to Brinley, begging her to text me back and let me know she was okay.

Because this? Where my mind circled to… it couldn't

happen. Life couldn't repeat itself. I couldn't lose Brinley too.

After throwing on a shirt, I ran into the living room where Bert, the chief of police stood by my aunt's worn couch.

I stared at him, my heart thundering in my ears, pounding behind my ribs. I couldn't bring myself to voice my concern. Couldn't stop myself from worrying about the worst.

Clenching my phone in my hands, I unlocked it to see if she replied. She didn't.

My limbs shook, anger and dread rose with bile.

"What is it?" I croaked out. "Is Brin okay?" I finally managed to ask.

"Brinley's fine," Bert said.

My shoulders sagged forward. Relief felt like a gift. Whatever else he had to say I could handle.

The man rubbed his round stomach. "I'm sorry to tell you, son. There's really no easy way to say it." He huffed out a frustrated breath. "Last night, someone defaced your parents' headstones."

I jerked back as if he'd struck me.

He looked sorry. He sounded sorry.

It didn't matter. Not when my body throbbed with a pain I was too familiar with.

"What do you mean?" By my sides, my fists clenched, grabbed at nothing but air. Because as usual, when I needed someone, I was alone. No one was there for me to hold onto.

"We have the persons of interest in custody," he said, "but I'm truly sorry, Roderick, the damage has already been done."

I nodded, a quick dip of my chin to my chest.

"How bad is it?" I swallowed hard.

"They spray painted both headstones and knocked them over." He paused. "That's the worst of it, but they also painted the grass surrounding it. They dumped trash everywhere. It's," he scrubbed his face, "it's a mess, but it'll get fixed."

"Fixed?" A scornful laugh erupted from my lungs.

Fixed. There was no fixing what was irrevocably broken. And this broke me in a way that I'd never be able to be pieced back together.

"It can be cleaned up. Your…" He opened his mouth to continue, but I held out both palms to him. I didn't want to hear anymore.

My parents. I had to see them. Had to see the damage that was done to them. To the only parts of them that I still had.

Without socks or shoes, I ran out of the house and didn't stop until I made it to the cemetery my parents were buried at. My vision blurred, my chest screamed. I rushed through the paved path in a blur of movement and when I reached the top of a hill, I saw my parents' resting place. Saw several people working to clean it up.

On shaky legs, I made it to them. My breath hitched when Brinley looked up, seeming to search for something until her gaze met mine. Almost as if she could feel my pain, her shoulders slumped forward.

Defeated.

Slowly, carefully, she took the few steps to reach me. The beautiful girl I loved. The girl I couldn't breathe without.

"What are you doing here?" I tucked her messy hair

behind her ears.

"I heard what happened. Bert came to my house a few hours ago to talk to my dad about it." The tremor in her voice hit me in the gut. "I didn't want you to see what they'd done." She looked behind her to her friends—our friends, who had stopped cleaning up to watch me.

Danny was the first to wave.

"When Bert told me we could start cleaning up, I called our friends and they met me here," she continued. "My dad left a little while ago."

"Your dad was here too?" My tone was low, my voice shaking with each word.

"He likes you," she said touching my face. I leaned into her palm. "He cares about you."

I swallowed hard, past the lump in my throat. Tears burned the back of my eyes.

I wasn't alone. Brinley, Danny, Seth, Ari and her dad – I had them.

Needing her more than I needed anything else in my entire life, I pulled her in for a hug, rested my head on her shoulder. Her fingers curled into the back of my shirt, and she pressed a sweet kiss against my throat.

"Why?" A sob tore from me, caught in my throat. "Why would someone do this?"

Tender fingers weaved through my hair, touched me with such delicacy, I was afraid I'd break.

"Because they're assholes," she said.

"Did Bert tell your dad who did it?"

Her body jerked, her back straightening. When I edged away, she had her eyes shut tight. She sucked in a breath through her parted lips, drew it out while a tear fell from the corner of her eye.

"Who did it, Brin?" It came out harsh, volatile.

I had a good guess who it was. Had an even better guess why they'd done it.

She blinked her eyes open. "Jacob and Joseph." She said it so low, it felt like a whisper of the passing wind.

My heart, it couldn't take anymore. Not when the pain felt insurmountable.

"You need to leave," I said.

She nodded, her eyes sad but understanding. She knew this was her fault. Just as their assault on Seth was her fault. It all fell back on her, who she was, who she used to be. Now they wanted to punish her for calling them out while she managed to redeem herself.

"I'll go after I finish cleaning up."

"No!" I roared, the veins on my neck tightening with the exertion. "Now, Brinley."

She turned back to her friends, who had started working again.

"I'm almost done cleaning your mom's headstone." She hesitated. "I can't get all the paint off, but most of it…"

"Don't touch her headstone." Heat rushed to my head, made me dizzy. "This is your fault. You did this!"

She bowed her head. Another tear spilled. "I know," she whispered.

"Doesn't matter how much you change, Brinley." I spat out. "You're still the school's princess. You can't move from that, when you've lived it for so long. When you try, this is what happens!"

She flinched at my words. Nodded again. "I won't touch your mom's headstone. The stuff my dad brought for me to use to clean it, it's all there." She jerked her head toward my parents' headstones. "I wasn't able to start on your dad's." Her chin wobbled. "I won't touch it though. Just let me help pick up the trash."

I didn't answer her, couldn't answer her. Not after everything I'd said. Not with all the emotions churning inside of me.

When I reached my parents, I touched my mom's headstone first. Her vase no longer there, but it'd been replaced with one similar to it. Fresh flowers rested in it, each of them neatly placed with care. There was a crack down the center of the stone, much like the crack that tore through my chest.

Comparing my dad's headstone to my mom's, Brinley had done a good job cleaning up my mom's. An incredible job. I shot her a look over my shoulder, but found Danny standing behind me.

"Want me to finish your mom's while you work on your dad's?" he asked.

He should've been angry with me, with the way I'd spoken to Brinley. I was sure he'd heard us, was sure all three of them had heard us. But he showed me nothing but compassion.

"Yeah, whatever." I brushed him off, wanted to brush everyone off, so I could be by myself. Alone with the ghost of my parents.

Brinley worked as far from me as she could, picking up the multitude of trash that Jacob and Joseph had spread, tossing the never-ending strands of toilet paper that they had flung everywhere in her trash bag. The hateful words Joseph and Jacob sprayed right over their grave glared at me. I couldn't get rid of them. Couldn't wash them away. Instead, I had to wait for the grass to grow so it could be mowed down. But even worse than that, were the words they used to cover the plaque. Brinley had been able to clean away the words on my mom's plaque but my dad's…

I leaned my head against his headstone, dug my fingers in the dirt beneath me while my other hand clung onto the large chunk on the top that had fallen off completely.

Cheater

I scrubbed the words with a hard pad, wished the lie into inexistence. They didn't just deface my parents' plaque and tombstone, their resting place, but defamed their character with an untruth that cut me to my core.

If Roderick were my son I would've killed myself too

My parents had loved me. I knew that, felt it in my bones. But those words, they made me wonder. Made me think of my mom's sister, who cared for me but barely tolerated me. And I wondered if they were happier without me.

The words I tried to cleanse myself of slithered into my mind, wrapped around me and made it all true.

Brinley's words from so long ago crashed in my head, reminded me that I'd killed my parents. Because if they hadn't gone to get me ice cream, maybe…

The thought pierced my heart, ran my soul straight into the ground. Her words had been tossed at me callously; they still clung to me like a cloak. And every time I remembered it, I felt the spike of pain her words delivered.

She and I knew the weight words carried. They could save. They could destroy. Us? We played at saving, but chose to destroy.

We were both victims, both perpetrators.

By the time Danny finished with my mom's headstone, the others had also finished. I stood up from my place in front of Dad's headstone. He gripped my shoulders, squeezed them before letting go.

"I'm sorry about this," he said. "It's all so screwed up, but it isn't Brinley's fault."

"Danny," she said his name, a warning not to continue.

He nodded his head. "If you need anything, man…" he trailed off.

"I'm good. Thanks for…," I couldn't finish, didn't want to finish, but I met all of their gazes, except Brinley's.

With nothing else to say, I knelt back in front of my dad's headstone and got back to work. When I was sure they'd all left, I let go of the spray bottle and the scrub pad. Placing a hand on both of their headstones, I dropped my head and cried.

Tears for them, for the life that was stolen. Tears for me, for the life I couldn't have. Tears for Brinley, and the promises I broke. Because regardless of the words I'd said, I still loved her. I still needed her.

It didn't mean I could have her though. It didn't mean we'd ever stop hurting each other. It didn't mean I deserved her.

My fingers hurt by the time my dad's headstone was as clean as I could get it. It wasn't perfect, would never be perfect, but nothing in my life had ever been perfect. At least not since my parents' death.

After placing a kiss on both their headstones, I stood up and looked over their grave. The words were still painted on the grass, but all the trash was gone. When

I started making my way back up the hill, I noticed Brinley's figure facing me from beneath a tree.

Anger pulsed. I didn't want her here, hadn't wanted her or anyone to see me when I broke. Fury grew with each step and when I reached her, she stood up.

Her eyes were red, her face pale. When she crossed her arms over her stomach, her hands shook. And damn, I wanted to go to her. To apologize and make her feel better.

Instead, I glared into her, straight through her the way I'd seen her do multiple times throughout the years.

"What are you doing here?" I demanded.

She jutted out her chin, threw her shoulders back. "I didn't want you to be here by yourself."

My resolve wavered. The unconditionally way she cared for me was insane. And stunning.

"I wanted to be alone," I replied.

"You were alone." Her voice remained steady while her eyes glistened with tears she tried to hold back. "I just watched over you."

"I don't want you watching over me," I barked out. "We, us? We're no longer together. We were a mistake."

"Don't say that!" Her scream startled me. In all the years she'd been mean and hateful, I'd never once heard her raise her voice. "You can't say we were a mistake. You don't want to be with me anymore, fine." Her voice broke and she hugged herself tighter. "I get that, but you don't get to say we were a mistake. Not when you're my only truth."

"I can't be your truth, when you're my lie."

She cried out. It was a painful sound that chipped at the wall I was so desperate to build.

"You were a flaw that should never have happened."

A sob ripped through her. And I left her there. Shattered.

I finally got it. I got why so many times Brinley had told me she hated herself. Because in that moment, when I lashed out at the person I treasured the most, I hated everything about myself, especially my words.

Bare feet carried me forward while my heart stayed behind, with Brinley, with my parents. I walked with purpose, with heat slamming through my limbs. The need to destroy, to hurt, grew stronger.

When I rounded the corner, I paused. Took in a sharp breath. Taking out my phone from the pocket of my shorts I clicked on Danny's name.

> Me: Call Brinley. Make sure she's ok and take care of her.

The thoughts were final. We were done. A beautiful tragedy that I already missed. The memory of her touch, of her lips, of her breath on me would carry me. It had to.

A block away from Jacob and Joseph's house, a car pulled up beside me. I walked faster, not knowing or caring who it was. My only concern was the twins. Was making them pay for vandalizing my parents' headstones and for taking away the girl who was supposed to be my forever.

"Roderick!"

I kept walking, ignoring the voice that belonged to Brinley's dad. A few beats later, and he was in front of me gripping me by the shoulders.

"Think about what you're doing," he said.

I shrugged out of his hold, or tried to, but he kept me fastened in place.

"I know you're pissed, you have every right to be, and if you really want to go after the twins, I won't stop you."

"I really want to kick their asses," I seethed.

"Think about your future for a second." His voice was calm, his hold on me tight. "You go up there, you kick their asses, and then what?"

"I feel better."

"Yeah." He nodded. "Until you're arrested for assault without cause."

"They destroyed my parents' headstones!" Rage drummed through my veins and poisoned my heart.

"I know they did." His hands slid to the sides of my neck, continued to ground me. "And their punishment isn't fair, a fine their parents will pay isn't justice, but neither is you fighting them. You'd hurt them, sure. They'd end up back in the ER for a few hours, and then they'd get better. But you? Roderick, you'll end up in jail. You're better than that. You deserve better than that."

I looked back at their house and then back at the man who apparently knew I'd wind up coming here and tried to save me from myself.

This man, whose daughter's heart I'd shredded, took me in his arms. I held onto him while I let the tears fall. For the second time today, I broke down, covered myself in grief.

So many things in my life had gone to ruin. So many times my life had collapsed.

CHAPTER 42

Brinley

THE PERSON WHO wound up hurting me the most was the one who promised me he never would. It made sense though. I'd hurt him first.

At school, he was a shadow of the person he was before. Or maybe not a shadow, but a looming cloud. Destructive and angry.

No one was safe from his wrath. Jacob and Joseph smartly stayed away from him until one day they quit coming to school all together. I learned from Nicole that their parents had transferred them to another school to finish out the year. I was happy to see them go, but miserable to see how deeply Roderick rooted into himself.

Days passed, blurred together and when a new week started, I still couldn't shake the misery. But today, I had to fake my smile. Had to put on a show as our cheer captain when we went to a nearby middle school to perform and encourage future freshmen to join the cheer squad.

After changing into my outfit in the girls' bathroom, I ran across the empty gym, hoping I'd make it to the bus that waited for me in record time. Already I was three minutes late.

I came to a stop when someone grabbed me from behind by my ponytail and tugged me back. I yelled in surprise, in sudden pain, but that kind of hurt was nothing compared to the poison that lurked in my heart. Falling on my bottom, I looked up at the face of one of my old friends, one of Jacob's best friends. Ethan's smile was twisted, his eyes narrowed.

His big body loomed over me. I crawled back, my chest heaving as fear gripped me. He smacked his lips and when his hand reached for me, I scooted back further.

A scream tightened in my throat, stalled on my tongue. I couldn't get it out, couldn't yell for help.

Hands gripped my wrist and I threw my leg up in a kick. He stumbled back on a laugh. Twisting my body, I jumped to my feet, but the same hands grabbed my waist and pulled me to him. My back hit his chest hard, and I shuddered out a scared breath when he ran his nose across my neck to my chin.

"Stop." My voice trembled, but I'd managed to say it. To tell him to stop. Not that he would listen.

A dark chuckle fell from his lips on my neck.

I stomped on his foot, dug my heel against his shoe. He let me go for only a second, not enough time for me to run.

"Let her go!" A familiar voice, one I loved and dreamt

about roared.

Ethan shoved me away, and I spun around to watch them, knowing I should run for help. Roderick was nothing but a blur of motion when he ran to us. His fist connected with Ethan's face on a loud crack. Blood splattered everywhere.

Finally, the scream came. It wasn't a call for help though, but a plea for Roderick to stop. He didn't hear me. Fists rained across Ethan's face while Roderick crouched over him, pinning his body to the floor. The fight in Ethan had already stopped, and I was scared what would happen if I couldn't get Roderick to quit.

I pulled on Roderick's arm but fell back when he shrugged me away. At least that seemed to get his attention. A pained expression looked back at me.

"Roderick," I whispered.

He stood up, came to me with slow movements. Behind him, Ethan dragged himself up and after swearing at Roderick, he stumbled out of the gym, never uttering a word why he would attack me. My guess was he was finishing Jacob and Joseph's work, their ridiculous vengeance on me. At least they finally stopped hurting the people I loved and were finally focusing that attention on me.

"Are you okay?" Roderick asked.

I took his hand when he reached for me. I loved his warmth, loved the feel of his skin on mine.

"Did he hurt you?"

I shook my head. Ethan wasn't the one who hurt me.

"I'm fine." I brushed my skirt down and then went to work on fixing my ponytail.

"Your bus is waiting for you."

I nodded.

"No one's gonna hurt you again. You're safe."

Lie. Every day Roderick hurt me. Every day I felt less and less secure.

He smirked. "Even when I try to hate you, I'm still going to make sure you're okay."

He was back to trying to hate me. We'd made a full circle, back to where we started.

My coach's whistle blew in the distance. I chanced a glance away from Roderick, hoping he wouldn't disappear.

"You should go." His voice sounded distant.

I took a step away from him, away from us and it hurt. God, it hurt.

"Are we ever going to be okay again?" I held my breath, waited for him to answer.

"No." He breathed the word, stole my oxygen.

With my head bowed down, I ran from him, from the boy who held my heart. Our coach rushed me when she saw me, and I sprinted faster.

On the bus, I sat next to Nicole. Our friendship was still a work in progress, but I was glad to have her back.

"You guys wrote poetry together?" she asked me while I continued to stare out the window.

"Yeah."

The reminder of the messages we'd written to each other, for each other haunted me every day. I hadn't been able to write since, and wondered what I'd do at the art school if I could no longer write. If writing had become painful, instead of healing.

"So write him a poem," she suggested.

She made it sound easy. Write him a poem, send it

to him through text or on a note that I could tuck in his locker.

"Brin." She touched my hand. "You're sad without him. Get him back."

"He doesn't want me back." Finally, I turned to her, showed her my despair at losing the boy I loved.

"Fight for him, Brin," she urged. "Your words have power, use them."

Once we reached the middle school, I ambled out of the bus with enthusiasm I didn't feel. I shouted, went through all of our routines with a smile I couldn't feel.

I was numb. Lifeless.

I pretended for the kids though, and for the girls on my team that relied on me.

In the cafeteria, I watched my team talk to the girls that approached them. They were loud, rang with a joy that draped over me like a protective arm. I felt it, felt their happiness.

Looking around the room, I saw a girl sitting in the back. She watched us in quiet wonder. I went to her, took the empty seat beside her.

"Hi," I said.

She brushed a strand of hair out of her face. "Hey."

"I'm Brin."

"Gabbie."

"What'd you think, Gabbie? Are you going to cheer for us next year?"

A deep blush spilled over her cheeks. "Oh no." She shook her head. "I couldn't do that. Not in front of so many people."

"It's kinda scary, isn't it? Having all those eyes on you?"

Her mouth gaped open. "You were scared up there?"

"Every time I'm scared. But you know what that means, don't you?"

She shook her head again.

"Whenever you're about to do something you want to do that scares you, it means it's something important. Something that matters." I licked my lips as my heart clenched in my chest. "Don't let it stop you. Instead use it to move forward. And when you do it, Gabbie, do it with your whole heart."

She perked up, nodded her head. "I'm a pretty good dancer."

"Yeah? Then let's see you cheer." Standing up, I extended my hand.

With a shy smile, she took it. I called my team to me, told them we were going to teach the girls one of our more basic routines. It wasn't part of what our coach told us to do, but it was something I had to do, for Gabbie.

"Stand with me," I instructed Gabbie when we all lined up.

I took the girls through the moves, one at a time. My team encouraged them, helped them make slight adjustments. After a half hour, the girls were jumping in excitement to put the whole routine together.

"Can you lead them?" I asked Nicole. "I want to watch."

Nicole grinned and after clapping her hands to get their attention, she started.

The girls followed suit, and to my delight, Gabbie was really good. A bit timid in her movements, but she would do well. I took a picture of the girls, and made a mental note to give our coach Gabbie's name and show her what she looked like. Because if Gabbie wanted to join the team next year, I was going to give her a solid, fighting chance to get in.

"You did good, Gabbie," I told her before we left the cafeteria.

"You think so?" she rushed out, her cheeks flushed.

"Yeah, girl. Try out next year," I said.

Her face fell. "What if I don't get in?"

I bumped my arm against her shoulder. "At least you can say you tried."

DINNER WITH MY dad was always entertaining. Even when I didn't want to laugh, he pulled it out of me.

We hadn't spoken about Roderick since Danny had brought me back home after Roderick fully and thoroughly broke my heart. I didn't even have to say anything to my dad about it, he just knew. Roderick and I were over.

I thought he still clung to hope that we might get back together. And after my little talk with Gabbie, a small flicker of hope sparkled to life.

It might not work, but I had to try. In the end, at least I could say I had.

When I went to my room after dinner, I dug my phone out of my pocket and clicked on the Instagram icon. Tagging Roderick, I added a picture Seth had taken of us. In the photo, I stared up at him, a secret smile on my face while he laughed into the camera. Putting my fingers to the phone's keyboard, I bled. For him, for us.

It is love
that ignites
the beats in my heart

A breath stuttered against my lips. I hit post and sent up a small prayer that it would reach Roderick and remind him of what we had. Of what we could still have.

CHAPTER 43

Brinley

THE HOPE I felt last night when I posted on Instagram vanished as I made my way to school. Countless people had liked it, commented on it, but not the one who counted the most.

Danny met me at my car when I pulled up. When I stepped out, I rushed into his arms.

"He doesn't love me anymore," I said.

"He does, he's just hurting or too stupid to see it."

"I thought if I wrote to him like we used to, if I put it on Instagram for everyone to see my truth, he would see me again."

"What you did last night was brave." Danny smoothed a hand over my head to my back.

"It wasn't enough."

"We'll see. Maybe things'll get better before the day

is over."

I nodded. It wouldn't.

Danny walked me to my classes, stayed with me in the first few until I made him leave. He had his own classes to attend, and I was determined to save myself. I finally understood the need to be alone. The solace found when no one was around. But I couldn't have that. I was after all, the school's princess and everyone had to talk to me about my poem, about my break up. As if seeing my heart bleeding on the floor wasn't enough.

When the bell rang for lunch, I didn't bother going into the cafeteria or sitting at my normal table. Instead, I sought seclusion and headed toward the library. To my relief, there weren't very many students there.

I dropped into a bean bag and reclined my head back. When my phone vibrated in my hand, I unlocked it. The reaction was instantaneous. My heart beat wildly in my chest and a smile crept over my face.

Roderick liked my post. He read it, hadn't ignored it, and let me know he liked it.

I hugged the phone to my chest and suppressed a squeal.

Fight for him, that's what Nicole told me to do. Don't let fear stop you, that's what I'd told Gabbie. Despite the fear, I had to do what was most important to me. And Roderick, he was still everything.

SITTING ON THE floor in my mom's room, I scrolled through the various pictures of Roderick and me, while my mom painted. It wasn't a good day, but it wasn't bad either.

We didn't talk, but still I enjoyed her company. Although I wished I could speak to her, ask her for her advice.

Once I found the right picture to post, I went to Instagram and added it after tagging Roderick.

The weight of your love
carried me.
The weight of my fears
drowned us.
You're still my home though.
My truth,
my heart,
and world.

A few spaces beneath the poem, I wrote, "I'm sorry." And I was. If I hadn't befriended Jacob and Joseph our freshmen year, if I hadn't egged on Jacob and then ridiculed him in front of everyone none of this would've happened.

While Seth wouldn't accept my apologies, saying it wasn't my fault, I knew he was wrong. I was the cause of his assault, just as I was the cause for Roderick's parents' grave being vandalized.

It was me. All me, but still I hoped he forgave me.

Waiting to see if I would get a reaction from Roderick, I scrolled through Instagram. A few people had shared my post from yesterday. Nicole had shared the pictures from our visit at the middle school. Seth had posted a picture of him and Sammi.

And then I saw it. Picture after picture of Danny and Ari kissing, leaning onto one another, touching, embracing. It was endless.

While I'd thought about unfollowing Jacob and Joseph from Instagram, I never did. Never made the final leap and now I was able to see them spread malice in other ways. It wasn't enough that they'd gone after Seth and Roderick. They were bent on hurting me by hurting everyone I loved.

My stomach dropped. Not bothering to say anything to my mom, I left her room and after clicking out of Instagram, I dialed Danny. He didn't answer so I tried again. This time, he picked up after the second ring.

"Brin?" His voice sounded low.

"Where are you?" I asked.

"I… I'm just walking around."

"Where?" I asked again. "I'll come pick you up."

He stayed quiet for a moment. "I was walking to the cave."

"Okay." I pushed out of bed. "I'm on my way."

I raced out of my house and jumped in my car. It didn't take me long to reach Danny and when he got in my car, I took him in. His face was beaten, already the red bruises were turning purple while the blood dried on his skin.

"You should see the other guy." He grinned but it fell just as quickly as it appeared.

Reaching for his hand, I held onto him, needed him to know I was here. He wasn't alone. I drove us to the cave after making a stop at the gas station where I picked up ice and some first aid stuff. It was dark by the time we made it to the parking lot, but I used the flash light on my phone to guide us.

At the cave, I cleaned up Danny's face, put antibacterial cream on the open cuts. Once I was done, I patted my lap. He came to me quickly, dropped his head on my lap. While I ran my fingers over his short hair, I held ice over his cheek where the bruise looked the worse.

"Guess my dad didn't like the pictures on Instagram," he joked.

Anger surged. I did my best to temper it down, but I felt it brewing, boiling just beneath the surface.

"You're not going back home," I said. "No way in hell I'm letting you go live with your dad again."

He gave a humorless laugh. "Doesn't matter. He said I couldn't go back home anyway."

"Whatever." It came out bitter. I softened my tone. "You're coming back with me. I'll explain it to my dad, he'll understand."

From my lap, he met my gaze. Sadness permeated from his face. I wanted to make it better, but didn't know how.

"He's cutting me off," he said. "Not paying for college, not helping me pay for anything. I have no money." He hesitated. "Even though he never went to my games, I played sports to make him happy and never had time to get a job. What the hell am I supposed to do?"

I touched his cheek, careful not to get near any of the cuts or bruises.

"I have a two bedroom apartment in San Diego." It wasn't much of a solution, but it was all I had to offer. "You can live with me after we graduate."

"I don't have money to pay rent."

My dad wouldn't make him pay anyway.

"We'll talk to my dad tomorrow morning. He gets off his shift before I go to school."

He sat up, twisted his body so he could hug me. "Thanks, Brin. Even if it doesn't work out and your dad doesn't want me living with you here or in San Diego, thanks."

"He won't mind," I promised.

But he didn't believe me. I knew my dad though, knew he wouldn't turn Danny away. Wouldn't mind him living with us or with me in San Diego. Because my dad? He was a hero.

"Mind if I write something on your wall."

"Go for it."

I watched him stroll to the wall, dejection pulling his shoulders down.

"Brin?" He looked over his shoulders to me.

Although I didn't want to see the wall, see the poems Roderick and I had written to each other, I went to him. Right now, Danny needed me more than I needed to protect my heart.

"Let's just go." Danny turned to me quickly, his eyes wide with worry.

I furrowed my forehead and tried to peek around his broad shoulders. "Why? What's going on?"

"I'm tired," he said. "My dad beat my ass, and I just want to lie down."

"Okay." I took his hand in mine and tugged when he didn't move.

He raked a hand through his hair and hissed. "I can't do this."

He pulled me to him, covered my shoulders with his

arm. He stared at the wall so I turned my attention to it.

A gasp spilled from my heart. The wall, it was white. No poems, no marks of Roderick and me. Just white paint.

My bottom lip trembled and I pushed my head to Danny's side. "He did this." My voice quaked. "Roderick erased us."

"I'm sorry, Brin." Arms that had always been there for me wrapped around me.

I found the greatest love in this cave. I didn't know it then, but I knew it now. After love, came the greatest sorrow.

CHAPTER 44

RODERICK

I WOKE UP early to read Brinley's poem again. And again.

She was still my home, my truth, my heart, and my world.

It was a wonder she still loved me though. Still wanted me.

I had to talk to her today. Had to make things right again. I just didn't know how.

She'd given me the chance to do that when I found her with that prick Ethan trying to hurt her. I should've told her everything I felt, everything I still wanted for us.

But fear had a way of twisting my heart against my mind, and I wound up spewing words I didn't mean.

She was ready to forgive me, that wasn't the problem. Hell, maybe she'd already forgiven me. It was me who didn't know how to get past the words I'd flung at her at the cemetery to hurt her the same way Jacob and Joseph had hurt me.

What they did, it wasn't her fault. She believed it was, thought it to be another one of her truths. When that was the biggest lie.

Or not the biggest. I was the one who'd said the biggest lie when I told her she was a mistake. When I told her she was my lie.

The pain in my chest magnified, and I rubbed where my heart throbbed with intensity. She thought she'd destroyed us, when it was me. All me.

I could make it right though. I had to. Because living this life without her for almost two weeks was unbearable.

As I left my aunt's house, I sent her a text.

Me: Can we talk at school? Please

She didn't reply right away like she normally did. By the time I reached our school, she still hadn't text me back.

I waited for her, sitting on the picnic table beside the parking lot. Even by myself, I knew something was wrong. Around me, everyone talked too loudly, anger and sympathy colored their voices. When one of them mentioned Danny's name, I again reached for my phone.

Although, I'd kept my distance from the people who had proven to be amazing friends, I only texted with Danny. He was my last tie to Brinley, and I wasn't ready to give that up.

With my phone in my hand, I sent him a quick text, asking him if he was okay. Just like Brinley, he didn't answer me.

I couldn't stay here, not knowing what was going on. Even if I hadn't been acting like a good friend, that's exactly what Danny was.

When I reached Danny's house, I knocked on the door, then rang the doorbell when no one answered. Again, I didn't get a response.

I sent him another text, and then asked Brinley if she knew if Danny was okay. Not expecting them to reply, I wasn't surprised when my text remained unanswered by the time I reached Brinley's house.

I was surprised to see Ari's car and Seth's bike parked outside her house. Just as I reached the front steps to her house, the door flew open.

"You!" Brinley screamed. She ran down the steps and shoved my shoulders hard. "How could you do that?" Her voice got louder. "How could you do that to me?" Louder. "How could you do that to us?" Her scream rang in my head, echoed in my chest.

Danny stepped beside her, put an arm over her shoulder. He edged his body in between her and me, a gesture meant to protect her. From me. It was only then that I saw the dark circles that ran under her eyes. The redness of her nose and eyes. The puffiness of her cheeks. The pale pallor of her face.

"Baby, I'm sorry." I couldn't stop myself from calling her baby, even though I no longer had a right to. "I was waiting for you at school to talk to you, to apologize. So we could talk."

"You're sorry?" she whispered. "I thought you loved me. I thought if I fought hard enough…" She shook her head. "You erased us."

Sad eyes met mine. I reached for her, and when

Danny took a step to the side, I touched her face with my palm. God, I missed her.

"I screwed up," I said. "I know I did, and baby, you have to know how sorry I am. Please tell me you know how sorry I am. Tell me we're not over."

"But," her bottom lip trembled, "you erased us. You erased everything."

"What do you mean I erased us?" I trailed my thumb over her cheek. "How did I erase us?"

Her eyes searched mine. I didn't hold anything back. Not the sorrow of pushing her away, the guilt of hurting her, the fear of losing her, or the loneliness of not having her. It was all there. I showed it to her, hoped she saw it. Saw me.

"Roderick?"

I stepped in to her, waited to see what she would do. She took a step back. Her rejection hurt, left me breathless.

"You were ready to fight for us." I knew I sounded desperate, but I didn't care. I couldn't lose her. The past week had been hell without her. "Your poems, you said you still loved me."

"I did. I still do but…" she trailed off.

"But what, baby? Tell me what I have to do to fix this."

"You can't. Can't you see, Roderick? Some things can't be fixed."

"What happened between yesterday's poem and today?"

With her head bowed, she shook her head and left me. Danny hung back. I'd forgotten he was there, but of course he was. He was always there for Brinley.

His bruised face mirrored my own sorrow. A good friend would've asked him what had happened, asked him how I could help. But all I could think about was Brinley. Getting her to see me, getting her back.

"You like look shit," I said to him.

His lips twitched. "You look worse."

Yeah, I probably did.

"What the hell happened, Danny?" My voice sounded as desperate as I felt. "She put up those poems on Instagram, she tagged me on them with pictures of us. I thought I had a chance to make things right."

"We went to the cave last night."

I waited for him to continue, but he stayed quiet.

"Okay, you guys went to the cave last night. Then what happened?"

His brows shot up. He winced but quickly covered it up. "You didn't do it."

"Didn't do what?"

A grin took over his face. He grabbed my wrist, dragged me inside her house. Ari and Seth jumped from the couch when they saw me.

"Brinley!" Danny yelled. "Brin!"

"What's wrong?" She stepped out of the kitchen. Her breath caught when she saw me in her living room.

"What's with all the yelling?" her dad asked, trudging out of his bedroom. I knew he'd gotten off his night shift only a couple hours earlier and felt bad for waking him. "What the hell happened to your face?" he asked Danny.

"Dad found out I was gay, he beat me up." He waved her dad away.

"What?" her dad roared, veins on his forehead making an appearance.

"Not important," Danny pushed away his concern and then turned to Brinley. "Roderick didn't do it."

Shock made her pretty green eyes widen. Her attention bounced from Danny to me. She wanted to believe him, wasn't sure if she could.

"What didn't I do?" I asked.

"Why does my daughter look like she's been up all night crying?" her dad asked.

"That's my fault, sir," I said. "I hurt her. I've been hurting her for almost two weeks. I hate how much I've been hurting her."

"Call me sir again, and I'll come up with a clever punishment as soon as I'm awake to think straight." He walked to me, put his hands on my shoulders. "What are you going to do to fix whatever's wrong with you and Brin."

"Whatever I have to."

He nodded. When he reached the hallway, he looked back at all of us. "Keep your voices down. Superhero at sleep here. Wait, Danny?" he asked.

Danny shuffled on his feet, waited for her dad to continue.

Phil looked at Danny with a serious expression on his face. "Which is better, Star Wars or Star Trek?"

Danny turned his head in confusion. "Star Trek."

"Good answer," her dad said. "The guest room is yours. Brin, use my card to order the man some Star Trek sheets for his bed."

She smiled. "Thanks, old man."

I suppressed my own smile when he turned to wink in my direction. He'd asked me the same question, only when I replied, Star Trek wasn't the right answer.

Brinley's dad wasn't conventional, but he was good to his core. He cared about people, just like his daughter did. Now I just had to win her back, fix what she thought wasn't fixable.

Although lost, she'd found me in the darkness. She'd breathed life back into me.

I thought I was helping her save herself, when it was Brinley who wound up saving me.

She was the girl who'd cleaned my clothes and fed me. The girl who'd written to me in the hopes of dragging me out of my loneliness. The girl who'd taken care of me, given me a place where I belonged with friends who'd stayed by my side even when I was wrong.

She was the girl who'd given me a home.

CHAPTER 45

Brinley

HE DIDN'T DO it.

Danny's words echoed in my hollow chest. I clung to them, needed them to be true.

"I'm sorry about your face," Roderick broke the silence. Although he spoke to Danny, he looked at me. Only me. "I'm sorry about your dad, but right now I have to talk to my girl."

His girl.

"If you hurt her again…" Danny said.

"I'll give you the knife to stab me," he finished.

"Morbid." Danny grinned. "I like it."

Roderick fought back a smile and tilted his head to the hallway. Wringing my hands in front of me, I made my way to my bedroom. I sat on my bed and watched him close my door.

My sheets and pillows still smelled like him. I'd been too scared to wipe away his scent and lose him entirely to wash them.

He sat beside me, braced his hands on his bouncing knees.

"At the gym, you asked me if we were ever going to be okay again."

"No," I said. "You said no."

He roughed a hand through his hair and pulled.

"I didn't mean it. I haven't meant anything I've said since the day at the cemetery. Brin." He stopped to clear his throat. "You're my heart, my home, my truth. You're my girl. I know I messed up. I told you I'd never hurt you."

"My dad said it was an impossible promise to keep." I didn't realize the truth behind those words until Roderick broke my heart at the foot of his parents' grave. "You promised him you'd never hurt me on purpose."

"I did that. I hurt you on purpose." He jumped from my bed, paced in front of me.

I felt his anguish, his frustrations as if they were my own, but I couldn't go to him. Because last night, between my fits of crying, I promised Danny I'd start saving myself. Even if it meant saving myself from my own heart.

"Seeing what Jacob and Joseph did to their headstone, to their grave…" His voice cracked. "It brought everything back. Their death, the loneliness, the way you held onto me, the way you let me go. It was too much, but worse than that was the moment before the chief told me what had happened. When my aunt…" He paused, rubbed the back of his neck while his eyes

327

danced across my face. Dropping to his knees in front of me, he pushed his face on my lap while his hands circled around my waist. "When my aunt came to my door, her eyes red and puffy from crying and told me Bert wanted to speak to me, I thought…" he sucked in a breath, "I thought something had happened to you. I thought my past had repeated itself and taken you from me." A sob tore through him, and he drew himself closer to me.

My fingers went to his hair slowly, tentatively.

"The idea of losing you… it's too much. It hurts too damn much. So I pushed you away. I used words I didn't mean to make you leave me."

Running my fingers over his face, I touched his cheek, his lips. I traced over his forehead and his eyes, that he kept shut tight. Wanted to smooth the lines from his pinched expression.

"When I saw you and our friends cleaning up their grave, I can't tell you what that meant to me," he said, his voice as pained as his expression. "The love I felt, the loneliness that melted away. It was all because of you."

"What Joseph and Jacob did to you, to your parents, was because of me too," I said.

His eyes popped open. "It wasn't," he said. "I know I said I blamed you, but I didn't. I don't. They did that because they wanted to."

"They went after you, Seth, and Danny to get back at me." I wiped my nose on a sniffle, and then went back to petting his hair. "And our wall, that wasn't you, but another gift to me from them."

He looked up at me, his eyes red from the tears he'd spilled. "What happened to our wall?"

"They erased us." It came out low, sad. That wall,

that cave, it was more than a sanctuary. "They painted over our poems."

An angry red spread over his neck to his cheeks. His touch was soft though and when he cupped my cheek, I turned into his hand.

"You thought I was the one who painted the wall? Over our words?"

He brushed away a stray tear that fell down my face. I nodded.

"I wouldn't do that. Baby, that wall means everything to me. *You* mean everything to me."

I felt his words, knew he meant them. Still, I held myself back from him, couldn't give myself freely back to the boy I loved. Because if he broke me again, I wasn't sure I wanted to live through it.

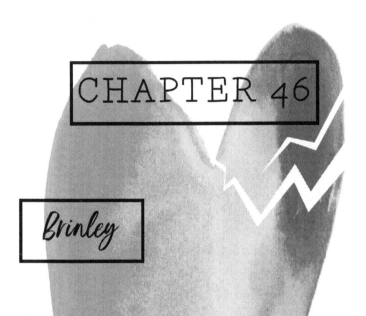

CHAPTER 46

Brinley

Roderick stayed at my house the rest of the day along with our friends. When they left, Danny and I curled into my bed together and fell asleep watching reruns of the old Star Trek episodes.

I'd wanted to be there for him, to be the strength he needed, but as usual he was my strength. My foundation. I didn't know what I'd do without him.

And I didn't know what to do about Roderick and me. I wanted to get back with him. It's what I fought for, why I started posting poems on Instagram and tagged him. But the devastation I felt over our wall was all consuming. Even if he hadn't been the one to paint over our poems, it was the thought that I'd really lost him that destroyed me.

"You should post this picture today." Danny handed

me my phone back before he dug in to the scrambled eggs I put in front of him.

The picture was taken in our cave on Roderick's birthday. The happiness that emanated from that moment reached into my chest, made my heart beat a steady pace.

"I wasn't planning on posting anymore pictures or poems."

Danny cocked his head to the side. "Why not?" he asked between mouthfuls of toast.

"Because..."

Because we both wanted to be back together but didn't know how to get there.

"You're still fighting for him, and he's fighting back." Danny wiped his mouth, stood from his chair and smacked a kiss on top of my head. "Desperately together, right? That's what you guys say. You guys fight with your words, show him he still has something left to fight for."

"I hate how smart you are." I smirked.

Danny looked better. It would take time for the bruises to heal, even longer for the scars we couldn't see to mend.

"When I called you the other night, I meant to be there for you, not the other way around. But thanks for taking care of me." I looped my arms around his waist, leaned my head against his shoulder. "Thanks for being my best friend."

"We took care of each other." Another kiss against my hair. "Besides all your crying distracted me from the fact that my dad kicked my ass."

He poked my side and I snorted.

"You're an idiot," I said.

He pulled me back. His expression was serious, his eyes tender. "You took care of me, Brin. You were there for me when I needed you the most. Thank you for being my best friend."

I stepped on my tiptoes and kissed his cheek.

"Nine kids, three cats, fourteen ferrets, and a squirrel monkey, right?" His voice was nothing but a tease.

"You forgot about the big slobbery dog." I grinned.

"Stupid dog. If he chews on my shoes one more time, we're taking his manhood away," he teased.

"He's already neutered," I played along.

"No." He gasped. "Why would you do that to poor Rufus? Now he'll never know the pleasures of life."

"Rufus is pretty happy just drinking out of the toilet bowl."

We continued teasing each other on the drive to school. Seth and Ari waited for us on the picnic table under the tree. I looked for Roderick when I stepped out of the passenger side. He either wasn't here yet or he wasn't meeting us at our regular morning spot. Maybe he hadn't meant what he said yesterday. Maybe he did but didn't want to be seen with me in public.

"Seth broke up with Sammi," Ari said as a way of greeting.

"What?" I pulled Seth into a hug that he returned. "I thought you liked her. Did she hurt you? I swear I'll..."

He laughed. "Slow down, Terminator," he teased. "She didn't hurt me. I just didn't want to be with her anymore."

"Okay," I said slowly.

"How come?" Danny asked.

"We heard her talking crap about Brin to some of her

friends," Ari answered.

That stung. I'd liked her, thought she and Seth were good together.

"Seth went up to her, told her all the reasons why Brin was the better person and broke up with her," Ari continued.

"Seth." I searched his face, looked in his expression for remorse or sadness, but all I saw was Seth smiling back at me. The boy I'd made fun of through the years, the boy who had become one of my closest friends. "You didn't have to do that."

"Of course I did." He draped a heavy arm over my shoulders, which reminded me he'd been working out with Danny and Ari for a few weeks now. "We're friends. That's what friends do for each other."

That's what friends did for each other. It felt good to have friends who looked out for you, who showed up at a moment's notice to be there for you. For years Danny had been the only one who stood by me. But now I had three, and although I wasn't sure about Roderick and me, I still felt whole.

I sat on top of the picnic table with Seth and Danny on either side of me, and Ari sitting between Danny's legs. Turning my phone over in my hand, I thought of the past year, of my final year in high school. So much had changed. I had changed, or I'd finally flourished into who I truly was. I was proud of the person I'd become, excited to see how else I'd grow.

"You gonna write to Roderick?" Seth asked, glancing at my phone.

"Yeah." I smirked.

Choosing the same photo Danny told me to post, I

went to Instagram and tagged Roderick.

The broken shards
shattered quicker
than I could piece them.
My universe
was in chaos
with false truths
I believed.
He bore
the weight
of my universe.
Made it lighter,
with the most beautiful
love
the universe
has ever seen.

This time it didn't take long for Roderick to like my poem after posting it. Just like before, my heart soared that he'd read it, that he'd reacted to it. It was a step forward, a step toward us fighting for each other. Desperately together.

When the bell rang, I went to homeroom with Danny after saying bye to Ari and Seth. Although I felt bad about Seth breaking up with Sammi because of me, I also felt lighter, freer. Like maybe things might actually work out.

In homeroom, I kept a good distance from Mariah and the group she hung out with, and stuck next to Danny. Sometimes we talked to other people, but on the days we didn't I was okay without the noise of extra people. Besides, Danny was enthusiastic enough to keep my mind busy.

Danny knelt in front of the desk I sat behind. "I was thinking I should go see the counselor to see what I need to do to transfer to a school in San Diego." He hesitated. "You're sure you want me to move in with you?"

I groaned. "Stop making me repeat myself. Of course I want to live with you."

"While you were in the shower last night, your dad offered to buy me a Millennium Falcon bed for my room in San Diego."

I giggled. "I'm not even surprised. I didn't even know he liked Star Trek so much."

This time, it was Danny's turn to groan. "Millennium Falcon is not Star Trek," he corrected. "Get your Star Wars intel straight, little Padawan." He gasped. "Does this mean he secretly likes Star Wars more than Star Trek?"

"Probably."

"Poor soul." He shook his head.

"Whatever. Go see the counselor, get everything set to move to San Diego when we graduate."

"What if it's too late to get into a college over there?" Worry crept into his tone, made the lines around his mouth deepen when he frowned.

"Then you'll get in next semester," I said, rubbing a thumb over the wrinkles on the bridge of his nose. "I'm not starting until summer is over anyway. I wanted to enjoy some time away from school and just lounge on the beach."

"That does sound pretty awesome." He stood, turned toward the door. "You gonna be alright by yourself?"

I grinned. "Alone isn't such a tragedy," I quoted the first of Roderick's poem that I had read.

I read a book until the bell rang, alerting us we should make it to our next class. My phone vibrated with a notification when the teacher started my first period class. I unlocked my phone, hugged it to me when I saw an alert that Roderick had replied to my status. I clicked on it, tried to steady the erratic drum of my heart to no avail.

You are a heaven
I would go to hell for.
The sparkle of fallen stardust
I would search eternity to find.
The greatest love
I dove into.
The girl who found me in the dark
And revived me with her light.

Butterflies took flight, went completely crazy in my stomach. I couldn't contain my smile, didn't want to.

I wished first period would end, so I could see Roderick in our English class. Of course, it dragged on what seemed like forever. But as soon as the bell rang and Danny met me so we could walk together to Mr. Scott's class, anticipation settled in my gut. Danny's knowing smile didn't help, not that I could hold back mine. Anticipation grew when Danny opened the door for me.

Then… it disappeared.

In the back of class, sitting in his usual spot was Roderick. He stood from behind his desk when I walked into the room.

"Hi," he said.

"Hi," I breathed. "I read your poem."

He reached for my face and before he could drop his hands to the side, I took hold of his wrist to press a kiss against his palm.

His lips kicked up in a beautiful smile that wrapped around my soul. "I read yours too." He paused. "I've missed you." The broken tone that fell from his lips tore into me.

His body seemed to relax when I stepped into him and hugged my body to his. He circled his arms around me, squeezed me tightly into his embrace.

It felt good to be in his arms. He felt good, a lot like home.

CHAPTER 47

RODERICK

"LOOK AT THIS!" Danny turned his phone to Brinley and me to show us an R2D2 lamp. "This is gonna look so kick ass in my room."

"Yeah." Brinley rolled her eyes. "Along with your Death Star poster, Darth Vader bookshelf, and BB8 lamp."

Pride shone behind Danny's eyes, and he put a hand on our shoulders to stop our hike to the cave. "Look at our girl naming characters we've taught her about. All grown up." He wiped away a pretend tear.

"How could I forget when you've only brought them up a thousand times in like a five-minute time period?" she shot back.

"It's your dad's fault," he accused. "He shouldn't have mentioned anything about a Millennium Falcon bed.

What kind of bed are you guys gonna get?"

Silence fell between us. It ran deep into the ground, pummeled through the depths of hell I'd trek to get Brinley back. But we hadn't talked about whether she still wanted us to live together. And seeing as we'd only sort of been back together since second period, I didn't want to push her. Or I did, but the familiar hands of fear held me back.

"So Ari and Seth are already at our cave?" She tilted her head to the side to look at me.

Our cave. I loved when she called it that. It was ours. More ours than anyone else's.

"Yeah."

I'd asked Danny to go ahead with them to get the final touches of my surprise done, but he insisted we needed to get enchiladas to help us recover after such a long hike, and hung back with Brinley and me. In truth, he simply didn't trust me with Brinley anymore. I didn't blame him. So, I stayed quiet when he stopped at the Mexican restaurant and came out with the two large bags of food he and I now carried.

A pretty hue of orange cast over the mouth of our cave, like a final cry before the sun set. Light would fade soon, and although darkness would invade every part of this forest, it wouldn't reach me. Not anymore. Not after what I'd fought through.

When we got closer to the cave, I held out my hand to Brinley. With a soft smile, she took it. We walked in together where Seth and Ari watched her carefully to see her reaction.

"Roderick." Her eyes danced in wonder as she looked around. "This is incredible."

The same lights we used to adorn the walls and low ceilings draped across the spans of our cave. Tea lights flickered everywhere with rose petals spread throughout.

But it was our wall she had yet to see. Giving her hand a gentle tug, I gestured to it. She pulled her bottom lip in, but nodded.

She was scared. I knew she was because according to her even if we rewrote our poems, it wouldn't be the same. Wouldn't carry the same sentiment.

Of course she was right, but I hated the idea of our poems no longer coexisting on the cave's wall that brought us together. So last night, after I left Brinley's house, I came here. Poured hours into rewriting our poems, including the ones we put up on Instagram. When that wasn't enough, I walked back to town and bought every single tea light our local drugstore had in stock, along with other things I wanted to do for her. Then this morning before school started, I bought five dozen roses to cover the floor with their petals.

Even with the lights Ari and Seth had strung up for me, it didn't feel like enough. Like I'd done enough to be worthy of winning back the girl.

It wasn't my words that drew a gasp from her pretty lips though. She went to her knees and with outstretched fingers, she traced over the first frame. Then the other.

"When did you do this?"

"Last night I went to the drugstore," I answered. "Pretty sure the manager thought about changing their twenty-four-hour policy when he realized I was printing out so many pictures from their automated photo printer. The frames aren't great." A breath hitched in my throat. "But I can get you new ones if you want to keep the pictures."

"This is perfect. Better than perfect."

After touching another picture of us that I'd printed — this one a selfie of us on her bed, she stood up and came to me. Framing both sides of my, she pressed her lips to mine.

It was soft, tasted like forgiveness, like love, like home.

"They'll look great in our apartment," she said when she broke from our kiss.

My face must've shone with the shock I felt. She laughed, kissed my chest before she snuggled into my hold.

Tipping up her head, she said, "We're still moving in together, aren't we?"

"Yes." A thousand times yes. A million times yes.

"I love this." She stepped out of my embrace, made a couple small twirls in front of me. "I love everything you did for me. I love you, Roderick. So much."

I hugged her again, never wanted to let her go.

"This, what you did for me…" she trailed off. "A thousand thank yous will never be enough."

Inside my chest, my heart stuttered before it leaped forward, straight toward Brinley and our future.

"I love you, Brinley." I grazed my nose over her throat to her shoulder, kissed every inch that I covered.

"So Roderick," Danny called out, but I didn't move or let Brinley move away from me, "did you invite us so we could witness your love fest, or are we going to eat?"

Brinley laughed, her breath tickling my throat. "We should probably eat." She kissed my jaw, right where my pulse throbbed hard and fast. "If we don't, he might die or mutate or something." Her lips moved to my lips.

"Maybe we should just kick them out," I said against her lips.

"Heard that!" Danny shouted. "Brin, if you don't get over here, I'm eating all the chips and queso dip."

She twisted in my arms, her eyes wide with mock horror. "Oh no, not the queso dip," she deadpanned.

Ari and Seth laughed while Ari took out the containers of food and spread them across the ground and over the petals.

"Great, you're back to being in love and losing your priorities." He took out a chip and made a big show out of dipping in the queso. "Mmm," he said when he took a bite.

"We really should grab some before he eats them all," she suggested.

I laughed. My heart fluttered in my chest when she took my hand in hers.

When I sat down, I extended both arms to Brinley. She came to me, crawled in my lap and nestled her head against my chest. Right where she belonged.

"My grandpa called me after school today to let me know he rented the limo for us," Seth said after a few moments of silence.

"Cool," Ari said.

"Thank him for us again," I added.

"Yeah," Ari agreed. "And I was thinking, Brin, do you have your dress yet or an idea of what you're wearing?"

"I have my dress from the Fall Ball that I only wore in Roderick's room," she said.

Memories of that night flooded me. I almost lost that, threw away what we had. And for what? Fear? It wasn't a good enough reason. Nothing was.

"I was thinking about wearing that," she continued.

"What color is it?" Ari asked.

"Silver."

Silver that clung to her body with a dip in the back. Reaching beneath her shirt, I caressed her back. She shivered.

"Okay, so guys, what do you think if we all get tuxedos to match Brin's dress?" Ari asked.

On top of me, Brinley jerked in surprise. Her lips parted as she watched her friends through wide eyes.

"That's kind of a great idea," Danny said.

"Yeah," she agreed, "I think it's amazing and absolutely would love for you guys to do that. I mean, everyone already knows you're all my favorite guys," she smiled, "but, Seth, what about your date? She wouldn't want to match me or have you match me instead of her."

"This date you're talking about is totally fictional," Seth said. "And look, I just talked to her and she says she thinks it's an awesome idea."

"Shut up," she griped. "Right now you don't have a date. That could change."

"Prom's two months away," he said. "I'm not gonna find someone before then. Besides, everyone already has a date."

"Nicole doesn't," Brinley said.

Seth's laughter boomed in the cave, echoed off the wall. All while Brinley watched him through narrowed eyes. When he finished, he smoothed his hands over his face.

"Don't look at me like that," Seth said. "We both know Nicole would rather not go to Prom than go with me. I don't need a date, Brin. I'm just happy I'm going." He paused, licked his lips. "In the beginning of the year, if you'd asked if I were going to Prom, I would've laughed. I don't go to school events. Hell, up until we all became friends, I hated going to school. Hated being there."

"I guess it works out better this way." Brinley's smile was slow. "Just means I don't have to steal you away from someone to dance."

"Dance?" He gave a nervous laugh. "I don't think so. I don't dance."

"Like hell you don't!"

With her foot, she pushed away her uneaten food and stood up.

"One of you guys, put on some music we can dance to," she ordered.

"Like shake your ass kind of music?" Danny asked.

"Exactly!"

Danny was the first to reach for his phone. A fast beat spilled from it, filled our small cave, vibrated in my muscles.

Brinley nudged Seth's shoe with her foot. When she reached down to him, he put his hand in hers.

Her body moved to the music as she danced in front of him, swaying and bouncing to the beat of the song. When Seth finally started shuffling his feet, she brought their joined hands over her head and spun with her head tipped back in a laugh.

She was stunning to watch. Beauty in motion.

The way she moved her hips sent adrenaline pulsing through my body. My gaze followed her every motion, swept over her enchanting body and beautiful face.

As if she sensed my searing gaze, she tipped her head

to me. When our eyes clashed, she smiled. It was the only invitation I needed.

While Seth danced in front of her, I put a hand on her waist and moved behind her. Not close enough to hinder her movements. Free, that's how she was meant to be.

From the corner of my eye, I saw Ari and Danny start to dance alongside us.

It was liberating, captivating.

The beating rhythm of one song bled to the next, and for hours we danced. We laughed. We chased away the troubles of the past few weeks.

We lived.

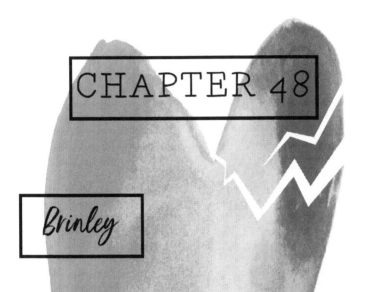

CHAPTER 48

Brinley

My MOM SNAPPED another picture. It was at least the millionth one of the night. Not that I minded when it meant I had my mom back. At least for a few hours, she was herself.

"You look so handsome, Roderick." She smoothed the front of his suit. "You all do." Her eyes jumped from Roderick, Danny, to Ari.

The only one missing was Seth, but he'd be here any minute with the limo his grandfather rented for us.

"Your daughter's standing right here," I teased my mom. "She wants a compliment too."

My mom winked. "You look very handsome too, sweetheart."

"This house is full of nothing but smart mouths," my dad quipped, putting his arm around my mom's waist and pulling her to him.

"I love that your suits all match Brin's dress," my mom said. "That was such a great idea, Ari. If you guys can suffer through a few more pictures, I'd love to take some more when Seth gets here."

"We should take some in front of the limo!" I squealed.

I couldn't believe I was going to Prom in a limo with my four favorite guys. If that didn't make me the luckiest girl in the world, I didn't know what would.

When the doorbell rang, my dad shouted, "Get in here, Seth."

Beside me, Roderick laughed. And because he couldn't seem to help himself, he pressed a kiss to the side of my head. I turned my face to him and captured his lips with mine. His palm pressed against my back and he stroked a finger over my skin. He ended the kiss quickly, his eyes bright, his smile wide.

"Be right back!" Roderick shuffled to the door, following Danny and Ari through it.

I went to follow them, but my dad stopped me with a hand on my shoulder. He pulled me to him and my mom reached across him to put her hand over mine.

"I'm proud of you, Brin," my dad said. "You've turned out to be one hell of a good woman. Exactly the kind of daughter I always hoped for."

"I have pretty awesome parents to thank for that."

"Brin." The way my mom said my name, filled with so much insecurity and doubt, pricked against my skin.

"Both of you," I continued. "I have the best mom and dad."

She tightened her hold so I bent down to kiss her hand.

Shouts and swearing came from just outside the door. Ari came in first, walking backwards as he carried part of what looked like a heavy box wrapped in pretty yellow wrapping paper. Seth and Danny took either side of the object while Roderick carried the far end.

"What's this?" I asked.

Seth beamed at me. "A present for you. Well, I guess it's for Roderick, Danny and you since you're gonna be living together, but I originally made it for you."

"You made it?" I asked. "Ohmygosh! Seth! You made me something."

I flung my arms around his neck, squeezed him tightly to me. The hug didn't last long. Not when I needed to see what Seth had created with the wood he loved to work with. The table he'd made for my mom was stunning, and she used it every day. But this? This was for me from one of my best friends. I knelt in front of the large box and after sending Seth another grateful smile, I tore in to the wrapping paper.

"Don't take your time savoring the moment or anything, Brin," Danny teased.

I was too busy to shoot him the middle finger. When I finished unwrapping it, I sat back. Took in the beautiful bookshelf Seth had made. On unsteady legs, I stood up, trailed a finger over the intricate carvings, made several sweeps over the poems he'd cut into the sides. Poems the five of us had written together and apart.

They were all in our cave, but now I had some of them to keep with me forever on my bookshelf.

Emotions caught in my throat. I blinked several times to keep the tears away. When one slipped out anyway, I laughed as I fanned my face with a hand.

Turning back to Seth, I hugged him again. Thanked him a thousand times, but like Roderick's mom had once told him, it wasn't enough.

"It's perfect," I told him.

It was. Everything about this moment was perfect. And while our high school years were mostly not perfect, we had plenty of moments that were. Those were the moments we had to hold onto.

"Okay," my mom said. "I need more pictures. I want a good one of the five of you so when you all go off to college, we still have a photo of Brin and her guys."

Sometimes I felt like I'd lost my mom, like the distance between us was too big, too grave, and she'd never understand me. Tonight she proved me wrong. She knew me better than I thought. She saw me, saw my best friends were also my guys. They were mine.

On the stage, Mr. Scott cleared his throat into the microphone. "Every year," he started, "I get the honor of announcing your Prom King and Queen. And every time I stand up here, I reflect on the years I watched not just them, but all of you grow into the young men and women standing before me." He paused, his gaze falling on us, the prom court standing beside him before he looked out to the sea of students.

I reached for Danny's hand and he squeezed. Just like the Fall Ball, I hoped he'd win the title of king. Not because the title was some prestigious thing, but to further show how much he was loved because of who he was, even if his father couldn't see it.

"I'm proud of all of you," Mr. Scott said into the microphone. "Proud to have gotten to know each of my students. That being said, I must tell you I have deep rooted respect for your future king and queen. I've watched them stumble, watched them be pushed down, watched them rise with a resiliency and strength I admire. Before I announce them, I want to read something to you." He took out a piece of paper from the front pocket of his pants and unfolded it.

My heart kicked up, beating hard against my chest. I looked out into the crowd, looked for Roderick. He nodded his head, and I felt the calm seep into my system. Slowly, from limb to limb.

"This was written by one of your nominees, Ms. Brinley Crassus with Mr. Roderick Roher. They were partnered together to create a blackout poem in my class. With her permission, I'd like to share it with you." He slipped his glasses over his face.

"Afraid to show my depth
I use my shallow
as a shield."

Mr. Scott looked at all of us, seemed to take us in. "In life, we will wear several masks, carry numerous shields. Despite that, students, I want to ask you to remember to be true to you. Remember to always be someone you are proud of. Don't be afraid to show your depth. Don't be afraid to show the world who you really are. The world needs you to be you. No one else can do what you're capable of. Give us your talents, show us your passion. I promise you, you won't regret it." He took another long pause. "Okay," he laughed, "enough with that! It's time to crown your Queen and King." He smiled at the court. "Graduating class, I'd like to present your King and Queen, Danny Reyes and Brinley Crassus."

Cheers and applause erupted in the large dance hall. I grinned up at Danny, who held our joined hands in the air. When he led us to the center stage, I gave him a quick hug before I turned to Mr. Scott. He nodded, handed me the microphone and waved me to move forward with the request I'd made in case I won.

I licked my lips and smiled when Danny gave me a curious look. "I know as Queen and King, Danny and I are supposed to share the first dance to kick off Prom," I said into the microphone. "But I'm not gonna dance with Danny, at least not right now. Maybe later?" I turned my head to the side in question.

He stayed quiet, his brows drew together as even more confusion crossed his features.

"Instead, I'm going to give my spot to someone else." I turned to the silent crowd, found Ari's face and with a finger signaled for him to come to the stage. "Ari," I said, "you wanna take this dance?"

He nodded, a smile so wide it made me dizzy with happiness. Or maybe the dizziness came from Danny spinning me in circles in his arms. When Danny put my feet back on the floor, he kissed my temple.

"I love you, Brin," he said before he stepped into Ari's arms.

To the thundering applause of our peers, they started

to dance. Danny's hands clasped behind Ari's back, and Ari's arms around Danny's neck.

I got off the stage and with my heart soaring, I stepped into Roderick's embrace. He held me from behind, swayed our bodies in tune to the music while I watched my best friend show our class one of his greatest truths without fear.

When the song ended, Danny leaned over to Mr. Scott and shouted into the microphone, "Let's party!"

Music emanated in the air, infused our souls with dreams and hopes that reached beyond our little beach town. We danced as if the yesterdays never existed, as if the tomorrows would never come.

And in a sense, it was true.

Our yesterdays could hurt us, could mold us, could drive us, but they were only as valuable as the importance we gave them. They only existed if we gave them the power to. And the tomorrows, of course they would come. Or at least, I hoped they would. But worrying about it, about what might or might not happen, stole us from the todays. And the todays… they were far too important for them to be ripped away from us by our own fears.

When the song finished, and a slow one started, Seth shouted that he was going to grab something to drink. Danny and Ari turned to each other, went into each other's arms, and held each other close.

With my arms around Roderick's neck, we danced the first slow song of the night. His nose inched across my throat to my ear where he nipped.

"Are we all really spending the night in our cave tonight?" he asked.

His warm breath hit my skin, set me ablaze. I pulled myself closer to him.

"My dad bought us some sleeping bags," I replied. "You don't want to disappoint my old man, do you?"

"Are they Star Wars bags?"

"No," I giggled. He wasn't far off. "He got me Thor, Danny Yoda, Ari Captain America, Seth Spider Man, and you Superman."

"Superman?" He laughed.

"He says you're the greatest superhero of them all. I agree."

I twined my fingers through his hair. He murmured something against my neck. I didn't hear him but it didn't matter. I heard his heart. Every day it got louder. But it always said the same thing.

Home.

Home.

Home.

We were home. No matter where we lived, as long as we were together, we were home.

The song ended and when another slow song came on, I asked if I could ask Seth to dance with me. He kissed my cheek and led me to where Seth sat at our table drinking a soda. Cocking my hip to the side, I held my hand out to him. He looked at it and then at me, before a slow smile began to build on his lips.

Holding onto me, he led me to the dance floor. When his hands met my waist, I circled my hands behind his neck.

It was different being in his arms. Not bad or uncomfortable, but a type of ease and comfort that melted into my skin. He swayed us back and forth, his hands light on my waist. Since we were the same height with my heels on, I tucked my chin onto his shoulder.

I kissed his cheek when the song ended. "Thanks for the dance," I said.

His dimples popped out with his grin.

The next song was faster, had a fun beat. The guys circled around us to dance, while Roderick gripped my waist from behind.

The night was ablaze with laughter and dancing. It was perfect. The perfect night. A memory that would stay with me forever.

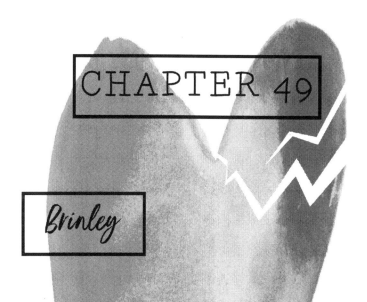

CHAPTER 49

Brinley

Although I had my own sleeping bag, it was much cozier to sleep with Roderick. Not that sleeping on the hard cave's ground was cozy.

I didn't know how Roderick had slept in this cave at all. He'd done it, though, and never once complained.

When his fingers touched my face and spread into my hair, I closed my eyes. His lips caressed my cheek, moved to my nose, before they started to massage my lips. I ran my tongue over his lips and when he parted, he took me in. It was slow, as if he were exploring my soul.

"I can hear you guys kissing!" Danny shouted.

Ari and Seth laughed.

I groaned.

"You're gonna be hearing a lot of that in San Diego,"

Roderick said.

"So get used to it," I added.

He kissed me again. Long fingers pushed beneath my shirt. I stuttered out a breath when he trailed a feather light touch from my stomach to my chest. Pushing down my bra, he rubbed a thumb over my breast. I moaned into his mouth and felt him smile against our kiss.

A few feet to the side of us, music started to play. It wasn't a song I recognized, but something with just instruments playing in a cheesy melody. Something that sounded a lot like what I imagined music in porn sounded like.

Digging my face against Roderick's neck, I laughed. The laughter got louder until we were all cracking up.

"I can't stand you," I told Danny. "Seriously, you're like this parasite that refuses to leave me alone."

"I'm not the one making babies while people around you try to sleep."

My cheeks heated. "We're not making babies."

"Well then you should be. I mean, you have to start soon if you want ten kids, three dogs, eight seahorses, and a llama."

"Oh." I scoffed. "You're passing our future to Roderick?"

"Damn right," he replied. "I hate seahorses. Freaky little animals."

"But you're okay with the three slobbery dogs?" Seth asked.

"I mean I don't want them," Danny clarified. "It was a sacrifice I was willing to make for Brin, but then she threw in seahorses and that's it. I'm out. She's all Roderick's."

"Okay," Ari said. "When we get married, I won't ask for seahorses."

I bit my bottom lip, snuggled closer to Roderick as joy slammed through my veins. It was like a warm blanket, secure and protective.

"I'd get a seahorse for you," Danny replied. "I'd never look at it and would probably slip poison in its tank, but I'd get one for you."

Ari laughed. When it fell silent, the sound of kissing sounded in the air.

"Ohmygosh!" I yelled. "Can you guys not kiss while I'm trying to sleep?"

A pillow hit my side. I grabbed it, put it under the pillow I was already using.

A few beats later, Danny asked, "Can I have my pillow back?"

"Nope," I sing-songed.

Roderick pulled the pillow out from beneath me. "He'll probably end up in our bag if you don't give it back to him." He tossed the pillow back to Danny.

"He's right," Danny agreed on a laugh.

"When we get married," Roderick whispered, his breath falling on my lips, "I'll give you anything you want."

"You," I replied. "I only want you."

The people I loved surrounded me, joy followed. I found happiness in them. Found love in them. The love I felt was different for each of them, but just as potent. Together and apart, we'd been through a lot, but this moment – our moment – outweighed all the bad. Outshined the dark. Proved that love was greater than anything else.

That love always won.

EPILOGUE

Three years later

"WHAT THE HELL is that?" Danny looked at the large dog I led into our shared apartment.

"A big slobbery dog," Brinley replied. "The first of the seven you and Roderick promised me."

She was big, at least seventy pounds, and she was only six months old. From what the shelter worker told us, she'd get a lot bigger.

"Holy crap." Seth walked into our living room, folding thick arms over his wide chest. It reminded me that the boy who was once picked on could now fend for himself thanks to friends who'd given him the tools and confidence to learn how to fight, which then grew to a love for working out. "Did you guys buy a small horse?"

Turned out college wasn't for Seth, not like it was for Danny, Brinley, Ari and me. Instead, he'd started an online store to sell the furniture and other things he created with wood. It did so well, he was thinking about expanding to have an actual, physical store. The first place he was looking at real estate was in San Diego.

Brinley, Danny, and I loved it out here, and had decided we didn't want to move back to our sleepy little beach town. We visited often since Brinley's dad insisted we stay at her old house for a long weekend every three months. Sometimes Danny came with us, but most of the time he stayed away. When he did come, we'd all go to the diner where Nicole worked full time. She wound up moving back home and doing online courses after getting pregnant with Jacob's baby. A baby he never saw or cared for. But Nicole's baby was loved beyond measure by her mom, her grandparents, Danny, and Brinley, who would never abandon Nicole the way she once left Brinley.

After graduating from college, Ari planned on moving here too. It would be the five us again. Friends that had turned into a family that reminded me I would never again be alone.

Life wasn't perfect though. Rosie's brain continued to deteriorate and no matter what tests the doctors ran, there was no real explanation behind it. It just was. Despite the struggles, Rosie and Phil had become my family. A family I'm sure my parents had set in my path when they realized my aunt would never be what I needed. Hell, it only took three months living in San Diego for her to stop returning my calls and texts.

I missed her, but I also didn't.

"She's a puppy," Brinley replied.

"A puppy?" Danny pet the dog's large head, and when she shoved her nose between his legs he screamed. "She's a man eater!"

When I unhooked the dog's leash, she sniffed the floor for a few seconds before she ambled away, turning straight into Danny's room.

His mouth fell open as he pointed toward his room.

"You should probably check on her," Brinley said with a smirk. "I'd hate if she chewed on one of your shoes."

He took off after her.

"I think this is going to be fun," I told Brinley.

She giggled, wrapping her arms around my waist and kissing my chest. Still after three and a half years together, the feel of her against me filled me with love and hope. And her kisses... they grounded me with a home I never thought I'd have.

"What's her name?" Seth asked.

"Leia!" Danny shouted from his room.

"I second that choice," I said.

Brinley arched a brow at Seth. "What do you think?"

"I vote for Leia too."

"You hear that?" Danny asked, still in his room. "You're name's Leia."

I laughed. For all the fuss he'd made about not wanting a dog over the years, he sure had warmed up to her quickly.

Brinley sat on our couch and I followed her. When I put an arm around her shoulders, she nestled into my side.

"Did you find anything that would work for your

store?" I asked.

With a grin, Seth joined us on the couch. "There's this place a few blocks from the beach that gets pretty good traffic. Not a lot, but it's not bad. The place itself is big with two stories. I was thinking the upstairs could be my workshop and keep the store downstairs." His voice vibrated with excitement. "There's a section I want to frame your poems, try to sell them too along with the book you guys wrote together."

I drew myself closer to Brinley, keeping my fingers trailing over her arm.

It'd taken a little over a year to get the collection of poems we'd wanted together. And when we pitched our book to agents we'd gotten six rejection letters before one finally took a chance on us. To our surprise and joy, the book did well. So well, our readers wanted more. Not just more poetry, but more of us. Our story.

Brinley's social media was the first to blow up, which made sense since she was the more active and engaging one. Me? I just posted pictures of my girl with poems as captions, just as she'd done so many years ago. When she fought for me, for us.

So much had changed since then. So much had stayed the same. One of the many truths that remained was the way we fought desperately together, every single day.

"It's not just the store that I love though," Seth continued. "Behind the store is a three-bedroom house. It's kind of a fixer upper, but it has so much potential." His eyes danced, the passion he had for creating and fixing things evident in his expression. "And the backyard is huge, big enough for ten Great Danes to run around.

And there's a pool."

"A pool?" Danny asked. "I'm so in!"

"Why don't you come over here and talk to us like a normal person?" Brinley asked. "Instead of shouting across the apartment."

"I can't move!" he yelled back. "Leia has me pinned to my bed."

I shook my head on a chuckle.

"What do you think?" Seth asked.

"I think it's fantastic," Brinley said. "The store, the house, everything. And I think I'll be spending every chance I get in your new pool."

"I think I'm ready to move in yesterday," Danny said.

He strolled into the room with Leia walking beside him and sat with us.

"Are you gonna get it?" I asked.

"I think so," Seth answered. "Yeah." He nodded. "I'm gonna put an offer on it tomorrow." He reached for his phone. "Or tonight. I'll email the realtor." He hesitated, peered back at the three of us. "If I get it, you know you guys don't have to look for another apartment when your lease is up in two months. I think it'd be pretty cool to have you guys as roommates."

"Seriously?" Brinley asked, hopping up and down on the couch next me. "Yeah! I mean… but wait, Seth." She hesitated. "We can't just move in with you."

"Why not?" Danny and Seth both asked.

"Because." She waved her hands in the air. "It's your place. You'd be buying it, not renting."

"And whatever apartment you rent, would be owned by someone. What's the difference?"

"Think about the pool, Brin," I said, thinking about

her in a tiny bikini. Thinking about living in a houseful of two of my best friends and my girl.

Eventually, Brinley and I would have our own place, but for now, I loved living with her and Danny. Loved the noise they brought with them. Adding Seth to our crazy little world would be even better.

"Think about all the movie nights and weekend barbecues we would have," I added.

"It does sound really awesome," she agreed. "You really want to do this, Seth? Live with all of us?"

"Yeah," Seth answered. "When I saw it, I thought of you guys, and could see us in there. And then, you know, when I'm ready to settle down with my future hot bikini model girlfriend, I'll kick you guys out."

Brinley giggled. It was a pretty melody that I'd never grow tired of listening to. Of trying to bring out.

"How thick are the walls?" Danny asked, sending Brinley and me an accusatory glance.

"Yeah," Brinley piped in. "I swear if I have to keep hearing Danny and Ari in their bedroom whenever Ari comes to visit, I'm gonna cut my ears off."

Danny gave her a wink. "Just returning the favor."

Brinley pushed up her middle finger while I kissed her shoulder.

"If the walls need more insulation, I can do that." Seth laughed.

"So it's settled?" I asked.

"And then there were four," Danny sang.

"There's five of us," Brinley corrected him. "Oooh, I'm gonna tell Ari you forgot about him."

Danny stood up with a pillow in his hand that he smooshed into Brinley's face. She screamed. Leia barked.

"This is what you're getting into," I warned Seth.

He nodded. "The house would be pretty boring without you guys."

He was right.

My life was loud, full of motion and chaos. Full of words my girl and I shared with the world. Full of friends and the woman I loved.

My life? It was pretty damn good.

ACKNOWLEDGEMENTS

Always I have to thank God first. Without you, none of this would be possible. Thank you for giving me peace when I need it the most, for whispering in my ear to try one more time, for giving me a life I love with people who make the hard times worth going through.

Derrick, Dustin, and Chase – this book consumed me, took me away from time I normally spent with you. Thank you for giving me the time I needed, for being patient with me. I promise I'll make it up to you with all the movie nights you want. I love you guys with every part of who I am, even when you annoy the crap out of me.

Marisol and Kiara – I finally wrote a book you can read. If you hate it, don't tell me lol

Alyssa and Caitlin – in a couple of years you can pretend to love this book too.

Jill Sava – omg, right? I was about 99.9% sure you were going to call it quits and smack me upside the head.

But damn, you did it! You created a cover that is beautiful beyond words.

Mady Valle – you're an AH but I love you anyway. Every best friend is written because of you.

Denise Sedlacek – thank you doesn't feel like enough. Thank you for believing in me, making me believe in myself. Thank you for reading my crazy stress-filled messages and calming me down. You're an incredible woman and an even better friend.

Tessie Afzal – having you on my side is one of the greatest gifts. I can't wait to squeeze you when you make it from the other side of the moon.

Lee Casey – I'm not sure I can ever write a book without you by my side. Which pretty much means you're stuck with me forever.

Talon Smith – you were the boost I needed to go through with publishing Shallow. Would you judge me if I told you your messages made me cry lots and lots of happy tears?

Eli Peters – your input was invaluable, your suggestions spot on. I couldn't have done it without you.

Jen Van Wyk – as always, you made my baby shine. If I ever try to write a book without you, I give you full permission to beat me with a baseball bat. Also, I'm sorry for naming the twins after your kids lol

Megan Luker – the love you brought while working on Shallow is humbling. I'm so grateful to have you on my team and as a friend. Thank you for seeing the magic behind the mess.

Ella Maise – thank you for not once shooing me away when I continuously messaged you with all my crazy anxiety. You're a true gem and I'm grateful to have you as a friend.

Kasey Metzger – you are sunshine. I love your heart, your personality, and you.

Mary Johnson – every girl needs a Mary in their life. Not you specifically because I refuse to share you with anyone but Lee.

Shannon Harrell – giiiirrrrl, you are my most favorite f(h)airy godmother! Thank you a thousand times over for everything you do for me. I especially love talking sharks with you haha

DND authors – never have I met a group of authors so willing to help, support and encourage one another. I'm proud to be part of a group of women who are truly amazing. Every day, I learn from you. Every day, I'm grateful for you.

My reader group – I've made some incredible friends in this group. I love going into Yessi's Sadistic Sweethearts and talking with you guys. Thank you for accepting me in all my weird awkwardness.

Bloggers – where do I even start? I hope you realize how special each and every one of you are. Your selflessness in promoting authors and our work is awe-inspiring. Not a single one of us would get very far in chasing our dreams without your help. There aren't enough words in the English language to accurately say how thankful I am for you but I hope this will do.

Readers – if one day I show up on your doorstep to give you a hug, please don't call the cops on me. I'm so grateful for you, for giving my books a chance, for your messages that seem to lift me up when I need it the most. You're the reason I'm living my dream. I can only hope my words make you proud, bring you a sense of belonging, let you know you matter. And if you ever need a reminder of how incredible I think you are, message me. I'll fangirl so hard on you, I'll probably embarrass us both.

ABOUT THE AUTHOR

YESSI SMITH is a South Florida girl living in Texas with her husband and two sons.

She has a Bachelor's degree in Business Management and a Master's in Human Resource Management and has held several jobs, from picking up dog poop to upper management positions. And now she hopes to leave the business world behind so she can live full time in a world that does not exist until she places her fingers on a keyboard and brings them to fruition.

If you'd like to hang out with Yessi, join her in her reader group on Facebook: https://bit.ly/2LxSjxo

All of her books are available for free on Amazon with your Kindle Unlimited subscription:

viewAuthor.at/YessiSmith

Made in the USA
Columbia, SC
15 June 2018